An Amish Christmas Star

Center Point
Large Print

**This Large Print Book carries the
Seal of Approval of N.A.V.H.**

An Amish Christmas Star

Shelley Shepard Gray
Charlotte Hubbard
Rosalind Lauer

CENTER POINT LARGE PRINT
THORNDIKE, MAINE

This Center Point Large Print edition
is published in the year 2022 by arrangement with
Kensington Publishing Corp.

The text of this Large Print edition is unabridged.
In other aspects, this book may vary
from the original edition.
Printed in the United States of America
on permanent paper sourced using
environmentally responsible foresting methods.
Set in 16-point Times New Roman type.

ISBN: 978-1-63808-538-6

The Library of Congress has cataloged this record
under Library of Congress Control Number: 2022944033

Contents

Buggies, Trains, and Automobiles

Shelley Shepard Gray

For Jean Volk, who went above
and beyond when I asked
for train station help
Thank you for being such a loyal reader
and an even better friend

By day the Lord went ahead of them
in a pillar of cloud to guide them
on their way and by night
in a pillar of fire to give them light,
so they could travel by day or by night.
—EXODUS 13:21

Even if you're on the right track,
you'll get run over if you just sit there.
—AMISH PROVERB

Chapter 1

December 20
11:46 p.m.

Rap, rap, rap. "John! John Miller!" *Rap, rap.* John's eyes flew open, but the rest of his body couldn't seem to move. The clock said 11:46. He'd been asleep for almost two hours.

Lying in bed, staring at the door, he wondered if he'd just dreamed his landlord had come knocking in the middle of the night. In the five years that he'd lived in the house, John couldn't think of a time when Curtis had done much more than thank him when John paid his monthly rent.

Rap, rap, pound. "Wake up, John. This is important."

At last making sense of what was happening, John climbed out of his bed. Not even bothering to shrug on his robe, he crossed the room, unlocked the door, and opened it a crack.

"*Jah*, Curtis? Is everything all right?" But, of course, he knew it wasn't. Curtis wouldn't be knocking on his door if everything was good.

"I'm sorry, John. You've got a phone call." With a sad smile, his fiftysomething landlord thrust the cell phone into John's hand. "Here, son. Take your time, and feel free to use it as much as you need to. You can return it to me in the morning."

As Curtis walked away, John placed the phone to his ear with a feeling of dread. "Hello?"

"John, this is Susan Dee."

He had no idea who she was. "I'm sorry. Who is this?"

"I'm your father's caregiver at the Healing Hearts Nursing Home in Berlin."

"Oh. Yes, of course. I'm sorry. It's the middle of the night, and I fear I'm not at my best."

Her voice turned warmer. "I'm sorry for the time of the call, but I didn't want to wait. I understand you live in Florida. Is that correct?"

"*Jah*. I'm in Pinecraft."

"That's what I thought Angus told me." She took a deep breath. "John, I am very sorry to tell you that your father has taken a turn for the worse. The doctor said it's likely he only has a day or two left."

"I see." He swallowed. As another second passed, John struggled to think of something appropriate to say. It was difficult, though, since all he felt was dismay. It was obvious that this Susan Dee person was expecting him to visit.

John wasn't sure if he should. Did a final visit even matter? He hadn't spoken to his father in years. Almost fifteen years.

Susan cleared her throat. "Obviously, that is why I'm bothering you so late at night. Every second counts at this point. I mean, I'm sure you're going to want to get here as quickly as possible."

"Is my father awake?" He wasn't sure which would make the visit easier, his father being awake or asleep.

"He is drifting in and out. I feel sure he is waiting to see you."

"Really? Has he been asking for me?"

"Well, no," Susan replied. "But I feel certain that if he was in his right mind, Angus would be doing so."

"I see."

"So, will you be coming? If Angus knows you are coming, he might just hang on a little longer."

Susan sounded so hopeful. Sweet, too. Far too sweet for John to say what was really on his mind, which was that if his father was in his usual right mind, he would've said that John needed to stay away.

Feeling as if he didn't have a choice, John made his decision. "I'll do my best to get there soon," he said at last. It wasn't much of a promise, but it was the most he was willing to say.

"Do you have a pen and paper handy? Write down my phone number. You can give me updates."

His room was dark, and he was standing in his bedroom with only a pair of pajama bottoms on.

"Hold on." A minute later, he had a pencil and the back of an envelope. "I'm ready."

She promptly gave him her phone number. "Remember, my name is Susan Dee. Feel free to call me at any time during your journey. Day or night."

"*Danke.* Thank you for calling."

John hung up, carefully placed Curtis's phone on the dresser, and sat down on the edge of the double bed. The bed was in the corner of a room large enough to also hold a couch, bookshelf, and desk. A kitchenette with a tiny fridge and hot plate took up one corner. A small gray-tiled bathroom took up another. It held a narrow shower stall that not only provided as much hot water as he could ever desire but also the best water pressure in the world.

He looked down at his bare feet, so comfortable on the cool tile floor. When he'd first arrived, he'd thought the white-tile floor and yellow walls were the strangest things. Now he would likely find carpeted or wood floors foreign.

He thought about how much he'd gotten used to living in this spacious room on the third floor of Curtis's house. He'd gotten so comfortable there, he'd almost forgotten that it wasn't home.

Home, for him, would always be the sprawling farmhouse he'd been born in. It would be the kitchen in which his mother baked nonstop—as well as her sprawling garden outside filled with giant sunflowers in late summer. They'd towered over him when he was a little boy. Home was rain in the spring, red leaves in the fall, and piles of snow in the winter.

It had also become a place of darkness after his mother had passed away, a feeling of loneliness when his older sister left the order and never returned. Home had also been where his father had become so bitter and isolated that the smallest infraction by John drew swift criticism. It had been constant enough that his pity for his father's grief had turned to impatience and finally anger. There was only so much abuse he'd been willing to take.

And so he'd left.

Oh, not like his sister, Jo. Jo had never become baptized and had argued with both of their parents from an early age. He, on the other hand, had been baptized in the faith but had searched for someplace else to live. Someplace where he'd never have to see his father again. Somewhere that didn't have the memories Berlin, Ohio, had.

He'd found that haven in Pinecraft.

Had he ever thought about returning? Not for a single day.

"Lord, I'm ashamed of myself. I'm ashamed of my feelings. Ashamed that I don't want to interrupt my life to go back to the man who made me so unhappy."

He was ashamed of his first thoughts when he'd

realized why Susan was calling. He wasn't brave enough to apologize for those thoughts yet—after all, there were some things that couldn't ever be forgiven.

He knew that to be true.

Chapter 2

December 21

Ellie Coblentz was wearing her favorite traveling dress. It was a sage green and didn't show stains or lint easily. It also had long sleeves, which would keep her from getting chilled by the Pioneer Trails bus's air-conditioning.

On her legs were black stockings and a new pair of black tennis shoes. They were slip-ons, so they were easy to take off in the middle of a road trip. On her shoulder was her Florida purse. A lightweight cloth purse made out of a bright red, pink, and yellow print. The strap was long enough for her to sling over one shoulder. And the inside was deep and roomy. It held all sorts of things—reading glasses, tissues, lip balm, sunglasses, a wallet, an emergency sewing kit, a book, a mini Bible, and several snacks.

On her journey down to Florida, she'd learned that bus drivers didn't always pull over for meals when they said they were going to. Her stomach had been rather grumpy about that.

All in all, Ellie was well equipped and well prepared for the bus trip to Berlin, Ohio. From there, it would be a short buggy ride to her grandmommi's *haus* in Charm.

Except that the bus had left thirty minutes ago. Without her, thanks to a mistake on the booking agent's part and a woman traveling with her five-year-old.

It seemed that the agent had mistakenly written down months instead of years for the child's age. Which meant that the little boy had needed his own seat. No one with a heart was going to make a mother and her son wait for another bus. Ellie understood that.

But she was still annoyed that everyone's kindness toward the mother and child in need meant that she was standing in the parking lot with a suitcase, her favorite traveling outfit . . . and nowhere to go.

"This is just awful," she muttered to herself as she reached into her purse to get her reading glasses. Someone must have put a notice on the nearby bulletin board, offering a ride to Holmes County.

"What is?"

She started at the voice and turned to find a dark-haired Amish man with a deep tan looking at her with interest.

She pretended not to notice just how blue his eyes were. "Sorry, I didn't mean to bother you. I was speaking to myself."

"I gathered that much. But now you have me intrigued. What is just awful?"

Ellie opened her mouth, started to tell him that

he was being rather nosy, when she realized that he was giving her the perfect opportunity to get out of her shell. She had a difficult time speaking to people she didn't know well.

Which, unfortunately, was just about everyone.

Hoping she didn't sound quite as annoyed as she felt, she replied, "I had a reservation on the Pioneer Trails bus that just left. Unfortunately, a child took my seat, so I wasn't allowed on."

"I hate when that happens." A few lines formed around the outside corners of his eyes.

He was teasing her.

"I'm being serious. I mean, I do understand why the child needed a seat of his own. I'm not heartless. But because someone thought the child was five months instead of five years old, I'm now stranded in Pinecraft instead of on my way to Charm."

"So, you're looking for other means of transportation to Holmes County?"

"I am." She noticed that he, too, was studying the large bulletin board filled with tacked-on notes and messages to other Amish and Mennonite members of the Pinecraft community. "Just so you know, this bulletin board is a treasure trove of information. People put all kinds of things here. You can find anything from a new puppy to a fishing trip to where to meet the Lancaster County coffee klatch group. And it just so happens that it's the perfect spot to find rides up north."

19

He stared at her for a moment, seeming to weigh his words before speaking. She assumed he was digesting everything she'd said—after all, she did have a tendency to talk too fast. Ellie had been told that on more than one occasion.

"I appreciate your help," he said at last.

He didn't actually seem all that appreciative. Actually, she kind of thought he was acting as if she had pulled him over to the bulletin board out of the blue.

"It's no trouble at all," she said at last. "I like to be helpful."

"Indeed."

When he turned to stare at the bulletin board again, Ellie almost asked if he was looking for something specific. Then she decided against it. Instead, she went back to looking for a ride, scanning the messages as if she were scrolling through social media pages on her *Englischer* sister's phone.

And then she saw it.

I have room for two people in my van. I'm headed to Middlefield, just east of Cleveland. If you're interested, come to my house on the morning of December 21 and ask for Fred. I'm leaving around noon. If you ain't interested, then don't come by. I've got things to do.

It was followed by an address.

The note startled a chuckle out of her.

The man turned her way. "Did you read something funny?"

"*Jah*, but it is *gut*, too. I think I've just found my ride."

"You did?" His expression grew more intense. "Which note?"

She pointed to the small piece of notebook paper on the bottom right corner of the bulletin board. "There."

He read it slowly. "Are you really going to go to this man's *haus*?"

She nodded. "I need to get to Charm."

"But you don't know anything about him."

She couldn't deny that, but she wasn't going to let a small detail like that derail her plans. "I am sure he can't be bad if he is posting on our community bulletin board. It isn't like I have a choice, anyway. I've got to get back as soon as possible. I need to take care of my grandmother."

He raised his eyebrows. "That's why you're going?"

Ellie was getting tired of both his questions and his know-it-all, rather superior attitude. "That's what I just said."

When he continued to stare at her, she took a step backward.

"Good luck to you, with whatever you're looking for."

"Hold on. I'm going to head over to Fred's, too."

"Really?"

"Really. I was here looking for a ride. I'm in a bind."

"Where are you going?"

"Berlin."

"That's very close to Charm." She took a breath. "There are a number of small villages all side by side. Near Berlin are Millersburg and Charm. To the east are Sugarcreek and Walnut Creek. If you venture a little farther, you'll find—"

"Oh, for Pete's sake. I know how close Charm and Berlin are to each other."

"I see. Well, I was just trying to help you out."

"I'm starting to think you really just like to hear yourself talk."

He certainly had a lot of nerve.

"That is not true."

"It is. You prattle on like an old gossip holding court after church on Sundays."

The description was not complimentary. "You do not have to be so rude. All you had to do was tell me that you were already familiar with Holmes County."

He crossed his arms over his chest. "Fine. I already know where Berlin and Charm are in relation to each other. Just like I know about the bulletin board because I live here in Pinecraft full-time."

"Oh."

"Yeah. So you don't need to be so helpful."

Forgetting her usual good manners, she propped her hands on her hips. "Well, you don't need to be so surly. It's only four days to Christmas, you know."

"Believe me, I can also read a calendar."

Stung and more than a little annoyed, she said, "Just for the record, I found this ride first. I didn't have to tell you about Fred. I also had no idea you lived here."

He sighed. "That's true. I'm sorry I've been so rude. I fear I'm on edge."

At least he'd apologized. Feeling that she owed him something in return, Ellie said, "I do have a tendency to talk a lot. Especially when I'm *neahfich.*"

"I have a tendency to be gruff when I'm stressed out. Which I am right now."

They could either continue to debate, or she could reach out an olive branch. "Sir, would you care to lead the way to Fred's?"

His lips twitched. "What? You're not going to tell me how to get to Gardenia Street?"

"I'm tempted to pull out my map, but I thought I'd spare us both the bother. I'll follow your lead."

"If we're going to meet this Fred together, it might be nice to know each other's names first, don't you think?" He held out a hand. "My name is Jonathan Miller, but everyone calls me John."

"I'm Eleanor Coblentz, but everybody calls me Ellie," she explained as she shook his hand.

"It's good to meet you."

"For me, too. If we both have to get up north real fast, I'd rather have someone to travel with."

"So would I. Besides, I think it's best that you don't travel alone."

"I'm actually very capable."

"I have gotten that impression. However, the trip to Holmes County is a long one. And though this Fred person is most likely a good 'un, one never knows, true?"

Ellie nodded. "Lead the way, and I'll follow."

As he turned and started walking, she heard him laughing.

"What is so funny?" she asked.

"You are. I'm getting the feeling that you aren't used to following anyone. Except maybe a horse."

She smiled but remained silent. There was no need for John Miller to learn that she often liked to tell her horse what to do, as well.

Chapter 3

Fred Perry was what John's teacher back in Berlin would've called eccentric. Wiry, over six feet tall, and sporting a shaggy mane of silver hair, the man might be mistaken for a member out of an aging rock band . . . until he opened his mouth.

After that, John was fairly sure no singer or musician would have wanted to either perform or travel by his side. Fred had a nasally voice peppered with a heavy dose of hillbilly twang. He also seemed to be in need of a good shower.

Four other people already scheduled to ride were lined up in the man's hallway. They were sitting in plastic folding chairs with unhappy, worried expressions, looking as if they were about to get dental work done. If he hadn't promised Susan Dee he would get to his father's side as soon as he could, John would've turned right back around.

Ellie appeared to be as taken aback by Fred as John was. Instead of talking a mile a minute, she remained silent, only speaking when the bear of a man asked them questions.

"You two are all right with the hundred-dollar fee, ain't ya?" he asked in a surly tone. "I expect half of it to be paid now. You can pay the other half when we arrive."

"I am," John replied. "Ellie?"

"*Jah*," she said, though she looked as if she had just swallowed a frog.

"And do you both understand that I am in charge? I don't want to hear your opinions. Not about the temperature in the van, or the music I'm playing, or the way I drive?"

His question didn't bode well, but what could they do? The clock was ticking.

"All I need is to get to Berlin as quickly as possible," John said. "I'm glad you had two openings. I won't complain."

"Missy?"

Ellie blinked and then shook her head. "I won't complain, either," she whispered. "I'm not a complainer."

Fred eyed them up and down another moment, then shrugged. "You two might as well join the others." He waved a hand toward the four silent people lining the hall. "I'll be ready to leave in two hours."

"Wait, you want us to sit here for the next two hours?" Ellie asked.

"Are you complaining?" Fred grinned, but the amusement didn't really reach his eyes.

"*Nee*. Just asking."

"Good. Now take a seat," Fred said. He pointed to the two plastic folding chairs on the far side of an older *Englischer* couple who looked resigned to their fate.

Reminding himself that he needed to see his father one last time for reasons he wasn't entirely certain about, John picked up his backpack and Ellie's wheeled suitcase. "Let's go sit down, Ellie."

"Okay."

Only after they sat down did Fred walk out of the room. The other four passengers breathed a sigh of relief.

Ellie chose the seat closest to the other passengers. In the chair next to her was a sweet-looking old woman with pure white hair. "Are you going to Holmes County, too?"

After darting a look at the door where Fred had exited, the woman nodded. "We're going to be with Fred the entire trip. Our son is going to pick us up from Middlefield and take us to his house."

"So you'll be spending Christmas with your family."

"Yes."

Ellie's smile faltered. "How nice."

When everyone shifted, each looking as if they were afraid of getting in trouble, John's curiosity got the best of him. "Have any of you ridden with Fred before?"

An Amish couple about their ages raised their hands. "Fred has taken us back and forth twice before," said the man.

"Do you prefer riding with him to the bus?" Ellie asked.

The Amish man shrugged.

The sense of apprehension that John had been trying to shake settled in and intensified. "Ellie, are you sure you want to do this?" he whispered.

"I don't think we have a choice," she whispered back. "But this whole setup is odd, ain't so?"

Looking at the two other couples, John nodded. Leaning toward the Amish man, he said in Pennsylvania Dutch, "Any tips for the journey?"

"*Jah*. Don't talk if you can help it. Fred ain't exactly what one would call a chatty sort."

"Whatever you do, don't ask to stop," the older woman said. "He hates that."

"Or complain about his music," the Amish girl said.

John exchanged a look with Ellie. Though her eyes were wide, she only nodded. John figured he could put up with almost anything, as long as he reached his father in time.

Ninety minutes later, Fred appeared again, this time in a snug black sweat suit and matching tennis shoes. "Everyone needs to go to the bathroom now," he said. "The toilet's down the hall. Come out to the van when you're finished."

When he disappeared, the group stood up and the young Amish wife trotted down the hall. When she came back, her husband went, then together they went outside. John and Ellie stepped up in line as the older man took his turn.

"I never asked why, exactly, you are going to Berlin," Ellie said. "Can you tell me?"

"My father is dying. I got a call in the middle of the night with the news."

"Oh, my word. I'm so sorry."

"*Danke*." Seeing that they had a bit of time— the man still hadn't returned—John said, "To be honest, I'm not sure how I feel. I haven't seen my father in years. We didn't get along."

"How long has it been since you've seen him?"

"Not since I was fifteen."

Her eyes widened. "And now you are only going home because he's dying."

The way Ellie phrased it felt wrong, but he didn't correct her. He wasn't going to defend himself to a stranger. "What about you? You said you need to care for your grandmother?"

"*Jah*. I help my parents on our farm, but my main job is to watch Mommi. I needed a break, so I came down here on a holiday while my sister filled in for me. However, her baby just came early, so my grandmother needs some help. She doesn't do well being alone." She paused for breath. "I hope that man comes out soon."

"He has stomach issues," his wife said.

Ellie's eyes widened as John fought to keep his expression blank. He knew for a fact that he could have gone the whole trip without knowing that.

"Here he comes." The older woman hurried down the hall.

The man didn't say anything, but he did look a little green. John wondered if he felt well enough to travel but elected to keep that question to himself. He was beginning to realize that the Amish guy's advice about keeping quiet might have been the best advice he was going to get all day.

Like the announcement about the older guy's stomach ailment, there were some things that were simply better left unsaid.

Chapter 4

Several years ago, when Ellie had gone into Cleveland to do some shopping with her mother, their vehicle's driver had elected to take some back roads instead of the interstate. That was when she had seen a pair of prison vans.

She hadn't known what they were at the time. She'd stared at them only because the pair of plain white vans looked out of place on the country road. Then she'd spotted several men in gray shirts and pants with bright neon orange vests on. They were picking up trash on the side of the road. They didn't appear to be saying a word. It was a hot day, and each looked sweaty. Not a one of them had looked as if he was enjoying himself.

Of course, no one enjoyed picking up litter . . . but she'd been curious and had asked her mother and their driver if the men went around cleaning up Ohio open spaces.

The driver had enjoyed a good laugh at her expense.

"Oh, they're not do-gooders, young lady. Those men are from the state prison nearby. See those vans?" When she'd nodded, he'd said, "The guards take them around in those. You see them out here from time to time. Don't you worry about them hurting you, though. They've got on ankle bracelets, and there's plenty of guards around to make sure that they don't stray."

That had been the end of the discussion, but the image of those men and the vans had stayed with her for some time. She'd always wondered what they were thinking. Had they been pleased to get out of the prison and do something different—or had it been just another day in captivity?

Now, she had a pretty good idea of how those work details had felt to the prisoners: never ending. That was certainly how her journey in Fred's white van seemed.

The van wasn't all that roomy inside. Fred had the driver's seat for himself and the passenger seat for his belongings. Behind him were two rows of seats, each holding three of them. The far back section held all their luggage.

The bench seats did have seat belts, but they weren't up to safety standards. At least, that was what Lois, the older *Englischer* lady, whispered. Regulation seat belts not only fastened around one's hips but also across one's chest.

Ellie knew all about this because she was wedged next to Herb and Lois. John was behind her with the younger, smaller Amish couple. It turned out that since she and John weren't actually a married couple—and they were the last to join the party—they were the chosen ones to be split up. Ellie figured that made sense, but she still wasn't pleased about the arrangement. Herb's stomach was still acting up, and Lois liked to whisper a lot.

Ellie was pretty much the only person who dared to speak, which was just as well, since Fred had the radio playing a band called the Rolling Stones really loud. When she'd given Julie, the Amish girl, a look the first time she heard the music, Julie broke her silence long enough to tell her to count her blessings. It seemed Fred's favorite band, ACDC, played even more jarring tunes.

Unfortunately, neither the code of silence nor the loud rock-and-roll music was the worst part. The worst, by far, was Fred's driving.

Ellie, like most Amish girls she knew in Charm, had been in her fair share of passenger vans and had been transported by various drivers. It was a given that some drivers were better than others. However, she was fairly certain that there was no worse driver than Fred. He sped through small towns, darted in between RVs and semitrucks on the highway, and honked at everyone.

She would've complained—if she wasn't so busy hanging on for dear life. She wasn't the only one doing so. The first thing Lois had done after buckling her seat belt was grip the edge of the bench seat for all she was worth.

As "Under My Thumb" turned into "Honky Tonk Women" and then "(I Can't Get No) Satisfaction," Ellie tried different methods of taking her mind off the journey. First, she looked at all the other vehicles, but that became difficult because they either were passed in a flash or they were frantically veering out of Fred's way.

Plus, she was kind of starting to feel carsick looking at the passing scenery.

Instead, Ellie concentrated on thinking about Beth's baby and how sweet she must be. Then she thought about her sweet, dear grandmother. She loved her so much! Yes, her bones were getting frail, but her mind was still as sharp as a tack. Perhaps her grandmother would want to do a Christmas puzzle together. Sitting in Mommi's quiet, peaceful house would be enjoyable indeed.

"I have to go to the bathroom," Herb announced over the music. "You need to pull over."

"I already told you that I don't make no sudden stops," Fred shouted. "No."

Herb wiggled a bit. "You don't understand. This is an emergency. I need to go *now.*"

"I'm sorry, but he means it," Lois warned.

Fred's voice turned even meaner as he swerved around a giant white FedEx truck. "I told you that I would determine when we stop," he called out over the truck's blaring horn. "We've only been on the road for a few hours."

Herb's fingers were digging into his thighs. "Fred, I insist."

"If you've got to go so badly, go in a cup or something."

Ellie was not the only person who gasped.

"A cup ain't what I need," Herb said.

She wasn't the only person who gasped yet again.

As yet another loud song blared out of the speakers, Fred let out a stream of not very nice words.

And just like that, the trip went from bad to even worse.

Chapter 5

December 22
4:00 a.m.

John had never considered himself to be an argumentative sort. He enjoyed getting along with folks. It was a necessary skill to have, too, given his job in home construction. Building and remodeling were team projects, and it didn't serve anyone to be difficult. His coworkers at Six Pack Construction completely agreed.

The group had come up with the name after a long day's work, and it had stuck. The six of them were good at their jobs—and just as important—easy to get along with. They'd been together for five years now, and during those five years they'd worked out a lot of kinks. Now, they liked to think that they got along like a well-oiled clock. They just ticked along, doing what was necessary to keep their business turning.

Each of them had his own specialty in the crew. Jason was a master carpenter. No plumbing problem had ever given Benjamin pause. The others had their specialties, too. John Miller's? It happened to be working with challenging customers.

Oh, he was skilled at a lot of things. He knew

enough about carpentry, masonry, plumbing, and landscaping to lend a hand in any of those areas. But it was with customers that he shined the brightest. His friends were glad of it, too. It seemed not everyone enjoyed dealing with nervous Nellies or cranky customers. John took everyone in stride.

Actually, he got along with most people very easily. John couldn't remember the last time he'd gotten in an argument with someone. It had to have been ages.

Well, it had . . . until fifteen minutes ago.

John wasn't exactly sure what had happened. One minute he was telling Fred to be more patient with Herb. The next? He was arguing with the man at the top of his lungs. He wasn't sure, but John was pretty certain he'd used the words *ridiculous, autocratic,* and *bullheaded.* He might be Amish with only an eighth-grade education . . . but he read a lot. He had an excellent vocabulary and wasn't afraid to use it.

Unfortunately, his actions didn't go over well with Fred. It seemed he didn't take kindly to either being yelled at, told he was wrong . . . or having big words thrown at him. By the time John figured that out, it was too late. One minute he was feeling rather proud of himself for speaking his mind as a paying passenger . . . and the next, he was standing beside Ellie while the van drove off down the highway.

They were stranded at a rest stop in Jackson-ville, Florida, and it was all his fault.

At least Ellie wasn't yelling at him, though John was beginning to think that she was simply too stunned to speak. He had a feeling a long lecture from her was in his future. He wouldn't blame her, either.

Now that the passenger van was long gone, John started putting their things to rights. "At least Fred tossed out our bags," he said.

Sure, Ellie's suitcase, tote, and his backpack were strewn across the pavement, but at least each seemed to have survived the journey.

"I was worried that he was going to keep my backpack as a punishment."

"You are glad Fred didn't forget to toss out your backpack?" Ellie folded her arms across her chest. "John Miller, is that truly *all* you have to say?"

Hmm. So, Ellie wasn't feeling all that under-standing after all. Thinking maybe she would want to inspect her tote, he handed it to her. She dropped it on the ground.

Ouch.

He did feel bad, but he was just as taken off guard as she was. "What else should I be saying, Ellie? I surely didn't expect Fred to toss us out without a backward glance."

"Are you sure about that?"

Wait a minute. Did Ellie actually think that

he deserved the blame for this debacle? "That man was unreasonable and rude," he said as he walked over and slipped on his backpack. "You know I'm right."

She rolled her eyes. "And we both know how you love to be right, John." Looking as if she was getting even more irritated, Ellie strode over to her wheelie bag and grabbed the handle.

John picked up his last item and walked beside Ellie to the curb. "Okay, fine. I should probably not have been quite so frank with Fred."

"Oh, I'm not disputing the fact that Fred was a handful and not exactly pleasant to be around."

"*Not exactly pleasant?* He was impossibly rude."

Ignoring his outburst, she continued. "However, there's a time and a place to speak one's mind. It is not when the person you are yelling at is the one you are depending upon to take you across the country."

And just like that, some of the wind fell out of his sails. "I suppose you are right."

Ellie looked pleased by his statement. "*Danke.*"

Hmm. It seemed that he wasn't the only person who enjoyed being right. At the moment, it was rather too bad that being right wasn't going to get either of them any closer to Holmes County.

"I think we should sit down and figure out what to do next."

Looking wary but resigned, Ellie pointed to

a grouping of iron benches in front of the rest-rooms and a trio of vending machines. "We could sit down there."

"That sounds *gut*."

"What about our bags, should we bring them with us?"

It was four in the morning, and no one else was in sight. "There isn't anyone else here. I think they're safe for now."

"I suppose you're right." She led the way to the benches and sat down on the middle one.

John took the bench next to her. "For what it's worth, I am sorry. I never expected my complaints to be taken so badly."

"Oh, it wasn't your fault. Not really. That Fred was wrong. Poor Herb really did have to go to the bathroom. It isn't right that Fred made that poor man practically beg him to stop." She smiled slightly. "Thank heavens we did stop."

That was true. The minute the van pulled over, Herb raced out of it like a greyhound at the races. "It's really too bad that the moment Herb returned, Fred threw us and our bags out."

"It is. But don't forget how grateful the others were for your intervention."

John actually suspected that Herb was the only one pleased by his outburst. Honestly, the other Amish couple only looked afraid that they were going to be left behind, too. "I hope the rest of their journey goes well."

"You mean that sincerely, don't you?"

"I do. Herb is obviously ill. It's hard enough to take a journey without feeling bad, too. Plus, Fred is a menace on the road. If they survive it will be a miracle."

"I've been praying for them. I figured they all need the Lord's help."

"Fred, too?"

She chuckled softly. "Maybe Fred, especially, even though he did drive off with our money."

He chuckled, too. And as he did, he felt his spirits lift. They were stranded in Jacksonville; that was true. However, it was also fairly warm, and they had their things, vending machines, and bathrooms. They also had each other.

"I'm grateful for small favors," he said at last.

Ellie stared at him a long moment, then nodded, her blue eyes warming with humor. "I am, too, John Miller. As my father likes to say, it can always, always be worse."

John didn't think that was exactly the best news . . . but it had a good ring to it.

"Amen," he said.

"What do you think we should do now?" she asked.

"Wait," he replied, as he turned to face the quiet road just beyond.

Chapter 6

8:00 a.m.

The sunrise had been amazing. Maybe it was because she was sitting on a bench at a deserted rest stop, because she was feeling a little weepy, or because God was simply so good, but Ellie couldn't recall another sunrise that had been so glorious. The first rays had shone almost a burnt orange before they turned pink, then bright yellow. By the time the sun had risen and cast its rays of golden light across the horizon, both she and John had put on their sunglasses.

"Would you get mad if I admitted that I'm glad I had the chance to see that?" John asked.

"*Nee*, especially since I found myself giving thanks for this moment as well." Turning to face him more fully, Ellie added, "Back at home, even though I'm always awake for the sunrise, I never stop to watch it."

"Me either. I take it for granted, I suppose."

Ellie supposed she did the same thing. "I've been guilty of only thinking about chores that need to be finished. I've begun to stop appreciating small things."

John looked rueful. "To be honest, I seem to only stress about the small stuff."

"My grandmother always says not to sweat the small stuff and that it's all small stuff." She chuckled as John finished the last part with her. "I guess you've heard that expression before."

"I have, though hearing it often hasn't done me much good." Folding his arms across his chest, he turned to gaze at the cars zipping by. "Perhaps this experience will do me some good," he mused. "Maybe in the future I won't dwell on the things that don't matter and concentrate more on the things that do."

She held up the Snickers bar she'd just bought out of the vending machine. "I'm going to do the same. And, John, with you as my witness, I will never take a candy bar for granted again . . . or judge a person who eats one for breakfast."

Holding up his Reese's peanut butter cup, he smiled. "Me neither."

Feeling better, she was just about to tear open the wrapper of her candy bar when a big eighteen-wheeler truck exited the highway and slowly drove into their rest stop parking lot. It took another ten minutes, but eventually the driver shut down the engine and climbed from his cab.

"John, at last someone is here! I was beginning to think we were at the least-frequented truck stop in the state of Florida."

He smiled at her. "I was thinking the same thing."

Looking at the man, who seemed far more fit than Fred, she said, "What should we do?"

He got to his feet. "Say hello and hope and pray that he's more pleasant to be around than Fred."

Ellie got to her feet as well and then moved to stand a little bit closer to John. She could tell when the trucker noticed them. He was on his cell phone, scanning the area, then seemed to slow as he caught sight of the two of them standing there watching him.

"I'm gonna have to call you back, Sal," he said as he headed their way. "Something just came up that I need to take care of."

"Oh, my word," Ellie whispered. "He's coming our way."

"Yup."

Ellie thought John sounded rather calm about the situation—but then she realized that there wasn't much else for him to say. After all, there was nowhere else for the trucker to go.

Watching the man approach, Ellie noticed that he had on a black knit hat, several layers of knit shirts, jeans, and big tan boots. He was a large man, reminding her of a lumberjack. He also had a thick beard. It had a red tinge to it that she thought was rather eye-catching.

"Hey, you two," the trucker said as he approached. "Are you doing all right?"

Ellie nodded, then immediately felt foolish. They were definitely not doing all right.

"We're currently stranded here, I'm afraid," John said.

The trucker's brows pulled together. "What do you mean by that? Did your car break down?" He looked around the lot. "Hey, where is your car?"

"I'm afraid the driver we hired left us here," John said.

"Say again?"

There was something about the man's confusion that settled Ellie's nerves. She tried to explain. "We were in a van with four other passengers and a driver. But, um, the driver got a bit annoyed with us so he tossed out our bags."

"It's only eight in the morning. Did this just happen?"

"*Nee*. It was several hours ago," John replied.

"But you kids are Amish, right?" He pointed to Ellie's white *kapp*.

"We are," Ellie said. "We're both New Order Amish." Realizing that she'd probably told the truck driver far more than he was interested in, she said, "I mean, yes. We're Amish."

"Where are y'all headed?"

"Ohio," Ellie answered.

The trucker frowned. "I'm headed the opposite direction. Otherwise I'd take you as far as I could."

Ellie's stomach sank. "Oh," she whispered.

"You have any ideas about what we should do?" John asked.

"Well, the bus might be an option . . . I suppose I could take you two to the bus station. If you'd like."

John grinned. "That would be real helpful. Thank you."

"No problem. Let me, ah, use the facilities and then we'll get you in my cab."

Ellie pointed to their bags. "We have a couple of pieces of luggage. Is that okay?"

The burly trucker started laughing. "I'm driving a semi, darling. Of course it's okay. I'll have plenty of room for your stuff. No worries there."

As he disappeared into the men's room, Ellie grinned at John. "Taking a bus won't be too bad."

"I agree," John said, though it was obvious that he was looking at something on the horizon. "Or perhaps we could travel some other way?"

"Like what?" Though they could travel on a plane because they were New Order, she certainly didn't have enough money for a plane ticket.

"Look." He pointed to the train that was traveling on the tracks in the distance. "What about that?"

The train had several engines and a great many railcars.

"I've never been on a train before. Have you?"

"*Nee*, but I've always thought it might be fun."

"I've thought the same thing. Let's ask our truck driver if he knows anything about train schedules."

It turned out Kramer the truck driver didn't, but he had no problem figuring out where the nearest Amtrak station was and getting them there. He held up his smartphone. "I've got a computer in my hand, you know."

Ellie laughed. "I hadn't thought about your phone that way, but I guess it's true."

"Do you ever miss it?" Kramer asked.

"Miss what?" John asked.

Kramer waved a hand. "You know . . . technology. Cell phones. Being able to get whatever you want or information about wherever you need to go within seconds." He paused, then added with a look that said he almost felt sorry for them. "It'd sure make your life easier."

"Would it, though?" John asked. "I promise, we Amish appreciate technology as much as anyone else. The difference is that we don't want to depend on it. Your smartphone might make things easier for you, but it might also give Ellie and me a whole lot more to worry about."

"Besides, if we'd had one of those gadgets, we wouldn't have gotten to appreciate your kindness," Ellie added. "You've been very kind to two strangers in need."

Kramer's cheeks flushed slightly, as if he was embarrassed by the praise. "It's the least I could do, especially so close to Christmas. I mean, what kind of man would I be if I didn't stop to lend a helping hand?"

"I reckon you might never know," John said. "Thank you for taking us to the train station."

Twenty minutes later, Kramer pulled into a vacant parking lot in the center of downtown. There was a square green Amtrak sign with a white arrow on it pointing to the right.

"This is the best I can do, yeah?" He gestured toward the one-story white-brick building about two blocks in the distance. "There's the station. Sorry, but there's no way I can get this big boy any closer."

"No need. God gave us two legs. We can use them," John said. "Thank you again."

"Not a problem. I'll do some thinking about what you said, too. About that phone stuff. You made a good point. I might even put it away some on Christmas Day. Jill will be pleased."

"I hope you get home soon," Ellie said.

"I will. Ten more hours and then I'll be home, if the good Lord sees fit."

"We'll pray for your journey, Kramer," John said.

When they were getting out of his cab, Kramer asked, "Are you two kids gonna be okay? I feel kind of like I've abandoned you two in a bad part of town."

Ellie looked around. She saw some homeless men sitting on the curb of a bakery outlet. They were watching them intently. If she had been alone, she might have felt afraid, but next to John, she was almost at ease. She spied something in the men's expressions that signaled they were merely curious. Ellie couldn't fault them for that. She would have stared at the Amish couple getting out of a big silver eighteen-wheeler, too. "I think we'll be just fine."

Kramer reached for his wallet and pulled out a couple of bills. "Here." He held out his hand. "It's fifty bucks. Take it, in case you get stuck somewhere."

John shook his head. "Thank you; we don't need your money. Your help was enough."

Kramer's hand didn't waver. "Take it anyway. You two are on quite a journey. God might be in charge, but he might not have time to check your wallets first, right?"

With obvious reluctance, John took the money. Neither one of them had much cash left now that Fred had driven off with the money they'd given him. "Thank you." Instead of slipping the bills in a pocket, he handed the cash to her. "Ellie, will you take care of this for us?"

"Of course." After she slipped the money into her wallet, she looked up into Kramer's eyes. "I'll keep it safe. If we don't need this money, we'll pass it on to someone else who does."

Kramer gently patted her on the arm. "You're my kind of gal. Paying good deeds forward. I like that."

John shook the truck driver's hand. "Merry

Christmas," he said. "May God be with you."

"To you both as well. Now, get a move on. Trains are pulling in as we speak."

Ellie smiled and waved, then walked with John to the curb, passed the group of homeless men, and then finally reached the outside of the train station.

When she looked back for Kramer, he was gone, and the truck was, too.

"I didn't hear Kramer's truck leave. Did you?"

John stopped and stared. "It was like he vanished. That sure was strange, ain't so?"

"Usually I would agree, but I'm starting to think that he was our own guardian angel," Ellie said.

"If the Lord sent us an angel, I hope He keeps them coming during the rest of our journey. We've still got a long way to go."

Ellie chuckled as she silently said, *Amen.*

Chapter 7

Ellie had learned a lot about train travel during the last two hours. First of all, the station in Jacksonville was on the north side of town, and it had opened all the way back in 1974. The building looked a bit worn down but was rather nice inside.

Ellie especially liked how all the waiting areas were open to the air. She liked being able to see the sun instead of being in a dark tunnel underground.

Once they got to the ticket counter, she found out a whole lot more information. First, there were two different classes on the train, but they were called first class and coach. Every time she attempted to ask DeWayne, the kind ticket agent, about why that was, he guided her back to the schedule and encouraged her and John to make a decision.

Money was tight for both of them, and destinations from Jacksonville were limited. After much discussion, she and John had each booked a ticket to Charlotte, North Carolina. Once there, they decided they would look into buses and call their homes.

They doubted anything would have changed, but there was always the chance that they would need to ask for money to be wired to them.

They must have looked a bit like lost sheep, because a woman about Ellie's mother's age pointed to the vending machines in the terminal. "There's not a lot of choices once you get on the train, kids," she said. "The food is expensive, too. It's best to get something here and bring it on."

One of the vending machines was filled with limp-looking sandwiches, but she knew they would be better for her than another candy bar. Feeling that ham and cheese was a safe choice, Ellie put in her money and watched her triangular-shaped package slide down the shoot. John decided to get tuna salad.

"Are you sure that is what you are gonna order?" Ellie asked just before John punched in the letter and the number of his selection.

He looked annoyed. "Of course I'm sure. I wouldn't have told you what I was getting if I wasn't."

"No offense, but we don't know how long it's been sitting in there. It could've been a while," she warned. Plus, they were in Florida. It was rather warm outside.

"Ellie, don't worry so much. We don't know how long any of the choices have been sitting in the machine."

Still feeling that she was right and he was wrong, she added, "Tuna salad goes bad quickly, *jah*?"

He raised his eyebrows, then, with an extremely smug expression, smiled as his sandwich dropped down the shoot. "Good thing my food ain't your problem."

His refusal to heed her advice irritated her, especially since his meal choice *was* her problem. If he got sick, she was going to have to deal with him. Someone had to. "I hope you don't get sick, John Miller."

"I could say the same thing about you, Ellie Coblentz."

Peeved, Ellie sat down on a bench and watched the trains come and go. By this time it was near noon, and the Jacksonville, Florida, sun was warm. From here on, the days were going to be cloudier and colder. It was December, after all.

Eventually, at just a few minutes before five o'clock, their train arrived, they hurriedly got in line, got their tickets punched, and boarded the coach-class section. As they walked down the narrow aisle, she studied everything, wanting to be sure to be able to describe each detail to her grandmother.

Unfortunately, there wasn't much to see. The seats were cloth and looked like they'd hosted many a warm body. Perhaps too many by the looks of some of them.

To Ellie's surprise, most of the seats were taken, too. After reading the numbers on their tickets, she and John eventually found their spots in the back of the third passenger car they entered. Their seats were right next to the bathroom.

What felt like seconds after they boarded and stowed their belongings, the train's whistle blew, and a recorded message told them that the next stop would be in forty-five minutes. Finally, with a bit of a lurch, they were on their way.

Ellie had been glad to have a seat next to the window and eagerly peered out. She'd never been on a train before, and the only time she'd traveled any distance had been last week, when she'd taken the Pioneer Trails bus from Berlin to Pinecraft.

At first, everything looked rather disappointing. But then gradually, the city streets of Jacksonville gave way to palm trees, some retention ponds, and then finally the rural fields of northern Florida and southern Georgia. She soon saw many birds perching on oak trees and other types of shrubs and vegetation she wasn't familiar with. The sights, together with the knowledge that she would likely not see them again for some time made her feel wistful.

After a brief stop, the train picked up speed. Soon it was chugging along again, the motion encouraging her body to relax. Ellie looked out the window, half watching the vegetation and birds and half thinking about her sister and the baby and Mommi, and how her life, too, seemed to be speeding by while she sat snug and safe in a seat and didn't move much.

When the train stopped again, this time for only

ten minutes, she murmured, "Isn't this something to see, John?"

"Can't rightly say, since you've been blocking my view."

Embarrassed, she moved away and realized that John wasn't lying. He'd been forced to look at her back while she gazed out at the passing scenery. "Want to switch places for a spell?"

"*Nee.*"

That was when she realized there was something wrong with his voice. It sounded a bit like he had a frog in his throat. She turned to face him more fully. "Are you all right? You don't sound too *gut.*"

"I don't know. I'm feeling a bit woozy."

Alarms went off in her head. "You feel sick?"

"Kind of." He did a one-shouldered shrug. "*Nee,* I think it's more of a yes."

All she could think about was that tuna sandwich. "You ate that whole sandwich, didn't ya?"

"Hmm?"

"That vending machine tuna sandwich. You ate it."

"I ate part of it."

"And now you have food poisoning."

"*Nee.*" He sipped from his water bottle. "I've had food poisoning before. This ain't it."

"How do you know? I imagine one can have all kinds of symptoms from bad food."

"I know you need to be right, but I think it's the train," he said.

That hadn't occurred to her, but she supposed the motion could make one rather queasy. "Do you really think so?"

He nodded weakly . . . just before he reached for the little paper bag in the back of the seat next to them and vomited.

It was never pleasant to witness someone getting violently ill. But it seemed to be even worse when one was on a train and in close proximity.

Thankful that she'd forgotten all about her own sandwich, Ellie rubbed his back. "I'm sorry you don't feel well."

He inhaled and raised his chin. His face was flushed, his eyes were watery, and he looked a bit green.

"Get me another bag," he said weakly.

Ellie handed John hers right away and couldn't quite control her feeling of distaste when John promptly utilized it as well.

Getting to her feet, she hurried to another pair of passengers, asked for their bags, then took the soiled ones to the trash can down the aisle. She breathed a sigh of relief when she spied an attendant wearing a name tag. "Excuse me, Carol."

"Yes?"

"My friend is trainsick. What should he do?"

"Let's get him a can of soda and a washcloth, miss," the woman said. "Don't look so worried. If he's motion sick, it will pass eventually. I promise, it happens to the best of them."

"It would seem so." She followed Carol to the bar car, got a cold Sprite, and then showed her where poor John was half huddled in his seat.

"You poor dear," Carol said. "Train travel doesn't agree with you much, does it?"

"I guess not."

She looked at the clock above the door. "Here's what you need to do. The next stop is a long one. Thirty minutes. Get off and breathe some fresh air. Walk around a bit. I promise, you'll feel better."

"*Danke*," John said.

"He said thank you," Ellie explained.

"I got the gist of it. Get him off the train now. You both will feel better for it."

And with that, she treated them to a smile and then hustled back down the aisle just as the train's whistle blew again.

"That's our cue, John. It's time to get off."

"I can't get out of here fast enough."

Thinking that the look on his face was a bit like Herb's, Ellie tried not to smile as they descended the stairs onto the platform.

She was pretty sure John wouldn't appreciate the comparison one bit.

Chapter 8

Carol had been right. Ten minutes of fresh air had done him a lot of good. Walking around on the street side of the train station, John took a deep breath. It was cooler than he was used to and smelled vaguely like the exhaust from the train. It wasn't exactly appealing, but knowing that his feet were on stable ground and he was breathing fresh air went a long way toward settling his stomach.

Ellie had stayed by his side, offering support in a pleasing, low-key way. Even after he'd assured her that he didn't need anything, she walked by his side. It was obvious that she was still worried about him.

He wasn't used to being fussed over. He'd been embarrassed at first, though he told himself that there was nothing to be embarrassed about. To his surprise, Ellie seemed to sense how uncomfortable he was and didn't say much. She didn't offer suggestions or ask him questions, only stayed nearby, as if she knew that sometimes it was better to offer silent companionship and that there was nothing she could do anyway.

If John had been feeling better, he would have teased Ellie, saying that he hadn't realized she could last longer than two minutes without chatting about everything and anything that was on her mind. But, of course, he didn't. It wouldn't have been kind, anyway. He wasn't the type of person to tease someone who was attempting to give him a helping hand.

When they made another pass past the platform, she glanced at the large white clock hanging above them. "We only have ten more minutes."

If they hadn't been in such a hurry to get to Berlin, John would have prayed they could stay where they were for another two more hours. Instead, he said a small prayer of thanks for the break they'd been given and pulled himself together.

"I'd better call and check on my father. Just in case," he added.

Pointing to a phone cubicle in the station, he said, "I'll be right back." He hurried over, pulled out a calling card, swiped it, and was connected.

Ellie hovered nearby, and he wondered whether it was because she was still worried about him or because it was getting crowded near the platform. He smiled at her, letting her know that her staying close was good with him.

After a couple of clicks, the receptionist answered in a peppy voice. "Healing Hearts Nursing Home."

He bit back a sigh. He didn't particularly like the name of the nursing home. He felt it was a jab at his relationship with his father—

but that was just his imagination. "This is John Miller. I'm calling to see how Angus Miller is doing."

"Is he your relation?"

"Yes. I'm his son." Even that small admittance made his stomach feel sour again.

"Hold, please. I'll find Jerry. He's on shift right now."

John glanced around, saw that Ellie was still standing nearby, but no one else was waiting for the phone. One of the benefits of the *Englischer* dependence on their cell phones, he supposed.

"Hello, John?"

"*Jah*. Are you Jerry?"

"Yep. I was actually just sitting with your father when you called. Are you on the way?"

John clenched his hand and reminded himself not to be defensive. The nurse's aide was only asking a question, not judging him. "I am. I've run into some snags but I'm doing my best to get there."

"I hope it won't be too much longer. Yesterday, when he was coherent for a bit, he asked if you were on the way." He lowered his voice. "I think your father is waiting for you."

The sense of urgency that John felt didn't sit well with him. Why was he now feeling that he was in a race against time that he must win? "I see." He cleared his throat. "Well, um, there's not much I can do about my progress. There are a number of factors that are out of my control."

"I see. Do you have any questions?"

Jerry's voice had turned noticeably cooler. John couldn't blame him. He'd probably act the same way if he hadn't lived with Angus Miller for fifteen years. "I'll check in tomorrow some time. Thank you for the update."

"Do you want me to tell him anything in the meantime?"

That he loved him? That he forgave him for his transgressions? Maybe those things were on the tip of his tongue, but he wasn't ready to admit them even to himself, let alone say them to a total stranger. "No. I don't have anything to say." He hung up then, sure that he'd just made an enemy out of Jerry but unable to bring himself to care. There were only so many burdens he could handle at the moment.

When he turned back to Ellie, he noticed that she was looking at him strangely. "Thanks for staying with me. I'm feeling better now."

"Oh? Oh, good. How is your father?"

"Not good. He's dying."

She gasped. "You shouldn't say that, John."

He had so many swirling, warring emotions inside him, he wasn't interested in hearing her opinions, too. "Why not? It's the truth."

She squeezed his arm. "You don't know that. The Lord is in charge. He might have a different plan for your father. Why, he could recover on

Christmas Day." Her expression turned pleading. "You need to have hope."

Unfortunately, there was still a part of him that hoped he'd never see his father again. "We should get on the train."

Ellie looked as if she wanted to continue arguing but simply nodded. He thanked the Lord for small favors as they showed their tickets to the agent and then moved down the narrow aisle to their row. Another couple had moved into the seats next to them. They said hello but went back to their books while he and Ellie sat back down again.

"You know, John, even if you and your father didn't have the best of relationships, there's still time to mend fences," she said. "You can pray for hope and strength during the rest of your journey. The Lord will help you—I know it."

"And then?"

She smiled as if what she was suggesting was easy. "And then do your best to make things right with your father."

He knew Ellie believed her words completely. He couldn't fault her for her faith.

Unfortunately, they were so far off the mark for him, her tidbits of well-meaning advice felt intrusive. "You have no idea what you're talking about."

She blinked. "Of course I do. I have parents, too, you know."

The train chugged to life, and his stomach lurched with it. "Ellie, not everything that is wrong can be made right with just a few sweet words and a couple of prayers. You have no idea what my life with my father was like."

"All right." She shifted so she was facing him more fully. "Why don't you tell me about it?"

"*Nee*," he said as the train's whistle blew before they zipped through an intersection. He looked out the window, saw the hills fly by, and felt clammy all over again.

"That's it?" she asked. "Just, *nee*?"

"Listen, Ellie. I'm not trying to be rude, but you don't know me, and I don't know you. I'm not going to start telling you stories about my childhood while we're on this blasted train. Save yourself some time and worry and stop attempting to get into my business. Don't forget, in a couple of days, we'll only be bad memories for each other."

Her blue eyes widened. "I can't believe you said all that."

"Believe it." He closed his eyes and pretended not to notice that she was continuing to stare at him.

Thirty minutes later, he tried to sleep when Ellie started chatting with the new couple across the aisle.

But all he could think about was the fact that he actually did feel something for his father. That

Ellie probably had a point about God and prayer being able to help.

It seemed that not even time, distance, or a private promise to move on could change the fact that Angus was his father.

Or the fact that no matter how hard he tried, he was still always going to be his father's son.

Chapter 9

December 23

B renda and Tony Parelo were Italian, in their early seventies, and were experts at train travel.

At least that was Ellie's perception as their train chugged along, John Miller pretended to sleep next to her, and she privately fretted about the journey, what they were going to do next . . . and the exchange of words they'd just had.

Brenda had been intrigued by John and Ellie's journey and asked lots of questions. When Ellie told them about Fred's behavior, both Brenda and Tony acted just as appalled as she and John had been back at the rest stop.

"We're scheduled to arrive in Charlotte in thirty minutes," Brenda said. "What are you two going to do now?"

"I'm not sure."

"Why?" Brenda asked.

"Well, we have to rely on the Lord, our finances, and what's available, I guess." Ellie knew her voice sounded strained.

Whether Brenda's statement about being close to Charlotte had encouraged John to open his eyes, or he'd finally decided to stop pretending to sleep, Ellie would never know.

"Sorry," he said. "The train's motion has made me feel a little under the weather."

"Are you feeling better now?" Brenda asked.

"I think so. Thank you."

"I'm glad you are feeling better," Ellie said.

"Me too. I'm sorry for earlier."

His eyes were full of sympathy. Ellie swallowed, taken aback by his change in demeanor. "It's okay," she said. "I . . . I shouldn't have been so eager to share my opinion. I have a tendency to do that, you know."

"I know, but I'm getting used to it," he murmured with a smile.

His words eased her anxiety and reminded her again about how thankful she was to not be alone. Yes, they were imperfect people, but they were on this convoluted journey together. She wondered if the wise men all those years ago had felt the same way.

Unable to help herself, Ellie smiled back at him. When their eyes met, it was as if there were only two of them on the train.

"Young man, do you have any idea about what your next step will be?" Tony asked.

John seemed to shake himself. Turning to the older man, he said, "No. It is as Ellie said. Our journey has been a confusing and frustrating one, but we haven't given up hope. The Lord has kept providing us with opportunities. We're simply going to have to keep our eyes and ears open."

Brenda and Tony exchanged glances. "We're due to arrive in Charlotte real soon. Why don't you stay at our house for a few hours?"

Ellie was stunned by their generosity. "Thank you, but I don't know if we should do that. Every hour counts, you know."

"Plus, we need to find a way home," John said. "Figuring that out might take a while."

"You don't have to stay very long," Brenda said. "You could stay just long enough to take showers, eat a good meal, and maybe gather yourselves together."

"While you two are getting cleaned up, I can call some friends of mine to see who can help you on the next leg of your journey," Tony said. "There's got to be someone in our circle who knows someone who is heading to Ohio for Christmas."

"I make a great bachelor casserole," Brenda said. "A hot meal might be nice, right?"

Ellie couldn't help but chuckle at the name of the dish. "I'm sorry but what is a bachelor casserole?"

"It's noodles, hamburger, a can of soup, and some frozen veggies."

"She tops it with crunched-up crackers and cheese," Tony added. "It's real tasty. Filling, too."

The noodles, soup, frozen veggie concoction didn't sound especially appetizing, but it didn't sound horrible, either. And compared to what she and John had been eating for the last several days, it sounded like a feast.

"Ellie, what do you think?" John asked.

As awkward as it might be to accept the couple's generosity, she couldn't deny that they were in need of help. Plus, there was the appeal of a shower. Two straight days of traveling had made her feel rumpled and more than a little grimy. "I think I would be very grateful for a shower and the chance to wash my hair."

"I agree. We've been getting bounced around like rubber ducks in a river. A few hours to get clean, rest, and eat sounds *wunderbaar*. And if you could help us with travel arrangements, Tony, we would be so very grateful."

"It's been decided, then." Tony reached out for Brenda's hand. "You have made us very happy. Thank you."

"We're the ones who should be thanking you, Tony," Ellie said. "Offering your home to a pair of strangers is not something most people would do."

"We're not innkeepers, and you two aren't Mary and Joseph, but giving some travelers a warm spot to rest does feel like a rather Christmassy thing to do."

While the four of them chuckled, Ellie glanced

at John. She wished she was brave enough to reach for his hand. It would be so nice to have that connection. A nice reminder that even if they might not always be on the same page, they were definitely in this together.

Chapter 10

Ellie had had more than one moment of misgiving since she and John had accepted the Peralos' kind offer. As nice as the couple seemed, Ellie knew there was a chance they could be dishonest or maybe even hoping to get something from them. Why, they could even be secret serial killers or something else that was awful and strange.

Sure, she was Amish, but Ellie did read the paper from time to time. There were bad people in the world. That was something she knew for sure and for certain.

Ellie worried that going to someone's house might put them at a traveling disadvantage, too. If Tony and Brenda didn't turn out to be all that helpful, then Ellie and John would be away from public transportation and would have to figure out how to continue on their trip.

She also felt guilty about wanting to spend a few hours freshening up. She needed to go help her family, not concern herself with things like hot showers and hot meals.

But all those fears vanished when Tony's cousin picked them up at the train station in a black Suburban and deposited them at *Chez Peralo*, as Tony liked to call his home.

The house was truly lovely. Originally built in an older neighborhood in the fifties, the home had been lovingly remodeled over the last thirty years. The inside was open, homey, and filled with comfortable furniture and sparkling appliances. It also had the most amazing bathroom Ellie had ever seen. Broad brown granite tiles covered the floor. A shower with two showerheads was situated in one corner. A freestanding pedestal bathtub graced another. There was also a mirrored dressing table, two sinks, a heated towel rack, and a comfortable chair to sit down upon.

Ellie gingerly sat down on it as she continued to admire the space. And then she was glad to be sitting when she caught sight of her reflection in the mirror.

In short, she looked like a woman who had spent the last two days in a passenger van, an eighteen-wheeler, a train, and a black Suburban. She also looked—and no doubt smelled—like a woman who hadn't showered or changed clothes during that time.

"I think I smell," she murmured.

That was all it took to push every thought about serial killers, vanity, or future transportation from her mind. She turned the shower on high, smiled at the variety of soaps and hair products available, and stepped into the steamy confines of the stall.

Feeling clean and comfortable once again, Ellie

sat at the kitchen table two hours later. Not only was she grateful to be wearing fresh clothes, she was thankful to their hosts for offering to wash the clothes she and John had been wearing. After saying a quick, silent prayer, they'd dug into Brenda's bachelor casserole.

Tony and Brenda were sitting across from them and seemed to be watching her and John take every bite.

"So?" Brenda asked. "What do you think?"

"I think it's good," Ellie said. "Thank you so much."

Brenda still looked worried. "Are you only being polite? I appreciate good manners, but I don't want you going hungry."

John gestured to his almost empty plate. "I've almost cleared my plate. I was hungry, but I am enjoying it very much."

The line between Brenda's brows eased. "Bachelor casserole really is the best."

Tony winked. "However, it's not like he's a bachelor, right? You two are traveling together."

"We are traveling together, but we ain't a couple," John said. "We only met a few days ago."

"I find that hard to believe," Brenda said. "The two of you seem to be a good match. Before you two came down here to eat, I told my Tony that you two seemed like one of those Amish couples who know they're going to get married from the time they are six."

Ellie smiled at Brenda's words. Many times in her life, she'd heard *Englischers* spout off information about how "all Amish" do one thing or another. Long ago she'd given up trying to make them understand that all the Amish she knew not only had their own minds, they all followed different rules, depending on their church district.

Instead, she focused on Brenda's fanciful thoughts about her and John. "John and I do get along well, but I think our rapport has been forged through the challenges of our trip. We've become fast friends."

"We decided that we work better as a team than separately," John added.

"That seems to be the case for most everything," Tony said.

"Do you have plans to see each other in the future?" Brenda asked.

Ellie almost choked on her latest bite. Brenda was being awfully nosy, but Ellie couldn't find the gumption to tell her to mind her own business. After all, it was obvious that the woman was only trying to be helpful. "Like, when we get to Berlin?"

"Yes. Or when Christmas is over. What are you two going to do when your journey is done?"

That question brought Ellie up short, which was something of a shock, because she prided herself on always thinking ahead. When John seemed to be just as much at a loss as she, Ellie shrugged.

"I'm not sure."

Brenda crossed her legs. "Really? Do you even know what your plans are for the future?"

"Well, I suppose I'll continue living in Berlin and helping my grandmother. And now my sister with her baby." For some reason, neither of those things filled her heart with happiness or pride.

It actually sounded like kind of a lonely prospect.

"What about you, John?" Tony asked.

He put down his fork. "My future is certain. I'll be heading back to Sarasota. I have a business there."

"Ah. Yes. You told me on the train that you run a construction business."

John nodded. "I started it with five friends of mine. We're proud of its success."

"I think that's wonderful. A good, solid business is something to be proud of," Tony said with an encouraging smile.

"Thank you. We are proud of Six Pack Construction. We've worked very hard to make a go of it."

Brenda looked from one of them to the other. "Perhaps the two of you will be able to visit each other around New Year's Day or something."

"Yes. I guess we'll see," Ellie said. She knew her voice was faint, but she couldn't seem to help herself. Brenda's questions were making her reevaluate everything in her life that she'd accepted without question.

She didn't know if that was a good or a bad thing. Maybe the Lord was using Brenda to help Ellie see that she had more options than she was aware of.

When Tony's cell phone rang, he excused himself as he walked to the kitchen. Almost immediately, he turned back around and hurried toward them.

Placing a hand on the phone, he grinned at Ellie and John. "Guess what? My buddy Alan has a sister who lives next door to Nan Randall." Taking a breath, he smiled wider. "Nan is heading to Beckley, West Virginia, in two hours. She can take ya if you two would be willing to pay for gas."

Brenda clapped her hands together. "Now, isn't that wonderful? That sounds like a good trade to me."

"What do you think, John?" Ellie asked. It did sound like a blessing. But yet again, she was going to be putting her future into another stranger's hands.

"I think it's as good an offer as we'll get and it is the right general direction."

"Alan said that Beckley is just four or five hours from Berlin."

John leaned closer. "We do have that money

the trucker gave us," he whispered. "We could use that, if you agree."

"I think it will be fine, but do you think it's enough?" Raising her voice, she said, "We only have fifty dollars to pay for gas."

"Hold on," Tony said. Getting back on the phone with his friend, he said, "Do you think fifty bucks would do it?" Turning back to them, he grinned. "Nan drives a Prius. It should do just fine."

That was wonderful news! "We'd love her help, then," Ellie said.

"Kids, go pack," Brenda said. "I'll get your clothes out of the dryer and fold them."

"I hate for you to go to so much trouble. And the supper dishes!"

"Dishes and laundry are nothing, dear. Don't worry."

"My bride is right," Tony said with a sparkle in his eye. "We've got to hurry you over to Nan's. I guess she's anxious to get on her way. We sure don't want to keep her waiting." Lowering his voice, he added, "Nan can be a bit of a drama queen. She, uh, likes to make mountains out of molehills."

Ellie shared a worried look with John. She'd really hoped this Nan was going to be as delight-ful as Brenda and Tony had been. She was starting to think that wasn't going to be the case.

With the decision made, the four of them got

to their feet, folded laundry, packed bags, stacked dishes, and then hustled back to the Suburban. In John's and Ellie's hands were peanut butter and jelly sandwiches, bags of corn chips, and something called Ho Hos.

"Good luck, you two," Brenda said as she waved them off. "I'll be praying for you both. Merry Christmas and don't forget to write!"

"Merry Christmas!" John called out.

"Merry Christmas!" Ellie added, feeling a little lump in her throat. She was going to miss this happy couple.

"I'll have you there in no time at all," Tony said.

"*Danke*," Ellie whispered.

Sitting next to her in the back seat, John slipped his hand in hers. "It'll be all right," he whispered. "We've already gotten through so much. I feel certain that this next leg of our journey will go smoothly."

"I hope so."

"Come on now. Think positive."

"You're right. There is so much to be grateful for." She smiled at him as Tony drove down the highway. That was true. She was grateful. Though, at the moment, all she seemed to be able to think about was how wonderful his hand felt surrounding hers.

Chapter 11

It was toasty warm in the Prius. Maybe even a little too warm for John's taste, but he kept that opinion to himself. The important thing was that they were getting closer to their destination.

Well, that they were getting closer and that Tony and Brenda's friend Nan was still on the road.

"I'm not much for driving in the snow, but it don't seem to bother Miss Blue here in the slightest. She just keeps a'trucking as long as I treat her nice and easy," Nan said as she continued to follow two large trucks on the highway. "All the three of us have to do now is hope and pray that the weather doesn't get worse. 'Course, while we're doing that, we ought to spare a thought for these two trucks. They better not decide to veer off the road or do something else that's equally crazy!" She paused, then glanced at John. "Right?"

"Right," John said, though he wasn't actually agreeing with her. No, it was more like he was playing her game, which involved agreeing with whatever Nan said, no matter how outlandish.

The woman didn't exactly take disagreement well.

"Ellie? Ellie, I didn't hear you. What did you say?" Nan asked.

"I'm sorry, I guess I almost fell asleep back here."

"Don't do that," Nan commanded, her voice hard. "You promised to stay awake. You promised. Do you remember that?"

"Yes, of course. I'm sorry. I, uh, misspoke. And, um, I'll do my hoping and praying about the weather and the trucks, too."

"Good," said Nan.

Worried that Nan might quiz Ellie on more things she'd said, John intervened. "Nan, tell me about this stretch of road here in West Virginia. Have you driven on it many a time?"

"Well, this here highway is Interstate 77. On our right and left are some of the prettiest stretches in southern West Virginia. But you have to be careful, you know."

"Careful of what?" Ellie asked.

"Of deer running through like they own the place. That can be treacherous." She paused meaningfully. "Then, too, this snow can turn to ice real easily, which is something I've got to focus on as well."

"It's good you're such a careful driver," Ellie said.

"I sure am, but I didn't used to be. About ten years ago I got in a bad accident and had to have two surgeries. That taught me not to get distracted."

"You seem very vigilant," John said.

"I am. I have my eyes on everyone." She took one hand off the wheel and gestured with it. "It's too bad more people around here can't go saying that."

"I bet."

"Why—" She stopped abruptly as the two trucks turned on their blinkers and exited. "Now, would you look at that? They're leaving us."

Nan was sounding as if she took their departure as a personal insult.

"Is that a problem?" John asked.

"I just told you it would be, son. Their leaving me is going to be a big problem." She wavered for a moment, then turned the wheel to the right and exited the highway as well. The Prius's rear wheels squealed as they slid on a slick spot.

John was suddenly glad that they'd learned to hold on tight when Fred had been driving.

Ellie, unfortunately, did not take the unexpected detour with much grace. "What are you doing?" she called out.

"I'm exiting the highway. Obviously. My tank is on empty."

Nan barreled down the exit ramp as if she were depending on those two trucks for salvation.

John gripped the side of the door, then squealed when they came practically face-to-face with a pair of dark eyes and a sizable set of antlers. "Deer!"

"Where? Oh . . . oh." With a slew of poorly

chosen and rather colorful words, Nan slammed on her brakes and skidded. Barely missing the wayward deer.

The vehicle slid to the right, tires screeching, and at last came to a stop right across from a gas station. "Come on, Blue. You can do it," she coaxed.

Whether the car listened to her, or the Lord took pity on them, Miss Blue at last limped into the gas station before petering out to a stop.

"I'm gonna need your fifty dollars," Nan said.

"We already gave it to you," Ellie said.

"No, you gave me that fifty for the first part of the trip. This is now the second half."

John shook his head. "I was in the room when Tony spoke to you. He told you that we only had fifty dollars. You told him that was fine because you drove a Prius."

"That's true. It was fine—for each time we filled the gas tank."

"But we don't have any more money!" Ellie protested.

Nan unbuckled her seat belt, turned around to face Ellie, and sighed. "I'm afraid, my dear, that we now have a problem."

"I can't believe we've been left again," Ellie moaned, pulling her winter cloak more tightly around herself. "What is wrong with us?"

"Nothing is wrong. We're fine. We're better

than fine," he said. "It's practically everyone else who has problems. Nan was more addled than a cuckoo bird in a cuckoo clock."

"I used to think that. With Fred, I was sure that we were in the right, and he was in the wrong." She sat down on a plastic bucket that someone had been using as a chair. Above her, the neon sign naming the gas station flickered, casting a blue and red glow over her face. "But now? Well, I don't think it's just bad luck. We must be doing something that annoys people."

John opened his mouth to argue, then thought better of it. "Maybe not . . . but you might have a point."

She rolled her eyes. "It's big of you to agree with me."

"You don't need to get snippy. Come now. You have to agree that Nan Randall had a screw loose, and it had nothing to do with Miss Blue."

"I'll give you that. I thought Fred was difficult, but Nan was as unstable as . . . as . . ." She looked up. "As this flickering light above me. One moment she was bright and even. The next, she looked in danger of breaking down."

"I couldn't have described her better." He noticed then that the wind had picked up. On its heels was a scattering of snow, either flakes that were being blown off the top of the gas station or perhaps fresh snow from the heavens. "We need to find a place to take shelter."

"You're right. It's gonna get colder, and it's probably not too safe around here, either."

He held out a hand to help her up and kept her hand in his as they approached the road. It was a rural town, but there were sidewalks. Someone had even attempted to shovel them in the last couple of hours. That was a nice surprise.

By mutual agreement, they walked side by side, Ellie's sad-looking suitcase rolling awkwardly behind them. There was barely enough room for the two of them, what with the snow banks on either side of them, but they made it work.

"Are you doing all right, John?"

Her question, so full of concern, took him by surprise. "Of course. Why?"

"You've been in Florida for years now. The snow and cold take some getting used to."

Come to think of it, the frigid wind did seem to bother him more than it did her, but he wasn't going to admit it. "I'm *gut*. The backpack helps some. Take care now, the sidewalk is slick, *jah*?"

"I'll be careful."

They walked another two blocks, each scanning the area. John wasn't sure what they were looking for. Maybe a sign? Maybe someone standing on the street offering shelter?

Of course, there wasn't another person around. When the wind picked up, causing them both to shiver, he knew they had to do something, even if it was to hunker down in an empty barn. Anything would be better—and safer—than remaining outside in the elements.

He began to study some of the buildings they passed, trying to imagine if any of them could provide shelter even in a garage.

After they crossed the next intersection, he spied a few promising candidates. There seemed to be some occupied buildings to the left and right. "Ellie, it's your choice. Which door should we knock on?"

"It doesn't matter," she said. "Maybe . . . oh! What about there?" she asked, pointing to another building about one block up.

A burst of wind had come up, catching the fallen snow with it and temporarily swirling it in the air. For a few seconds he couldn't see anything; then, just when he was about to admit that he couldn't see anything, he spotted the steeple. "You found a church."

"I did." She sounded pleased. "How about we try to take shelter inside? People are supposed to keep churches open all the time, right?"

He wasn't sure if that was always the case or not. Unlike most other Amish communities, in Pinecraft there was an actual church building for Amish to worship in. But since it served several purposes, including something like a multipurpose center, the doors weren't always open. They'd learned the hard way that not every person who walked by the building was respectful of the property.

But he did seem to remember other people saying that they occasionally left their church's sanctuary open for those in need. That certainly described Ellie and him.

"I think it's worth a try. If the door isn't unlocked, then maybe there's a shed or something nearby."

"Or a stable," she murmured, humor lightening her voice.

How many other people would be making a little joke at this moment? Her quip had made him smile—and he hadn't thought that possible. "You are amazing, Ellie."

"Why do you say that?"

"Because we've had some of the roughest, most unsettled, frustrating days in our lives and are currently freezing in the middle of West Virginia, but you are still able to look for something positive."

She seemed to think about his observation before nodding at last. "It has been everything you've just described, John. But I can't help but think that hasn't been *everything*. There have been some good moments, too."

"You're right," he said. In fact, some of those moments were so sweet, he reckoned they'd stay in his heart for a very long time.

It took them another ten minutes, but at last

they reached the church. It was a stucco building, not all that big. Surrounding it were numerous flower beds. John imagined that it was something to see in the spring and summer.

"Look, John. Stained glass."

And there was a flickering light on the other side. The stained glass glowed in different shades of white, yellow, and gold. The light illuminating it made the glass sparkle and shine.

"Look at that star," he murmured.

Ellie looked up at the sky. "There are a lot out tonight."

"No, I mean the stained glass. Look at what's shining so bright for us."

She turned in his direction and gasped. "Now, isn't that the prettiest thing you've ever seen?"

He couldn't deny it. There was something about seeing that beautiful light shining through the glass so close to Christmas that did seem glorious.

Maybe even awe-inspiring.

"Let's go try the doors."

Ellie stayed by his side. It was as if she, like him, didn't want to be alone—whether the doors opened for them or stayed shut.

"Let's say a prayer first," Ellie said. Closing her eyes, she spoke out loud. "Lord, I know you are in charge and you've been looking out for us this whole time. But please help us stay strong tonight. I think we need you more than ever."

"Amen," he whispered before his hand covered hers on the door's brass handle. "Let's give it a try on the count of three. One."

"Two."

"Three." Together, they pulled.

The door opened wide without even a hint of a creak. Wordlessly, he followed her inside.

Chapter 12

The inside of the little church smelled like incense. It was an unfamiliar scent; Ellie couldn't even recall if she'd ever come in contact with incense before. But Ellie knew what it was all the same. The room had an appealing aroma clinging to it. Something rich and complex. Almost as if a myriad of scents and smells had decided to linger there, along with a good amount of prayer and hope.

No place had ever felt so welcoming.

Resting a hand on the edge of one of the long, padded pews, Ellie tried to get her bearings. They were inside a lovely, empty, open church. For the first time in days, she felt both safe and relaxed.

It was blessedly silent, too. After all the days of traveling, of being in the constant company of strangers, engines, cars, and everything else to be found in big cities, this quiet sanctuary was a blessing. The only noise she heard was the sound of the door shutting behind them with a solid *thunk* and their muted footsteps on the carpet runner covering the center aisle. John had returned from his exploratory walk outside.

As her eyes adjusted to the dim light, she noticed that there were three candles burning near the stained glass window.

"It's so much warmer in here than outside," John said. "Ellie, I was starting to think that I was never going to feel my nose again when we walked that last mile."

"Me too." She blinked, realizing that her skin was thawing. "I've never been so glad to be warm!"

John had unbuttoned his coat. With a look of distaste, he shook off a couple of drops of water and then rested it on the back of one of the pews.

"Are you that warm already?"

"I think my coat was that wet and cold."

Again, it was as if her senses were functioning about a minute or two after his. "I'm going to do the same thing."

She loosened her cloak's hook and eye, pulled it off her shoulders, and rested it next to his. Her skin still felt a little chilled but better. With a sigh, she sat down. "I was starting to get worried."

"Me too," he said as he sat down next to her. "I'm glad you spied this church."

"I wonder if the pastor here leaves candles burning in the window every night. What do you think?"

"Maybe just when it's so close to Christmas Eve?"

"That's what I think, too."

He opened his pack. "Hey, I have a couple of crackers left from Brenda and Tony. Do you want some?"

"How about we put our bounty together. I have a granola bar and an apple." She pulled out both and placed them on a bulletin that someone had left behind from a previous service. "Want to take the first bite?"

"Sure." He bit into the crisp Gala, then handed it back to her. She carefully bit into the other side. The sweet taste seemed to awaken her taste buds. "I don't think anything has ever tasted so good," she said as she passed it back to him.

Two more times, they passed the apple back and forth. The intimacy of the action only made her smile instead of being embarrassed. When there was essentially only the core left, she broke the granola bar into two sections while John divided the remaining crackers in the ziplock bag.

They were finished in just a few moments. "I'm going to look to see if there's a bathroom," she said.

"Great idea."

They were blessed again. There were two small bathrooms. Both of the doors were open, and both seemed to be lit by battery-operated candles. Ellie washed her hands and splashed some water on her face.

When they were sitting side by side again, John leaned back on the cushioned bench. "I'm so tired. Do you mind if I go to sleep?"

"I was about to tell you that I don't think I'm

going to be able to keep my eyes open for another minute."

John walked to the bench across from her, pulled off his boots, and lay down. She kept her boots on but stretched out as well.

Within minutes, she heard John's breathing even out; then he fell silent. To her surprise, she realized she now knew some of his sleep patterns. In addition, knowing he was nearby comforted her, and not because she felt safer being next to him in a strange place. No, it was more that she liked not being alone.

All her life, though she'd enjoyed being with her family and friends, she'd felt just as comfortable being alone. That feeling had intensified as she'd grown older, culminating in her solitary trip to Pinecraft. Ellie realized now that her choice to travel by herself hadn't come as a surprise to her parents. Instead of attempting to convince her to stay home, they'd given her their blessing.

Now, as she lay on a cushioned pew across the aisle from John Miller, she wondered if this journey they'd been on had all been a part of God's plan. It seemed he'd known that she needed an extra push in order to finally fall in love.

Fall in love?

The thought was so jarring, she jolted upright. So fast that a foot hit the floor with a loud clap.

The sound of it seemed to have been magnified.

John jerked awake. Propping himself up on an elbow, he called out, "Ellie? What's wrong?"

"Nothing. I'm fine. Everything's fine." Well, everything was not fine, but she certainly wasn't going to tell him what was on her mind!

While he shifted and fell back to sleep, she took off her boots, curled in a ball on her side, and finally pulled her cloak over her. It wasn't completely dry, but its weight warmed her.

She decided to concentrate on that. On the cloak's weight and the fact that they were safe and warm. Little by little, her body eased, and sleep drifted closer.

She was grateful for the rest . . . and at last dissolved into a light slumber, all while attempting to match each breath with John's.

Perhaps another time she would think about why it was so easy to fall asleep next to John. Or wonder how she would feel when he was no longer a part of her life.

Chapter 13

Christmas Eve, morning

"Jesus, Mary, and Joseph! Kyle! Trudy! Wayne, get over here!"

"Ellen, for Pete's sake. Stop being such a drama queen. It's almost Christmas morning, don'tcha know. You don't need to be yelling loud enough to wake the dead."

"I have every reason to be in a dither. There's a couple in here. They're asleep on two of the pews."

"A couple what?"

"What do you think? A couple of kids, that's what."

Half asleep, John struggled to get to his feet. When he turned around, he spied two couples in their sixties or seventies staring at him from the back of the church.

After checking to make sure that Ellie was all right, he swallowed. Tried to come up with something appropriate to say—even though it was a given that there actually wasn't anything appropriate to say in that moment.

As the silence continued, he stuffed his hands in his pockets. "Merry Christmas Eve."

A gray-haired woman blinked her eyes behind

a pair of gold wire-rimmed glasses. "Merry Christmas Eve to you, too."

One of the men, who was wearing dark blue overalls, a plaid flannel shirt, and a heavy-looking shearling coat over it, stepped forward. He stared at John; then his eyes widened as Ellie also got to her feet. "My word. Are you two kids Amish?" He'd obviously gotten a good look at her dress and *kapp*.

"*Jah*," Ellie said. "I mean, yes."

One of the women cautiously approached, as if she was worried either Ellie or John was about to bolt. "Are you all right, dear? Are you in trouble? Are you hungry?" She glanced at them both. "Are you two married?"

"Um . . ." When Ellie looked his way again, she was wearing a deer-in-the-headlights type of expression.

He crossed the aisle to stand next to her. "Well, uh, we are in trouble, in the sense that we were abandoned at a gas station in your town. It was a shame, too, because we're trying to get to Berlin, Ohio, by Christmas Day. . . ."

"But other than that, I'd say we are all right," Ellie said. "And we had something to eat yesterday. . . ."

"We were also grateful that your church was open and that you had a candle in the window," John added. "Your stained glass star led us to safety."

One by one, each of the visitors sat down nearby. After they introduced themselves, Wayne said, "Maybe, if you'd be so kind, you could tell us about this journey of yours."

John sat down next to Ellie and smiled at her. "Do you want to begin, or should I?"

Forty minutes later, after going back and forth with Ellie, John finished up the story. "So that's how we ended up here last night."

All four of the church members said nothing for several minutes.

"I promise, we're harmless," Ellie said. "We, um, have just had a very long journey."

"You two have been through enough. We need to get you to Amish Country, Ohio, stat," Ellen said.

"We need help to make this happen," Wayne agreed as he pulled out his cell phone. "I'm on it."

John must have been tired, because all he could seem to do was stare at them in shock.

Trudy walked to their sides. "First things first, though. You two need to get out of this sanctuary and into my kitchen. You need a good breakfast."

Ellie had tears in her eyes when she stood up. "Thank you. Thank you all for being so kind."

Kyle put his hands on his hips. "Young man, you aren't going to put up a fuss about this, are you?"

John realized then that he would do whatever it took so Ellie would stop crying. He'd come to care for her that much.

He'd also learned over the last couple of days that he had to trust in the goodness of strangers and believe that the Lord was directing him based on His will. After all, even Fred and Nan had helped carry them toward Berlin.

"Not at all," he said as he reached for his coat.

Trudy and her husband Kyle were impressive. They were able to give orders simultaneously, attend to numerous tasks, and somehow be comforting all the while.

As the minutes passed, John realized that he no longer felt the same weight on his shoulders as he had during the previous forty-eight hours. Kyle and Trudy seemed truly invested, sincere, and intent on helping him and Ellie get home.

And, he realized with some shock, after all these years, after all the time he'd spent pretending he didn't care, he now realized that seeing his father one last time was exactly what home had come to mean to him.

"John, are you sure you won't have seconds? There's plenty."

With some surprise, he noticed his plate was empty. He'd eaten a huge portion of Trudy's egg casserole along with two waffles and three strips of bacon.

And he was stuffed.

"Thank you, but I couldn't eat another bite." Suddenly realizing that it wasn't an accident she'd had so much food already prepared, he swallowed in embarrassment. "I'm sorry, did I just eat your breakfast?"

"Not all of it," the woman replied with a laugh. She shook her head when he started to apologize. "No, don't do that. It's too much for two people to eat anyway. Kyle and I are real pleased that you and Ellie are here. You've made us feel like it's really Christmas."

John didn't understand how that was possible. Coming upon two needy souls on the pews in their church wasn't anything anyone would hope or ask for.

But he didn't dare dispute her words.

There was something in her eyes that told him she was telling him the truth. He needed to respect that.

Chapter 14

Christmas Eve, 1:00 p.m.

You still doing okay back there, Ellie?" Trudy asked from the front passenger seat as her husband drove down the plowed highway. They were currently headed toward Columbus. From there, they'd drive northwest to Holmes County.

"*Jah*," she replied before realizing that she'd spoken Pennsylvania Dutch. "I mean, yes, I am good." It was almost hard to believe, but they were finally headed straight for Berlin.

Trudy turned to smile at her. "Glad to hear it."

Ellie smiled back, thinking that she was glad as well. She was currently sitting in the back seat of a dark gray Subaru Outback next to John. They'd begun the final leg of the journey just an hour after Trudy had served them breakfast. She'd invited them both to come to her house to shower and change so they'd be comfortable in the car.

That had been the first of many gifts the kind people had given them. After being served a delicious breakfast, Trudy and her husband had prepared the car for the road trip while John and Ellie had showered and changed.

When they'd entered the vehicle, John had chuckled. "These folks are as close to miracle workers as I've ever met. Look at everything they put in here for us, Ellie."

Someone had placed two pillows, blankets, and a little container of snacks and water for them. Tears had threatened to fall when she'd met the couple's eyes.

"*Danke*," she'd said in a hoarse voice. After all the close calls they'd had, it was hard to believe that this was the way they were ending their journey.

"Don't you get yourself all worked up, sweetie," Kyle had said. "This is just simple kindness."

A few minutes after that, they'd been on their way. The roads between Beckley in West Virginia and Columbus were windy and snow covered. Surprisingly, they hadn't passed any big accidents yet, and they'd been traveling for a little over three hours.

No, their caravan had been traveling for a little over three hours. Four vehicles filled with members of the small congregation had decided to accompany them. A young couple in their early twenties had jokingly told them that the tale of Ellie and John's adventure had spread through the congregation like wildfire.

"A group of us decided to make sure that nothing goes wrong during the last leg of your trip," the man had said. "We have backup vehicles in case anyone breaks down."

"We're grateful to you for that," John had said with a grin.

During a recent rest stop, Kyle had announced that they would likely arrive in Berlin by two o'clock. They'd almost made it.

Trudy and Kyle had begun playing Christmas music on the radio, giving Ellie and John a little bit of privacy to converse. Leaning closer, she said, "Are you ready to see your father?"

"I think so." After a brief pause, he added, "I'm ashamed about the way I spoke about both my *daed* and my plans to go back when we first met. I sounded selfish and uncaring."

She thought he was being too hard on himself. "It was more like scared and maybe bitter."

He shrugged. "Perhaps."

"Do you feel different about seeing him now?"

"I think so." He paused, obviously choosing each word with care. "I've come to understand some things during our journey, I think. I realized that just because I don't agree with someone about most things doesn't mean I can't forgive him. Or love him. More important, I've realized that love and goodness don't always have to be equal."

Ellie puzzled over his words in her mind, but they didn't make sense. "How do you mean?"

"I think all this time I've been in Florida, I kept putting conditions and constrictions on my willingness to forgive. You know, if my father ever came to Florida to see me, then I *might* listen to what he had to say. And, if his speech contained an apology, then I *might* think he was worthy of my forgiveness. Things like that." He lowered his voice. "Now, I find it hard to believe I was so judgmental."

"Oh, John." Ellie felt for him. Not only for the pain and bitterness he'd been keeping inside him but for his bravery in sharing his thoughts with her.

Nodding, he pursed his lips. "Even saying the words out loud embarrasses me, because I know that ain't how forgiveness or love works."

"My mother once told me that babies are God's way of proving that there's such a thing as unconditional love."

A line formed between his brows. "But everyone loves babies."

"Her point was that babies only take and take from the people who love them. When they are really small, they don't even smile at you. But still mothers and fathers love them unconditionally."

"Your mother is a smart woman." He shifted, smoothing a fold in the fuzzy knit blanket resting over his lap. "Now that I've witnessed so many people's efforts to help us, I'm even more convinced that life isn't about checks and balances. It's about doing the best you can—and being able to accept the consequences."

"I think one day you are going to be really thankful you went on this journey. You're going to be glad that you traveled so far to see your father one last time."

"I already am." After peeking at Trudy and Kyle again, he reached out and clasped her hand. "If we hadn't gone on this journey, we wouldn't have met each other."

His words warmed her insides. She'd been thinking that as well but had been afraid to be so bold. "We surely wouldn't have grown so close if we hadn't been through so much together."

"That's right. So that's a blessing right there."

"Ten minutes away, kids!" Kyle called out.

Ellie grinned. "We've almost done it."

He squeezed her hand gently. "The Lord has surely been guiding us. With His help, we have almost made it."

Two hours later, John was sitting next to his father's bedside in a small room that smelled of disinfectant.

Lying in the hospital bed, his father had made hardly a sound. John wasn't even sure if he realized his son was there. When John had first arrived, he'd asked the kind nurse for the latest prognosis. She'd only said that his father didn't have much time left.

John had been shocked by the changes that had taken place in the man. His memories of his father were of someone larger than life. Invincible, unyielding, harsh.

The man lying in the bed next to him was pale and fragile-looking. Frail and slight. John wondered if the changes had taken place because of the cancer or had happened slowly over the fifteen years while they'd been estranged.

Thinking about his earlier conversation with Ellie, John at last gave up his bitterness. He discarded his need for an apology. Instead, he let the Lord's will flow through him.

"I'm glad I'm here, Daed," he said out loud. "Even though we had our differences and maybe never saw eye to eye, I am grateful that you gave me life. I know Mamm's death and Jo taking off left you feeling wounded. I know you didn't realize how much you were hurting me—because your pain was so deep. I hope you did eventually recover. I hope the Lord will give you peace very soon."

The monitor attached to his father's body didn't change. Nothing in the room really did. Only the stillness that surrounded him felt eased, as if the Lord had heard his words, knew he was speaking from the heart and was pleased.

"Do you need anything, John?" The nurse asked when she peeked in the doorway almost an hour later. "Would you care for a cup of coffee?"

"Thank you."

"I'll be back."

When she left the room, John got to his feet, stretched his arms above his head, and rubbed his hands over his face. He walked to the door to meet the nurse when she returned with a cardboard cup filled with steaming coffee.

After taking a sip, then another, he turned to sit down . . . and saw his father staring directly at him. His brown eyes looked almost clear.

"You're awake," John said as he hurried back to his chair by the bed. "Daed, it's . . . it's good to see your eyes."

When his father didn't say anything, only stared, John added, "It's me, John. Your son. I came up here to see you."

His father stared hard at him, then seemed to summon every last bit of energy his body had. "John."

Emotion clogged his throat as he nodded. "*Jah*, it is I."

His father continued to stare. One minute passed, then two as he seemed to take in every inch of John's very being. Then, with a weak sigh, he closed his eyes again.

"Daed," John said. "Daed?" Afraid, he frantically looked at the monitor. Nothing had changed. The line was still jumping with every heartbeat.

For the first time since his journey began, John felt hopeful. If his father had woken up once and recognized him, he would do so again. John just had to wait. To wait and be patient.

He finished his coffee, set the empty cup on the table next to him. Kicked his legs out and closed his eyes. Prayed for his father. Prayed for everyone who had helped his father in the nursing home. Finally, as his body relaxed, he prayed for Ellie and gave thanks that the Lord had brought her into his life.

"John? Mr. Miller?"

He startled awake. "Yes?" he asked as he stood up. "I'm sorry. I must have fallen asleep."

"I'm so sorry, John," the nurse said. "Your father died just moments ago. He passed in his sleep."

"He's out of pain, then."

The nurse reached out and squeezed his shoulder. "He is. I feel certain that he's in a better place now. I'm sorry for your loss."

When she left the room, John stared at his father again. His eyes were still closed, but he seemed now to only be a shell of himself.

John knew there would likely come a day when he would cry and mourn, but at that moment, all he felt was relief. He'd made it to his father's side so he didn't have to die alone.

And the Lord had gifted his father with one last bit of energy. He'd enabled his *daed* to say John's name, so John would always know that his efforts had not been in vain.

He was so very grateful for that.

Chapter 15

Mere minutes after the caravan had dropped off Ellie at her grandmother's house, the rest of her family showed up at the door. Though Ellie was surprised, Mommi didn't seem to be. In fact, she seemed delighted.

When Ellie's aunt Esther arrived at the door with a cake in her hands, Ellie was even more confused—until she remembered that it was Christmas Eve. Of course, everyone would have planned to celebrate together.

For the next hour, they ate cake while Ellie told a very brief account of her journey. Eventually, most of the extended family members left and there was only her grandmother Martha; her sister, Beth; her brother-in-law, Luke; the newborn baby Leena, and her parents.

"Now that it is just us, I want to know what really happened," Mommi said with a grin.

"Oh, Mommi . . ."

"Come now, child. Let me hear about your adventure. I could use a good story."

"Well, all right. But to do the story justice, I'm afraid it's going to take a while."

"Those are the best kind," Daed said. "Start at the beginning."

"And don't leave anything out," Beth added.

After taking a fortifying sip of her grandmother's spiced tea, Ellie began. She relayed the whole crazy, convoluted tale—starting with the moment she'd met John Miller in front of the bulletin board in Pinecraft. Her family seemed to enjoy the tale, but Ellie realized that they were only hearing the events. Not how scary and emotional the journey had actually been for her and John.

Everyone had chuckled at the part when Fred had driven off, not seeming to understand just how terrified she'd been. Their unexpected reactions continued to surprise her as she told the rest of the story. When Beth had the nerve to quip that she'd always thought Ellie's habit of speaking her mind would get her in trouble one day, Ellie had been hurt.

"Our misfortunes weren't my fault."

"Of course, they weren't, dear," Mamm said as she patted Ellie's hand. "But you do have to admit it is noteworthy that more than one person thought you and John Miller to be a handful."

Her father chuckled. "Come now. It likely weren't their fault that Nan was so cross when they wouldn't give her any more money."

Likely? "It wasn't our fault at all. Plus, she left us at an empty gas station!" Ellie folded her arms across her chest. She was starting to wonder why she'd been asked to rush home if her family saw her as nothing but a foolish girl. She'd thought she'd been needed, but it felt as if everyone was just humoring her now.

"Don't be so sensitive, daughter," her father chided. "You know we are glad you are home. We were worried something awful."

"I prayed for you the whole time," Mommi added.

"I'm glad you weren't alone. Thank the Lord for that John Miller," Beth added as she held Luke's hand. "It's too bad we won't get a chance to meet him. He sounds like a wonderful man."

"I'm sure you'll miss him, Ellie," Mamm said.

"I was hoping I could invite him over for supper, Mamm. He doesn't have anyone here, you know."

"I would love that. When should we have him over?"

"I'm not sure. I guess I'll have to find out when he can leave his father's side."

"What home is his *daed* in?"

"Healing Hearts in Berlin."

"I have an idea." Getting to his feet, Daed said, "I'm gonna take the buggy over to the nursing home and make sure this fella is taken care of."

"John might not want to leave, Daed."

"If he don't, he don't," her father said. "But if John is in need of a break, then he can break bread with us. After all, it's almost Christmas. Ain't so, Ellie?"

Feeling a little stunned, she nodded.

After her father and Luke left, she leaned down to her grandmother's ear. "Do you want some more Christmas tea, *Grandmommi*?" she asked.

"*Nee*, I have had enough, especially if we might be hosting your young man later."

Feeling her mother's and sister's gazes on her, Ellie said, "He's not exactly that."

"He could be though, *jah*?" Beth asked gently.

Ellie had been through too much not to speak from the heart. "*Jah*. I think he could, if John felt the same way."

"I've always known you to be a *gut* girl, Ellie," Grandmommi murmured as she patted Ellie's hand. "But you are a brave one, too. Don't give up on your dreams."

"I won't."

"I hope not. If you can make it all the way from Florida to here, you can make other dreams come true. You must believe."

"*Danke*, Grandmommi. I'll remember."

"I hope so. The Lord always provides, but I've also always thought that He likes it when we do our part."

"Indeed," Mamm said with a smile.

Mommi nodded as her eyes slid closed. "He is always *gut* and true," she murmured before falling asleep once again.

Gazing at her grandmother, Ellie felt her heart soften. Her grandmother was such a good person.

So kind, too. One day, perhaps, she would be half as good.

When Martha's breathing deepened, they moved to the living room.

"Do you really think John might be the one for you?" Mamm asked. "You've only known this young man for a few days."

"I think he is. And you must remember, we spent a lot of time together. Many more hours than the usual courting couple."

"If he is the one, then I am happy for you, dear," Mamm said.

Ellie glanced at her in surprise. "I didn't expect you to be so agreeable."

"Hearing about your journey made me realize how much you've grown—and how much I fear we've all come to rely on you. It wasn't fair of all of us to ask you to hurry home just because Leena was born, and I didn't want to leave Beth's side."

"It wasn't fair of me to expect Mamm and Daed to drop everything, either," Beth added.

"I don't know if asking me to come home was fair or not," Ellie said. "It doesn't matter, anyway. I've realized that I like to be needed. Maybe sometimes too much." Thinking of how each incident had propelled her toward the next one, she added, "Besides, if you hadn't asked me to return, I wouldn't have been standing at the bulletin board at the same time John was, so we would never have met."

They spent the next hour cleaning the kitchen and planning supper. Just as her mother said that she should go home and start cooking, they heard the buggy arrive.

"Ah, your father has returned," Mamm said. "And look who he has brought with him!"

Peeking out the window, Ellie smiled. Her father and Beth's husband, Luke, were standing next to his buggy with John Miller, just as if they were friends.

Holding Leena in her arms, her sister said, "Let's go save your beau from Daed's pesky questions and stories. If we don't do something, Daed'll likely never bring him inside."

Her sister was joking, but she did have a good point. Ellie grabbed a cloak from one of the hooks on the wall and then hurried out the door.

Her mother and Beth, holding Leena, followed. Their laughter filled the air like pretty bells, brightening Ellie's spirits.

Chapter 16

After visiting with Ellie's parents, grand-mother, and sister, it was decided that John would spend the night in the guest bedroom at Ellie's grandmother's house.

The family had also decided to have their traditional Christmas Eve dinner the following evening, on Christmas Day. Everyone wanted to have some time to prepare the meal, to allow Ellie and John to recover from their journey, and to give John time to grieve his father. All of that was a blessing indeed.

To John's surprise, Ellie's parents left soon after her *mommi* had gone to sleep. They'd said something about needing to take care of their animals but would be back in the morning.

When John had shared his surprise that they would leave Ellie unchaperoned, she simply shrugged. "It's pretty obvious that we've been alone before."

After checking on her grandmother one last time, Ellie joined him in front of the fireplace. "She said to tell you Merry Christmas, John," Ellie said as she sat down on the sofa next to him.

He looked at the clock on the living room wall. "It is late, isn't it?"

"Just one hour until Christmas Day."

"I still can't believe we made it back in time."

"Me neither."

She smiled at him before nervously clasping her hands together. "Isn't this something? I feel kind of awkward and shy all of a sudden."

"I feel the same way. Part of me wants to treat you more formally, like I was a gentleman caller, and the other part of me needs you near." Scooting a bit closer to her, he added, "I'm glad you didn't take the chair next to the fire. I guess it's going to take some time to get used to being apart."

They sat in silence for a spell, simply watching the flames. John had been sure he would be feeling melancholy, but instead he felt at peace. He'd gotten to see his father one last time, and he would always be grateful for that.

Eventually, Ellie broke the silence. "I'm going to miss you when you head back to Florida."

"I'm going to miss you, too." He stared at the fire again, then added, "Back when we were at the truck stop in Jacksonville, I never could've guessed that we would be sitting here together at your *grandmommi*'s *haus* on Christmas Eve."

"I wouldn't have imagined that happening, either." She giggled. "For a while there, I couldn't even imagine being clean!"

He chuckled. "I don't think I'll ever take a hot shower for granted again." Growing serious, he added, "It turns out that I am very thankful for a lot of things. For the Lord giving me the opportunity to see my father one last time, for the many blessings and goodness of strangers on our journey . . . but most of all, for you."

Her breath hitched as she looked into his eyes. There, he saw the same things that were in his heart—hope, gratitude, warmth.

"I am grateful and thankful for you, too, John," she whispered.

He reached for both of her hands. "Ellie, I don't want to leave here without knowing when we'll see each other again. I think there's something special between us. I think the Lord intends for us to have a future together. I want there to be."

"I do, too."

His heart filled with happiness. Pressing his lips to the back of one of her hands, he realized that this was likely the first of many evenings they'd spend together. It was okay that nothing between them was settled yet—they had plenty of time to plan a future. All they had to do now was decide when one of them was going to travel to see the other.

And that thought, of course, made him smile. "Uh-oh."

"What?" Ellie asked.

"If we're going to be courting, then we'll be traveling between Pinecraft and Charm again."

Ellie giggled. "I feel certain that any other trip is going to be far less eventful."

"It has to be. I, for one, won't mind traveling to see you."

"I won't mind it, either."

"Yep, we'll continue seeing each other every couple of months until . . ." He stopped, hesitating to say what he was thinking.

"Until what, John?"

"Well, until we both feel that the only way we want to go through our lives is together, Ellie."

"I'll look forward to that day," she whispered.

"I will, too." Glancing at the clock, he noticed that it was after midnight. "Hey, it's Christmas. Merry Christmas."

"And so it is. Merry Christmas, John."

After a second's hesitation, he curved an arm around her shoulders. Ellie leaned close, eventually resting her head on his shoulder and a hand on his chest.

His body relaxed. They'd not only reached the end of their journey but had a new and better one planned for the future. At long last, everything felt good in the world. So right.

John realized that it shouldn't have come as a surprise. After all, it was Christmas Day.

Star of Wonder

Charlotte Hubbard

For Neal, always my brightest star

Chapter 1

After a deadly dull Monday morning of filling small plastic containers with colored sugars and Christmas jimmies, Lizzie Zehr loaded them onto her wheeled cart and headed into the main room of Promise Lodge's new bulk store. It was boring work, all that scooping and labeling— repetitive and downright lonely, being stuck back in the warehouse by herself.

But compared to slaving in her older sister Maria's bakery or, for years before that, running the household for their eldest, crippled sister, Malinda, it was a piece of cake.

And because Dale Kraybill was paying her, it was *freedom*. This job was her ticket to independence, an escape from the two bossy sisters who'd been running her ragged for most of her eighteen years. Their parents had passed when she was very young, so Lizzie's sisters had raised her as best they could—and they expected her to be grateful. She was, of course. But she was also *really* tired of being at their beck and call.

Lizzie's thoughts shifted into a higher gear the moment she spotted the guy who was talking to Dale. The two fellows were hanging wooden signboards, which caught her eye because of their sparkly gold stars—but the shimmer of their glittery paint paled the moment the younger man turned around. In his green paisley shirt, red jeans, and backswept black hair, he looked anything but Plain, and when he met her gaze through his red-framed glasses, Lizzie immediately knew they were soul mates. Like her, this free spirit was gnashing at the bit and refusing to conform to the religious limitations he'd been raised with.

Like her, he wanted *out.*

"Hey there," he said. His voice, barely audible from across the cavernous room, spoke volumes to Lizzie's restless heart.

Afraid to say something stupid, she merely nodded and held his gaze. She heard the secretive whisper of soft, small objects hitting a hard surface—or maybe it was the feathery swishing of angels' wings—

"Lizzie, watch what—you're spilling jimmies all over the floor!" Dale cried out.

She blinked. She had no memory of picking up a container, just as she didn't realize she'd been squeezing it so tightly that the lid had popped off. The sight of red, white, and green jimmies bouncing off her bare feet—she wore flip-flops year-round to show off her painted toenails—was suddenly the funniest thing she'd ever seen. As Lizzie sprinted into the warehouse for a broom, her laughter filled the store.

Her life was finally taking a turn for the better. She just knew it.

• • •

With the girl's laughter still dancing in his head, Raymond Overholt tried to refocus his thoughts. If he didn't convince Mr. Kraybill to sell his handmade plaques, his past several weeks of work would be for nothing. He'd have to return home to Coldstream with his tail between his legs and face a long, dreary lifetime of milking his *dat*'s cows. Running a dairy was honest, necessary work but Raymond didn't enjoy spending his early mornings and late afternoons in a smelly barn disinfecting udders any more than the Holsteins liked having him around. Worse yet, if he overslept, his older brothers did the milking and left the hosing down and mucking out of the stalls for *him.*

"If your customers like these plaques, I can make more," he assured the steely-haired storekeeper. "I—I really appreciate having the chance to sell them here in your new store. Our bulk market in Coldstream is dim and overcrowded with merchandise, and even if the owner there had display space, he wants nothing to do with *artwork.* It's that Old Order thing."

Mr. Kraybill smiled knowingly. "*Jah,* Amish stores don't usually carry much that appears English even if they have a lot of customers come in from outside their community to shop," he acknowledged. "But your plaques carry a solid Christmas message—'Wise men still follow

His star' and the lyrics to 'We Three Kings' are meaningful reminders about following our Lord's holy light. Thanksgiving always kicks off the Christmas buying season, so we'll give it a shot, Raymond."

He hoped his grateful grin didn't appear too adolescent—or desperate. Raymond gazed around the store, where a gal in a pleated Amish *kapp* was stocking shelves in the rear. A few early shoppers were pushing carts into the grocery section.

"If you need some extra hands when things get busy these next few weeks, I'd be happy to help, sir," he offered. "I've not worked in a store, but I'm *gut* at tallying sums, and I'm a quick learner."

"I'll keep it in mind," Kraybill said with a nod.

Raymond heard *probably not* in the storekeeper's words, but he'd dealt with people's dismissals before. If he'd dressed in dark broadfall pants with a plain shirt and suspenders—and if he'd chosen glasses with conservative frames—Kraybill might've taken him more seriously. But until he had no other choice but to submit to Old Order ways and join the church, Raymond was determined to wear clothing he liked.

"I'll be back in a few days to see how my signs are selling," he said. "*Denki* for giving me a chance."

As he stepped out into the crisp November air, Raymond shook his head at his pie-in-the-sky thinking. The computerized cash register on the Mennonite storekeeper's counter told him that *tallying sums* wouldn't get him a job there, any more than his artsy individualism would.

But he'd taken a chance. He'd crafted a dozen of his barnboard creations, lavishing his attention on their shimmering stars and their calligraphic lettering. If he sold some of them, at least his brothers and Dat would have to eat their words about how, at twenty, he should be devoting his time and effort to useful work and finding a wife . . . and taking on the Amish faith. Mamm, bless her, was much more encouraging about his talent. In her eyes, however, Raymond saw the soft, unspoken wish that her beloved youngest son would find a purposeful life.

"Hey there, Raymond! I'm Lizzie. Lizzie Zehr."

He turned to see her jogging from the back of the store with her hand extended. As he shook it, Raymond felt a determined grip. Lizzie's pale green eyes glimmered with mischief as she flashed him a smile.

"Your plaques are really cool, Raymond," she continued breathlessly, "and I hope you sell every last one of them! And I hope you'll keep trying for a job here, too, because this place will be *packed* with shoppers until after the holidays! Gotta get back in there and clean up my mess. Just wanted to say hi!"

Before Raymond could respond, Lizzie rushed back the way she'd come. The *flap-flap-flap* in her wake made him realize she was wearing flip-flops despite the snowflakes that were pinging against his face. Her blond hair was pulled back into a high bun, tucked under a small, circular prayer covering. She wore a calf-length dress that whipped around her legs as she ran—a colorful variety of print fabrics joined at the seams with strips of coordinating solid colors.

Lizzie is Mennonite, like Dale Kraybill.

She was a few years younger than he, and her sense of wild abandon made Raymond think Miss Zehr was at loose ends about joining the church, just as he was. He wondered if she'd designed and sewn that unusual dress herself.

The little trail of red, green, and white jimmies she'd left on the ground made Raymond feel happier than he had in ages. Something told him his life had just taken a turn toward *adventure!*

Chapter 2

A s the afternoon sunlight streamed through the front window of the bulk store on Wednesday, Lizzie stood in awe. Raymond's wooden plaques had taken on lives of their own— and blank spots told of two sales. Each sign was about a foot wide and two feet high, made of weathered barn board cut at an angle—but their stars stole the show with their shimmery-glimmery paint and glitter that seemed to pulse and shift as she gazed at them.

She especially liked the ones that read *Star of wonder, Star of night . . . guide us to thy perfect light,* because they inspired her to hum that Christmas carol each time she glanced up at them.

Behind her, someone cleared his throat. "Lizzie, have you forgotten that I've asked you to straighten and restock the canned pumpkin and evaporated milk? Folks will be making their Thanksgiving pies later today, after all."

Lizzie smiled apologetically at the storekeeper. "I'm on it, Dale! Just taking a moment to be inspired by—"

The sight of the young man entering the store chased away all her best intentions, however. With his windblown hair, shy smile, and those

127

outrageous, red-framed spectacles, Raymond appeared even cuter than she remembered him—and she'd spent a *lot* of time recalling their first encounter over the past couple of days.

"Do you need more plaques, Mr. Kraybill?" he said eagerly, although his gaze remained on Lizzie. "Looks like you've sold a couple—"

"We have!" Lizzie agreed. "Not an hour goes by that a customer doesn't remark on how wonderful they are. I think we need to keep several on hand—don't we, Dale?"

The storekeeper blinked. "*Jah,* interest in your signs has been running high—"

"And just this morning you were saying—again—that we need more help," she continued in a voice that rose with her excitement, "so you should probably offer Raymond a job, ain't so?"

She beamed her brightest smile at the young man, who was gawking at her in disbelief, just as Dale was. "Don't know where you're from, Raymond, but I left home to live at Promise Lodge, and you can, too!" she blurted out. "You could rent one of the cabins behind the lodge and eat your meals with us in the dining room, and—"

"Lizzie, *whoa!*" the storekeeper insisted, grasping her shoulder. Dale lowered his voice then, holding her attention with his purposeful gaze. "This is not the time or the place for such a discussion, while customers are here. How about if you get back to work and leave the running of the store to me, please?"

Lizzie noticed several nearby shoppers chuckling as they glanced at her, but she refused to feel embarrassed. "Just putting in a *gut* word," she said, and with fresh inspiration, she pointed at the wall where Raymond's plaques were hung. "If you folks are interested in those fine Christmas signboards, you can ask the artist himself about them, because Raymond's right here among us!"

With a parting smile for the young man, whose cheeks had turned very pink, Lizzie wheeled her cart to the baking aisle a few yards away. With great satisfaction, she heard Dale ask Raymond if he could remain until the store closed at six o'clock. A few moments after he agreed to do that, Raymond went outside and returned with an armload of plaques and a grateful smile on his face.

Wasn't it amazing, what a little enthusiasm could accomplish?

Somehow Lizzie managed to remain focused on her stocking assignment, quickly replenishing the pumpkin pie supplies. When she rolled her cart into the warehouse to reload it, she was pleased to find Raymond chatting with Marlene Fisher, another lodge resident who worked full-time in Dale's store.

"Are you sure you'd want to be here over the

Christmas holiday, Raymond?" Marlene was asking as she deftly stacked bags of marshmallows in her cart. "Your *mamm* would miss you something terrible—"

"*Jah*, but she understands why I want to get out and do something *different*," Raymond put in as he opened a large box with his utility knife. "You know how it is at our place. There's all these peas in a pod—and then there's *me*."

"You two know each other?" Lizzie interrupted.

Marlene looked up from her bags of fat white marshmallows. "We Fishers and the Overholts go way back—we've been members of our church district in Coldstream for several generations," she explained. "Being the youngest, Raymond has always taken special care of his *mamm*, getting her around in her wheelchair at church or for shopping, or wherever she needs to go—not that you could ever call Alma handicapped. But her other sons aren't nearly as patient with her."

"Ah," Lizzie murmured. She tried not to dwell on the image of a woman in a wheelchair, because her sister Malinda had spent several years in one of those contraptions after her MS had gradually rendered her powerless. "So you have lots of brothers, Raymond?"

"Enos, Elmer, Ephraim, and Ezra," he replied with a chuckle. "Mamm said she knew I'd broken the mold the moment I was born. Ezra and I are the only ones still at home, but the other brothers live close enough that they help Dat with the dairy cows."

"Dairy cows," Lizzie repeated, wrinkling her nose. "For all the wiping and disinfecting you have to do twice a day, they still *stink* their entire lives."

Raymond gazed at her in wonderment, as though she'd summed up his lifelong frustration in one sentence. "I knew you'd understand," he murmured as he began opening boxes again.

Lizzie glowed all over. "And hey, if I embarrassed you when I called you out to the customers in the store, I didn't mean to. Sorry," she added softly. "I get a little excited sometimes."

When he shrugged, his maroon shirt tugged against his shoulders. Raymond wasn't as muscular as most guys who farmed, but his tall, slender body appeared firm and fit. "It's okay. A couple of those folks did ask me about my boards, and I had the feeling they'd choose one if I wasn't watching. So I came back here, and Marlene put me to work."

"And although Dale was right about not discussing a job with Raymond in public," Marlene chimed in, "I'll certainly put in a *gut* word about hiring him—even though his folks probably won't like him leaving home. We really could use his help."

It was all the encouragement Lizzie needed.

Shortly after six, when Dale had locked the

131

front door and Marlene had left for her lodge apartment, Lizzie lingered in the warehouse. Her heart thrummed with hopefulness when the middle-aged storekeeper invited Raymond into his office, which was tucked behind the warehouse doors. When the two men were seated inside, she shifted her position so she could hear their voices through Dale's open door without being seen.

"I appreciate your sticking around so we can talk, Raymond," the storekeeper began cordially. "But if you drove a rig here, it'll mean a very late return to Coldstream this evening."

"I hired a driver," Raymond said, "so it's really no trouble. He's waiting for me over at the lodge."

"I'll be happy to pay for your round trip, then, because your Christmas plaques have generated a lot of interest."

Lizzie clasped her hands tightly to keep from applauding. It seemed Dale already had a favorable impression of Raymond, so it wouldn't be long before he was bunking in one of the Promise Lodge cabins. She and the new boarder could become close friends—

"It's true that I can use your help here, son— and Marlene gave you high marks on your reliability and work ethic," Kraybill continued. "But I have to say straight-out that although hiring you for the Christmas season will solve a big problem for me, I sense it'll create an even bigger problem."

Lizzie blinked. After a few moments of silence, Raymond responded.

"How's that, Mr. Kraybill? If I take up residence here at Promise Lodge, I'll bring a large supply of materials to make more of my plaques. I can work on them in the evening after the store closes—"

"But you're a huge distraction to Lizzie. I can't have you two getting moony-eyed in front of customers," Dale explained. "And I'm concerned that Lizzie won't get anything done—except maybe for spilling things. Do you see my predicament?"

Lizzie scowled, barely able to remain hidden behind the stack of boxes. Of *course* she'd spilled those Christmas jimmies the first time Raymond had entered the store. Who wouldn't have been distracted by his unconventional appearance? Not to mention his sheer cuteness. But otherwise, she'd proven herself to be a model employee for the two weeks she'd worked in Dale's store.

"I see what you're saying, sir. And because I'm somewhat older than Lizzie, I'll take responsibility for behaving properly while we're on the job."

Her smile returned. Raymond sounded so mature and responsible—and if it meant he'd lose his job, she would just have to focus on her work while he was around . . . even if her sister Maria had often complained that Lizzie had the attention span of a gnat.

"How old are you, Raymond?"

"I've just turned twenty."

"Marlene has told me your family runs a dairy farm," the storekeeper continued in a no-nonsense tone. "If I hire you, I'll need your assurance that your parents will approve of your working here and that your absence from home won't cause your family a hardship."

Lizzie swallowed hard. When she'd blurted out her suggestion about Raymond taking a job at Promise Lodge, it hadn't occurred to her that his family might be counting on his help at home to maintain their livelihood. All she'd known was that any guy who created such wonderful plaques had to be a creative, extraordinary person. And his unconventional appearance had proven that to be true.

"Truth be told, when I mentioned that you'd be selling my signs and that you might need another employee, my *mamm* and *dat* weren't over-joyed," Raymond admitted with a sigh. "But then Mamm suggested they could surely get along without me for a month or so if it meant getting real-world experience at something other than milking cows. She knows how—how frustrated I get doing farm labor when I'd rather be painting and creating unusual stuff . . . even if the Old Order will never consider my artwork acceptable."

"And what about your *dat*? Will he resent your working for me rather than helping with the family business?"

Lizzie sighed. Amish fathers had the final say about such things—and perhaps, because she'd been raised by sisters, she'd underestimated Mr. Overholt's expectations. It wouldn't be fair to plead with Raymond to stay at Promise Lodge, if it meant his *dat* nagged him about his absence from family responsibilities.

Raymond cleared his throat, as though he'd already come up against his *dat*'s disapproval. "I suspect that Mamm's been softening him up, suggesting that a chance to follow my heart for a short while might help me make my decision about joining the church," he said softly. "Dat keeps telling me that at twenty, it's time for me to declare my intentions one way or the other.

"Somehow Mamm usually manages to convince Dat to do things her way," he added with a chuckle. "She's always said that the older four boys were his, and she wanted one son for herself."

"Ah. So you're the favorite because you're her youngest?" Dale asked. "That's how it worked in my family, as well."

"It doesn't hurt," Raymond confirmed. "And sometimes, because Mamm's confined to a

135

wheelchair, she uses that to her advantage when they have different opinions."

"I see. Does this mean your *mamm* won't have someone helping her if you're not there? How will she get by?"

"My brother Ezra still lives at home—and because it's winter, the cows are confined in the pasture closest to the house. There's no gardening to do, either. Less work, in general."

During the pause that followed, Lizzie's heart began to pound. Would Dale decide he was causing the Overholt family a hardship by hiring their youngest son? Or would Raymond realize he didn't want to deal with his father's objections?

"Would you *like* to work here, Raymond?" the storekeeper continued. "If you'd like time to discuss it further with your family, that's probably a *gut* idea. And if you decide to come to Promise Lodge, I'd want you to start next Monday."

"Will I be able to stay in a cabin, as Lizzie suggested?"

"I suspect we can work that out—or you could possibly bunk with a family that has an extra room in their home," Dale replied.

After a short pause, he said, "Here's my number. Let me know as soon as possible if we should expect you to arrive at Promise Lodge sometime on Sunday, and we'll be ready for you to work on Monday, Raymond. And if you decide not to come, I'll understand."

"Denki for at least considering me," Raymond put in. "I appreciate your giving me the display space to sell my signs, too. You could've put plenty of other Christmas items on that front wall.

"And how about if you hold my sales profits until after Christmas, and—if I take the job— we'll put my paycheck toward the rent on one of those cabins?" he went on earnestly. "I wouldn't want my parents to pay any of my expenses, you see."

As Lizzie heard the two fellows coming from the office, it occurred to her that if the Overholt family forbade Raymond to take a job in Dale's store, she would never see him again.

Her pulse pounded into overdrive. Such a panic filled her soul that she could barely stay behind the stacked boxes until Raymond reached the back warehouse door. Once he got into his driver's car, he might be gone from her life forever.

With a desperate gasp, Lizzie shot out of her hiding spot. Never mind that she'd sent a stack of boxes tumbling to the floor behind her! She *had* to talk to Raymond.

Chapter 3

Raymond had jogged several yards across the store's back lot toward the rustic, timbered lodge building when Dale Kraybill's exasperated voice rang out behind him.

"Lizzie! You were *not* supposed to eavesdrop on Raymond's interview!"

The sound of a slamming door and rapid footsteps made him turn. Lizzie's earnest expression gave him pause.

Is this girl too nosy—or too pushy—for her own gut *and mine? Will she be such a pest that I'll lose this job?*

When he saw the determined look on her face, however, Raymond told himself to be patient. After all, when had a girl ever seemed so interested in him? The young women who'd grown up with him in Coldstream had written him off as a hopeless romantic who'd probably never be able to hold down a job or support a family. Most of them were already engaged, or at least courting somebody—as his brothers never failed to point out.

"Raymond! I wanted to tell you *gut*-bye—but no! I mean, what I *really* want is to see you back here working, and—"

Lizzie gazed at him with pale green eyes as she

caught her breath. "I hope your family will allow you to work here, because—well, getting to know you would be the best gift I could receive this Christmas."

His eyebrows rose. He knew next to nothing about this girl, yet she was making quite a play for his attention.

"I know how important it is for you to prove you can do this," she continued earnestly. "Or at least to give it a shot before you have to settle in as a dairyman for the rest of your days. You were born for brighter, finer things, Raymond!"

And how does she know what the Lord had in mind when He created me? So far, no one else— including me—has been able to figure out what I was meant to do with my life.

"I appreciate your positive thoughts," he murmured.

As he heard his driver's voice drifting from the lodge's front doorway, he glanced at the row of ten tidy brown cabins sitting alongside the weathered lodge building. Promise Lodge, once a church camp, was such a peaceful place with its nicely tended grounds and new off-white homes—not to mention a lake. This community would be quite a change from Coldstream, and— the way he'd heard it—could mean a shift into a new spiritual direction.

"I'm ready for this new adventure, and I intend to be working in the store, come Monday,"

Raymond stated with a nod. "Take care, Lizzie. See you soon."

By the time he'd spent most of Thanksgiving Day with his family, however, Raymond had the sinking feeling his new dream would never be realized. Mamm had cooked his holiday favorites, including a roasted turkey, corn casserole, and yams with melted marshmallows, but the wonderful food hadn't mellowed his *dat*'s attitude.

"Raymond, it's time to face the fact that *art* won't put food on your table, son," his father said as the women scraped the dinner plates before cutting the pies. "And why would you break your mother's heart by moving to Promise Lodge to work in a store? You could stay in Coldstream to do that, if helping with the dairy isn't your cup of tea."

"And let's not forget what you'll be setting yourself up for when Bishop Obadiah hears that you've left us," Enos, his eldest brother, remarked. He snatched the last biscuit from the basket and slathered it with butter and honey. "The Bender sisters and Preacher Amos left nearly three years ago, and we're *still* hearing sermons about how they abandoned the true path to salvation."

"He's saying the Peterscheims and the Fishers are headed to hell in a handbasket, too," Earl chimed in. "Apparently the bishop at Promise Lodge has gotten so liberal and progressive, it might not be long before *women* are allowed to preach!"

At the other end of the table, Mamm let out an exasperated sigh. "That's not true and you know it!" she said in a huff. When she focused on Raymond, her blue eyes softened. "When you went to the bulk store yesterday, could you tell if any of your signs have sold?"

"*Jah*, they have! Two were gone from the display when I arrived. And two or three more might've sold, as well, because Lizzie—she, um, works there," he clarified quickly, "encouraged shoppers to talk to me. It's a wonderful new store, too. So clean and well organized compared to the one here in town."

Mamm nodded, seeming pleased. "And if you went there to work, it's not as though you'd be living among total strangers," she pointed out. "Preacher Amos and Preacher Eli—as well as the three Bender sisters—will help you with anything you need. And if I wanted to know how you're doing, I could just call to find out, ain't so?"

Raymond flashed his mother an appreciative smile. Wasn't it just like her to take his side, trying to convince Dat to relax his stiff, starchy Old Order attitude?

"From what I saw during a quick visit last month," Elmer's wife, Sadie, said as she carried plates to the sink, "the new store at Promise Lodge would be a great place to work. That Kraybill fellow who owns it seems very friendly, and he's got nice bright lighting and modern freezer units—"

"*Jah*, because he's a Mennonite," Dat interrupted gruffly. He focused on Raymond, his expression somber. "I'd be terribly disappointed in you if you jumped the fence to sign on with *that* bunch, son. Mennonites are nice enough people to do business with, but they don't believe in shunning—they let their members off with a paltry mention of their sins, standing up in church, and then the folks around them say they're forgiven. How can you be held accountable to God if you don't acknowledge your sin and do penance for it?"

Raymond swallowed hard. Would Dat expect him to confess in church on Sunday, as though taking a seasonal job in Promise Lodge was a sin? His father had been quizzing him about his trip to the bulk store and his intentions ever since he'd first taken his plaques there, so it was a sure bet he wouldn't let up until Raymond gave in and stayed home.

But he didn't want to admit defeat. And every time Lizzie's face flashed through his mind, Raymond felt indescribably light and free—as though he were a bright red balloon.

His brother Elmer cleared his throat as though

they'd all been missing an important point. "It's no secret that Raymond's never been wild about the cows and that the feeling is mutual," he said quietly. "Not everyone's cut out to farm, after all. I say if he wants to do something else, the rest of us can keep the dairy running just fine."

"And maybe," Ezra chimed in earnestly, "Raymond needs a chance to try storekeeping, and if he fails at it, he's learned that lesson. Better to find that out now and get it out of his system, rather than to wonder all his life if he'd have been better suited to that line of work."

Raymond appreciated Ezra's point of view. As the only other Overholt son who still lived at home, Ezra—barely a year older than Raymond—had a better understanding of his youngest brother's mindset. The older boys, being married with kids and homes on small farms nearby, had always tended to see life through the same lens as their father.

That wasn't a bad thing. It just meant that Raymond often had to defend views and opinions his father felt were hopelessly impractical. Dat saw it as his life's purpose to shepherd his boys into the Old Order fold, and his youngest son's worldview often exasperated him.

"Enough of this discussion," Dat declared. He didn't sound angry, but he meant what he said. "It's not as though Raymond is the only member of this family worth talking about, after all. We'll trust him to listen to God and do the right thing."

Although his family complied and let the topic of his potential employment drop for the rest of the day, Raymond spent a sleepless night searching his soul. Would Dat believe he didn't love his family—especially Mamm—if he worked in the bulk store over the holidays? Worse yet, would *God* consider his stint in Promise Lodge a betrayal?

And what if Bishop Obadiah had it right? What if living in Promise Lodge's freer, more progressive church district made him want to move there permanently—and it cost him his salvation? It was an answer he'd never know until he died, of course, and met his Maker for a final reckoning.

Does God condemn Mennonites for their more lenient views on sin and confession? Is Lizzie headed for damnation and luring me down that slippery slope with her?

Such a drastic idea made Raymond sit up in bed, staring into the darkness. Lizzie was a distraction, for sure, but there wasn't an evil thought in her cute little head. And who could find fault with Dale Kraybill's friendliness—his willingness to offer a budding, rudderless artist a job in his bulk store? Surely that was the Christian message of acceptance and *love thy neighbor* that Jesus Himself had taught His disciples.

Nevertheless, when Raymond went downstairs

for a quick cinnamon roll before heading to the milking barn early Friday morning, he'd made his decision. He wasn't happy about it, but he couldn't bear the weight of his family's judgment, either.

"Mamm, I'm going to call Mr. Kraybill and tell him I'm staying home," Raymond murmured as he uncoiled his snack. He was glad Ezra and Dat hadn't yet come downstairs, so he could share his inner misery with Mamm before going to the phone shack.

In the dimness of the kitchen, lit only by battery lamps, his mother's pale eyes glimmered with a hint of mischief. She rolled her wheelchair to the table to sit beside him.

"Your *dat* has agreed with Ezra's idea. He thinks you need to learn the hard way that your artwork will never support you," she murmured, placing her hand gently on his arm. "Tell Mr. Kraybill you'll work in his store through the New Year . . . and prove your father wrong."

Raymond nearly choked in his surprise. "But—but deep down I *know* my signboards and other projects probably aren't enough to pay my way, much less support a wife—"

"Take this chance to work in a totally different environment, Raymond," she put in firmly. "It's not as though our family dairy can support all you boys and your families, after all. You—and probably Ezra—would be doing your older brothers a favor by finding other livelihoods, ain't so? Maybe your *dat*'s the impractical one, insisting you need to stay right here for the rest of your life."

His jaw dropped. Somehow his dear mother, frail though she might appear, must've talked so incessantly about Raymond's opportunity in Promise that Dat had finally given in. "How did you get him to change his mind about—"

"The rooster may crow, but the hen lays the eggs," Mamm replied with a chuckle. "I'm just as concerned about you boys as he is, but I especially want to see *you* get a chance at a life that satisfies your soul as well as supports you. Who knows what might come of working in the Promise Lodge bulk store for a while?"

Relief and gratitude washed over him. Raymond gently wrapped his arms around Mamm's slender shoulders. "And you're sure *you* will be all right while I'm gone?"

"Don't you worry a thing about me, sweetie. The best gift you can give me is finding your own way in the world—preferably joining the church, of course," she added with a nod. "Maybe working in Mr. Kraybill's store is an opportunity from God, after all."

Raymond's eyebrows shot up. He'd never considered that angle. If Mamm was suggesting it, however, who was he to question her wisdom?

"*Denki*, Mamm," he said softly, kissing her cheek. "You're the best."

Chapter 4

L izzie was so excited to be standing alongside Raymond on Monday morning that she could barely hold still as Dale spoke to them.

"Raymond, I'll be asking you to help with unloading shipments, stacking crates with the forklift, and arranging displays in the store—things that involve heavy lifting Lizzie and Marlene shouldn't do," the storekeeper was saying. "And because you have such a personable way with folks, I also want you to wait on customers and learn to use the computer at the checkout counter. Can you handle that?"

Raymond lit up like a Christmas candle. "*Jah*, that would be fine!"

"And that way, if customers ask about your plaques, you can tell them all about your process for creating them," Dale went on with a nod.

"Why don't *I* get to run the cash register?" Lizzie blurted out. "I did that for Maria in her bakery, you know." Never mind that Maria's cash register was just a step above an old-fashioned calculator rather than the computerized kind Dale used. "I could drive the forklift, too, you know. I drove here from Cloverdale on my scooter, after all."

The storekeeper didn't bat an eye. "For now,

I prefer to have you filling bags and restocking shelves with Marlene—which is vital to keeping the store running," he pointed out kindly. "But while we're on this topic, I must also insist that you kids keep your socializing to after hours, on your own time."

Lizzie sighed loudly. Filling and labeling bags back in the warehouse got *so* boring, because she usually worked in total isolation.

"Let's not forget that Raymond is a few years older than you, and he has some skills—and muscles—that you don't," Dale continued kindly. "But we also realize that you took to this young fellow the moment he walked into the store. Nothing wrong with that, but we're running a business here. I don't want to reprimand either of you in front of the customers, just as I hope I won't have to fire either of you because your work's not getting done. Understand?"

Lizzie was about to protest when the front door opened and Preacher Amos Troyer walked in, followed by Monroe Burkholder, the bishop of the Promise Lodge church district. Bishop Monroe was a big, burly fellow with deep dimples that winked when he smiled—and he smiled a lot.

"Thought we'd make a quick visit to welcome our new resident," Preacher Amos said as he shook hands with Raymond. "It's *gut* to have you with us, son. I'd like you to meet our bishop."

As Bishop Monroe grasped Raymond's hand, Lizzie sensed that because she was a girl, she would always be positioned a rung or two below Raymond on the employment ladder. It had been different when she'd answered to her sister—although Maria had constantly reminded her who was the boss and that things would be done her way.

"I also came to look at the plaques I've been hearing about," Bishop Monroe was saying.

Lizzie immediately felt better. If the bishop approved of Raymond's creative work, it would greatly improve his chance of success.

"You're here at the right time," Dale remarked as the men moved toward the front wall. "When the morning sun comes through the windows, Raymond's stars take on a life of their own."

"I can see that," Bishop Monroe said with a chuckle. "Great messages, too, about wise men still following His star and guiding us to His perfect light. So how'd you get those stars to shimmer and dance that way, Raymond?"

Raymond himself seemed to shimmer and dance as he replied.

"The plaques and stars are cut from old barn boards. I swirl a layer of spackle on the stars to give them dimension," he explained eagerly. "While the spackle's wet, I spray the stars with three different shades of gold paint. Then I add in small shards of a broken mirror and sprinkle the surface with glitter. My *mamm* taught me calligraphy when I was a kid, so the words look attractive, too."

Lizzie listened, fascinated. It was more interesting, however, to observe the glow on Raymond's face as he spoke about his work. At Maria's bakery she'd decorated many cakes and cookies, but she'd never felt the same excitement about her efforts as this guy obviously did.

Preacher Amos was nodding, following the conversation. Lizzie had heard about how he and widowed Mattie Bender Schwartz—whom he'd married—and her sisters, Christine and Rosetta, had all left Coldstream to start the Plain community at Promise Lodge. So they'd known Raymond his entire life.

"You do beautiful work, Raymond," Amos said gently, "but you probably understand that your plaques are more artistic than useful, *jah*? Your English and Mennonite customers don't mind that, but we Amish want the work of our hands to have a function. A purpose."

When the smile dropped off Raymond's face, Lizzie wanted to smack the preacher for his insensitive remark. Instead, however, she marched over to stand in front of the display, her arms tightly crossed as she gazed at those plaques with their swirly, sparkly stars.

"Raymond, what if you attached your Star of Wonder plaques to bulletin boards? Or they could have hangers on the bottom for calendars or key rings!" she declared. "What household wouldn't benefit from a reminder that we need to follow Jesus's star all year round? Maybe folks could even attach their list of family members' names to your plaques and place them by their front doors."

A moment of silence warned Lizzie that she might've overstepped. Nobody had asked for her opinion, after all.

Bishop Monroe, however, stepped up to grasp one of the boards that read, *Wise Men Still Follow His Star.*

"You make a fine point, young lady," he murmured. "Amos is right about the artistic angle, but I have a use in mind for this plaque just as it is. How about if you ring this up for me, Dale?"

Lizzie felt like a can of soda that Bishop Monroe had shaken, ready to explode with wild, fizzy bubbles. When she met Raymond's glance, his shy smile affirmed his appreciation that she'd spoken on his behalf.

"Can I watch you make your signs sometime?" she asked him softly. "I—I promise not to interrupt or ask too many dumb questions while you work."

Raymond's laughter sounded hesitant, as though he needed more practice at expressing happiness.

And wasn't she just the girl who could help him with that?

• • •

That evening, as Raymond spread his boards, spackle, and paints on the floor of cabin #2, he wondered why he felt nervous about Lizzie watching him work. She was as delighted to be with him as an eager puppy, after all. And more than once she'd stood up for him and his work when someone had dismissed it as frivolous—or worse, had declared that as art for art's sake, it had no place in the Old Order lifestyle.

I've never shared my process with anyone. I've always treasured the time I spent alone while I gave my hands and my instincts free rein.

"Can I help you with anything? Can I get you a table to work on so you're not crawling around on the floor?" she asked.

Lizzie sounded so ready to chatter nonstop, he was concerned about how this work session would go. But she'd made a very useful suggestion.

"You know where there's a table I can use? I asked Rosetta's permission to work in this unoccupied cabin, but I didn't think to ask her for a table—"

Lizzie waved him off, heading for the door. "Not a problem. I'll be right back—so don't start without me, okay?"

When she'd jogged off—with her flip-flops *flap-flap-flapping* as her pink calico skirt flew around her bare legs—Raymond closed his eyes.

He reminded himself to be patient and kind. He suspected that Lizzie had grown up without many friends and was just as socially needy and nerdy as he'd always felt, even though she never hesitated to speak her mind. When she returned with an old six-foot folding table, he had to admit that his work would be much easier if he could stand rather than subject his knees to the hard wooden floors.

"We start with these pieces of barn board and the stars, which I cut out while I was at home," he began. "I didn't want to drag my saws and equipment to Promise Lodge with me."

"You must've worked a long time to get this many signboards cut," she observed. "And it's so cool that some of your stars have curved points, like they're blowing in the wind. It gives them a whole different personality—especially because no two are alike."

Raymond blinked. If Lizzie had reacted to his stars with such insight, maybe her soul craved creativity as much as his did.

"I got my idea from Mamm's folk star cookie cutter."

"You and your *mamm* are close, ain't so? I bet she misses you a lot, Raymond."

He glanced up from opening the big tub of spackle, swallowing the lump that had risen in his throat. "In a world of men who tell me my work's not useful," he murmured, "it's Mamm who insists that I keep at it. She believes we need to—to feed our souls, just as we feed our bodies. What's your *mamm* like, Lizzie? I haven't heard you mention her."

"She passed when I was very young," the girl beside him replied with a resigned sigh. "I've spent a lot of my life with my eldest sister, Malinda—helping her because her MS confined her to a wheelchair. My older sister Maria also pitched in to raise me and then took me in after Malinda passed last year."

Raymond couldn't miss the longing in Lizzie's voice, although she refused to shed the tears that had formed in her pale green eyes. "I'm sorry—"

"*Jah*, me too," Lizzie put in quickly, "but don't let my story keep you from your stars, Raymond. I want to watch you make them!"

Just like that, she was her buoyant self again, grinning at him. After he'd covered the table with old newspapers, Raymond chose three stars to work on. With quick, lifting movements he spread spackle on the first one, starting at its center and moving outward.

"Ah, so that's why your stars seem to whirl," Lizzie murmured. "You flick your putty knife as you stroke on the spackling, and you follow the direction of the star's curved point."

"*Jah*. You're on it."

When he'd finished spackling the three stars, he removed the lids from his cans of spray paint and shook them. Raymond sprayed the darkest shade of gold first, using the same directional motion with which he'd spread the spackle, and he continued this technique with the other two colors.

"Wow, so that's why they look dimensional," Lizzie murmured, her gaze never leaving his hands. "I've decorated a lot of cakes in Maria's bakery, but the colors are static and flat because my pastry bag only holds one color. If I were to load the bags with two or three different shades . . ."

Raymond smiled. His companion was following his progress intently, yet she wasn't intruding. As he thought about it, her murmured encouragements inspired him, so he continued by carefully sprinkling little glass shards onto the wet surfaces with an old spoon. Three shades of glitter—gold, yellow, and cream—added the final effect.

As he was carrying the wet stars across the room to dry, Lizzie gazed at the paints, glass, and glitter on his worktable. Should he ask if she wanted to try decorating a star? What could it hurt if he invited her to share his craft?

They heard a soft knock at the door, and then Rosetta Wickey entered the cabin. Raymond had always known her as Rosetta Bender, because she'd remained at home caring for her aging parents until they'd passed. Shortly thereafter, she'd moved to Promise Lodge with her sisters to start this community. He wasn't surprised to see Christine and Mattie behind her, all of them smiling at him.

"Hope you don't mind if we peek at your work, Raymond," Rosetta said. "After I saw the plaque Bishop Monroe brought home to show Christine, my curiosity got the best of me."

"*Jah*, Amos was shaking his head a bit over your crafty products," Mattie put in, "but that's a man thing. We're so glad you decided to work in Dale's store for the Christmas season, Raymond!"

"And what did your folks say about that?" Christine asked.

The three sisters focused on him with eyes and intrigued expressions that were very much alike, although each woman had distinct features and physiques. He didn't want to carry on about it, but Raymond felt so happy when he saw their familiar, sincere smiles.

"Oh, you can probably guess that Dat tried to keep me at home," he began, raising his eyebrows, "but Mamm convinced him to let me give it a shot. Ezra had suggested that maybe I should take the job at the store so I could fail at selling my work and learn that lesson firsthand—"

Rosetta let out an exasperated sigh. "Not your biggest supporter, either, that brother."

"And that was Dat's rationale, as well," Raymond continued with a shake of his head. "Mamm at least reasoned that one or two of us Overholt boys will need to learn a different trade because the dairy won't support all five of us. So she insisted that I take the job."

As Rosetta stepped across the room to admire his freshly painted stars, Mattie held Raymond's gaze. "I wouldn't be surprised if you kick up a snit, where Bishop Obadiah's concerned," she said with a shake of her head. "He was *not* happy when we sisters and Amos left his Coldstream church district—"

"He's declared us lost souls on the path to perdition," Christine chimed in.

"And he's also let the Peterscheims—and most recently, Marlene Fisher and her brother, Mose— know how perturbed he is that they've come here to live in sin under Bishop Monroe's progressive leadership," Mattie continued. "So don't be surprised if your *dat* calls to let you know the bishop's pressuring him to bring you back home."

Raymond smiled ruefully. "*Jah*, I've been warned about that. You sisters and the others who have abandoned us are still the topic of his sermons now and again. I suspect Bishop Obadiah won't be happy that I chose to work here in Dale's store instead of taking a job at the one in Coldstream, either."

"Well, it's a sure bet Ralph Raber wouldn't display your plaques in his store," Rosetta pointed out. "Before they all sell out, put my name on one that has the lyrics from 'We Three Kings' on it. I think a certain husband will be getting it as a Christmas gift—but don't tell Truman!" she added with a laugh.

"Save one for us, too," Mattie said. "After Amos remarked to me that Old Order folks probably won't be buying them, I told him I wanted one to hang on the kitchen wall to hold our calendar. So there!"

After the sisters had chatted for a little while longer, they left the cabin. Raymond laughed, shaking his head as he picked up three more stars to work on. "*That* visit was a nice surprise," he said as he scooped spackle with his putty knife. "Maybe you're my *gut* luck charm, Lizzie."

She beamed at him, moving a little closer as he began applying the spackle. "Seems to me that the only way you can fail is if you stop making your plaques or give up working in the store, Raymond," she remarked. "You really don't need a *gut* luck charm. But I'll take the job if you're offering it."

Chapter 5

Friday after the store closed, Lizzie raced back to the lodge. She wanted to change to a fresh dress before Raymond came to the dining room for supper. And she wanted to be in the kitchen helping the two middle-aged Kuhn sisters, Beulah and Ruby, when he arrived, so she would appear *useful*. Skilled at something besides filling plastic bags.

Her job at Dale's store was so boring that she was tempted to quit. But if she returned to Cloverdale to work in her sister's bakery, she wouldn't see Raymond every day. Indeed, she might never talk to him again.

When Lizzie stepped into the lobby of the lodge, the rich aroma of beef and vegetables smacked her in the stomach. She'd been running behind this morning, so she hadn't packed a lunch—and buying snacks from the store wasn't an option, because she'd soon have to pay her apartment rent. She couldn't afford any extras on her wage from Dale's store, but the job still represented her freedom and independence, so she wasn't about to give it up.

"*Gut* evening, missy! How was your day?"

In a dining room big enough to seat a hundred, Beulah looked up from setting the table nearest the kitchen door. She and her sister were Mennonite *maidels* who'd lived in the lodge for a couple of years, and they did most of the cooking for the other tenants.

Maybe I should skip changing clothes and help with supper. I could eat a few bites while I fill the serving bowls, so I don't devour everything in sight when Raymond gets here.

"The store gets busier every day." Lizzie smiled at Beulah, whose dress fabric was printed with red poinsettias the size of dinner plates. "I bagged five different kinds of Christmas candies this morning, and by the time I left, most of them had been snapped up."

"Folks are getting into the spirit," Ruby remarked as she carried a fruity red gelatin salad to the table. She was slightly shorter and younger than her sister—and *her* dress fabric featured the animals and people in the song about the twelve days of Christmas. "Next time I visit the store, I intend to load us up with Christmas sprinkles, candied cherries, and everything we'll need to start baking our cookies and cakes."

"Oh, can I help?" Lizzie asked as she hurried between the long wooden tables towards the kitchen. "But then, I'll probably be working in the store whenever you do your baking."

"I suspect we can arrange to do some of it in the evenings," Beulah replied kindly. "If you've worked in your sister's bakery, you could probably teach us a trick or two—"

"And you probably have a steadier hand when it comes to decorating cookies," Ruby put in.

Lizzie laughed. "Depends on who you ask. Maria thinks *she* does everything better than I— Oh, would you look at that fabulous pot roast!" she said as she entered the kitchen. "I'm so hungry I could eat the whole thing!"

"I won't let you do that, because I'm starving, too," Marlene teased as she came down the back stairs from her apartment. "The entire lodge smells like beef and gravy."

Ruby joined Lizzie at the counter, hugging her shoulders. "Why do I suspect you ran off without any lunch again today?" she asked gently. "You're welcome to eat whatever you find in the kitchen, you know—it's what your rent money pays for. Maybe if you made a sandwich the evening before—"

"*Jah*, my sister's *gut* at telling me I should think ahead instead of rushing around at the last minute," Lizzie confessed with a sigh. "Being organized isn't one of my most notable talents, I guess."

The lines around Ruby's eyes curved with her sweet smile. She lifted the succulent roast, so tender it was falling off the bone, from the blue enamel roaster and placed it on a platter. Then she handed Lizzie a fork and the carving knife.

"Maybe you can be our taste tester—quality control—before we serve this dinner to Raymond."

Lizzie gratefully stabbed a chunk of beef that had fallen into the broth. Closing her eyes to chew, she realized how grateful she was that the Kuhns looked after her without hovering.

"Raymond's a long, tall drink of water, and it takes a lot of food to fill that boy up," Beulah remarked as she attacked the cooked potatoes with a masher. "I doubt he'll ever say he finds this dinner lacking in quality, either."

The four of them laughed, filling the warm, fragrant kitchen with a coziness Lizzie cherished. The two *maidels* were quickly filling in the empty spot her *mamm* had left in her life. Baking cookies with Ruby and Beulah gave her something to look forward to—*almost* as much as she yearned for a romance with Raymond.

Minutes later, steaming bowls of mashed potatoes, gravy, green beans, and glazed carrots joined the platter of pot roast on the table. A large rhubarb pie sat on the sideboard. Lizzie's heart thumped like a drum as Raymond came in the front door. He hung his snowy wraps on the coat tree in the lobby and came to sit down with them. They bowed their heads.

"Lord, we're grateful for the life and the love You've given us, and we thank You for this food," Beulah intoned. "Amen."

Lizzie wanted to start some sort of witty dinner

conversation, but her hunger won out. As she heaped two big spoonsful of potatoes onto her plate, Raymond glanced at her from across the table.

Will he think I'm a pig, eating such a mound of carbs?

Lizzie's worries about appearing fat dissipated like the steam from her plate, however, when the lodge's front door opened. Her sister Maria paused with her fist on her hip, gazing into the dining room.

"So, Lizzie. You're alive after all," their visitor remarked as she approached the table. "I bought you that cell phone so we could touch base, but you don't return my calls."

Lizzie suppressed a smile. *The best thing about a cell is that you can call, Maria, but my answering is optional.*

"Sorry," she said aloud. "I need to charge the battery—"

"For the past three weeks?" Maria demanded.

"Well, Maria, it's nice to see you," Beulah put in purposefully. "I'll fetch you a plate so you can join us."

"And how's your bakery in Cloverdale doing?" Ruby asked before Maria could continue her rant. "Promise Lodge isn't the same without you, dear."

Lizzie nearly choked on a laugh. Maria had moved a small white bakery building next to the Kuhns' cheese factory a couple of years ago, yet her business hadn't lasted long there. She hadn't admitted many details, but Lizzie suspected that Truman Wickey—a member of their Mennonite church in Cloverdale—had bought Maria a new building there because she'd been disrupting his relationship with Rosetta.

Disrupting was one of Maria's most notable talents. That was probably what the Kuhn sisters were remembering even as they graciously set her a place at the table.

Raymond put the meat platter near Maria's plate. "Hey there, Maria, I'm Raymond. It's *gut* to meet someone from Lizzie's family—"

"*Jah*, her *only* remaining family," Maria cut in. "Which is why it's so bothersome that Lizzie hasn't contacted me since she came here—against my advice—last month."

"Ah. You're lonely without her. I can understand how quiet your life must be without your live-wire sister," Raymond observed. He shot Lizzie a playful smile and went on eating.

Maria's eyes widened, as though she just now realized other folks—including a cute guy who liked Lizzie—were in the dining room with her. And they were behaving politely, inviting her to eat with them instead of acting spiky, the way she was.

She slipped out of her coat and hung it on the back of the empty chair beside her. Raymond's remark had pierced her shell.

"Too quiet," Maria admitted under her breath as she took a chunk of roast. "I haven't had a meal like this since you left home, Lizzie. No reason to cook."

"You're welcome to take some back with you," Beulah offered as she and her sister passed the gravy and vegetable bowls. "It's our mission to feed people, you know."

"And you do it well." Maria found a smile for the sisters as she finished filling her plate. "I was hoping Lizzie would come to the Cloverdale church with you ladies these past Sundays—or buzz up on her scooter for the day."

Lizzie sighed loudly. "You know how I feel about the minister there. His long-winded sermons leave you wondering if he ever intends to make a *point*."

"I've had that thought myself," Beulah confessed with a chuckle.

"I can understand why Lizzie prefers the Old Order services here," Ruby said with a nod. "No chance of drifting off while any of these preachers—or Bishop Monroe—delivers the morning's message."

"When I glanced at Lizzie during the last service," Marlene put in, "she was bright-eyed and hanging on every word, too. I'm Marlene Fisher, by the way. Nice to meet you, Maria."

As she chewed, Maria nailed Lizzie with a purposeful gaze. "Seems you've made yourself some devoted friends here, little sister. They haven't yet discovered your more exasperating habits."

Lizzie shrugged, smiling at her companions. "Maybe I've changed. Maybe people here let me live my life without pecking at me like a cranky hen."

When Maria's eyes widened, Lizzie braced herself for a lecture she probably deserved.

"So how's it going in Dale's store?" her sister demanded. "Don't tell me you show up on time, or that you never sass back at him—"

"We'd be lost without Lizzie," Marlene put in, gently nudging Lizzie with her elbow. "She's a fast learner, and she fills and labels hundreds of bags a day."

"Dale hasn't once chased me out of the store with a fly swatter, either," Lizzie pointed out sweetly.

"What else was I supposed to do when you—" Maria stopped midsentence. When she sighed, her shoulders slumped. "I was having a crazy-bad day. Can we please stop talking about what a monster you think I am?"

Lizzie set her fork down to focus on her sister. "I don't think you're a monster, Maria," she murmured. "But I don't like living by your rules. As you've said before, I'm scatterbrained and unreliable, and I insist on doing everything *my* way instead of yours. I know I can be a headache, and I constantly test your patience. I thought coming to Promise Lodge might be a solution for both of us."

The dining room went quiet. After a moment, Maria dropped her gaze.

As the meal continued, the Kuhns and Marlene kept the conversation light by updating Maria on the new residents and the things that had happened since she'd returned to Cloverdale. After they'd finished their pie, Beulah and Ruby packed some leftovers into containers while Marlene ran hot, soapy dishwater.

When Lizzie carried her sister's food out to the dining room, she was relieved to see that Maria and Raymond were still at the table, chatting about his Christmas star plaques.

At the sight of the large bag, Maria sprang up from her seat. "I couldn't possibly eat so much! I don't intend to take your dinner for tomorrow—"

Lizzie grasped her sister's shoulder, smiling. "Have you ever tried to make the Kuhns take back food?" she teased. She held Maria's gaze for a moment. "I'm sorry we traded insults—it wasn't my intent to get nasty. But I'm not going back to Cloverdale, Maria. Please try to understand that I'm eighteen and I have to live my life by my own rules."

In the doorway to the kitchen, Beulah was chuckling. "We can recall Maria behaving that very same way for the short time she lived here—ain't so, Ruby?"

"My thought exactly."

"Yet now Maria's new bakery is successful, and she's supporting herself and taking responsibility for her sister—because she's done some growing up," Beulah pointed out. "That's progress!"

"The way these Zehr girls pick on each other brings a couple other sisters to mind, ain't so?" Ruby asked fondly.

"*Jah*, when we were their age, we could barely stay in the same room together," Beulah recalled with a nod. "I'm grateful to God that we've mellowed—"

"And that He saw fit to keep us from killing one another," Ruby added with a laugh. "It's been *gut* to visit with you, Maria. Don't be a stranger."

"And if we don't see you again soon, Merry Christmas," Beulah said. "I know you'll be busy baking, but if you feel the itch to get away, we'll have a room you can stay in."

Lizzie walked Maria to the front porch and then stood there in the light snowfall, waving as her sister drove off in a rumbly red car that had seen better days. She lifted her face to catch snowflakes on her tongue, delighting in their sharp coldness. A deep sense of peace settled over her as she gazed up at the crescent moon. It looked like a smile in the night sky, intended especially for her.

She was still here at the lodge. She still had her job—even if sometimes she detested its monotony. She was still her own woman living life her way. And she and Maria were still on speaking terms, even if they weren't nearly finished squabbling.

Best of all, though, she had a new circle of friends who shone as brightly as one of Raymond's gold stars when the morning sunlight hit it. And for that, Lizzie felt extremely blessed.

Chapter 6

"On this first Sunday in December, as we start our journey to Bethlehem to discover the Christ Child yet again," Bishop Monroe said in his resonant voice, "I'm adding something to the lodge's seasonal decorations. This morning's fresh snow and the aromas of the Christmas treats the ladies have been baking remind us what time of year it is—and so do the fresh pine branches and red bayberry candles in our meeting room. Before I begin my sermon, however, I'd like to suggest the *direction* our hearts should take as we anticipate Christmas."

From his pew bench in the middle of the men's side—with the older fellows in front of him and the schoolboys behind him—Raymond shifted to see what the bishop was taking from behind a large sideboard.

His jaw dropped. Bishop Monroe was holding up the wooden plaque he'd bought in Dale's store earlier this week!

" 'Wise men still follow His star,' " the church leader read as he held the signboard up for all to see. "This isn't the time to elaborate upon the plaque itself or the young man who created it, but the words ring true. No matter what season we're in, God calls us to seek out His Son, Jesus, and to get better acquainted with our Savior."

Bishop Monroe strode to the nearest wall and hung the plaque on a nail there. "I'm putting this reminder here during the service, and afterward I'll hang it in the lobby so everyone who enters this lodge will know our Christmas mission. We're a close-knit bunch here at Promise Lodge—one big family—yet this journey to the stable will unify us even more if we focus on God's greatest gift to us: His love."

A lump of emotion rose in Raymond's throat. Bishop Monroe was including *him*—Raymond Overholt from Coldstream—in the Promise Lodge family, and the thought filled him with wonder and gratitude. He couldn't imagine Bishop Obadiah alluding to such a warm family relationship within his church district. Nor would the members there believe that such a sentiment described them.

It was a sad truth. Raymond suddenly rejoiced that he was spending this Christmas season at Promise Lodge rather than at home. He missed being with his parents and brothers, but he suddenly realized how much he did *not* miss the judgmental undercurrents of discontent and negativity Bishop Obadiah's personality inspired.

For Raymond, church service had always been something to *endure.* He tried to remain invisible whenever Bishop Obadiah came to the Overholt home—and the church district had felt even more closed and unfriendly since Preachers Amos and Eli, along with the Bender sisters and the Fishers, had left Coldstream. Maybe that's why he'd never felt compelled to take his instruction and join the Old Order, despite his parents' wishes that he would commit to their religion.

If I'm ever going to marry, though, I must take my church vows.

As he spotted Lizzie sitting among the ladies on the other side of the room, Raymond's thoughts bounced like Ping-Pong balls.

She's been raised Mennonite, but she doesn't seem inclined to join that church. If she refuses to follow her sister's rules and her more lenient faith, why would she comply with the stricter Old Order way of life?

Or maybe we could jump the fence and live English.

Raymond shook his head at his premature thoughts of marriage.

Why would Lizzie consider me *as a husband? I have no means of supporting her. She might encourage my artistic inclinations now, but when the kids come along, she'll expect me to earn a real living—and she won't want to live in a room at my parents' place forever, either.*

In reality, living English would be unrealistic, too. If they jumped the fence, he wouldn't have the option of living with his very disappointed parents, and both he and Lizzie would have to find steady jobs to support themselves in a world neither of them was very familiar with.

Across the room, Lizzie flashed Raymond a smile that lit up her adorable face. His heart skipped beats and his pulse rang like Christmas bells. For a brief moment he felt ecstatic.

You're in church, Overholt. Focus.

As Bishop Monroe preached about the long, difficult journey Mary and Joseph were required to make to pay their taxes in Bethlehem, Raymond found himself drawn in. Monroe Burkholder was a tall, burly man whose voice filled the room with a down-to-earth eloquence. He was talking about the faith Mary had in God, and the love Joseph had shown by taking her for his wife even though she was expecting someone else's baby.

"As we follow this couple to Bethlehem, let's not forget that they were ordinary folks called to participate in an *extraordinary* story," Bishop Monroe reminded them. "Would you ladies believe it if an angel said you'd been chosen to have God's own child? Would you men wake up from a dream and love Mary, because another angel had told you to?"

The folks around Raymond appeared startled as they considered the bishop's questions.

"And how would any of us know we weren't imagining the whole incredible episode?" Bishop Monroe continued urgently. "Most important, what if Mary and Joseph had said *no?* What if they hadn't believed that God was the One asking them to undertake such an astounding mission? What if they'd refused to have any part of God's plan for salvation and Joseph had cast Mary aside as unworthy and unfaithful?"

Raymond saw a light bulb come on in Lizzie's mind. Her eyes widened and her mouth formed an O as she followed what the bishop was suggesting.

If Lizzie had been shamed and was carrying another man's baby, would I love her enough to take her as my wife?

The preposterous thought nearly knocked Raymond off the pew bench. Not only was it too soon to consider such a situation, but he was once again daydreaming instead of following the bishop's compelling sermon.

Yet in that moment, he knew that he was desperately in love with Lizzie.

The rest of the service passed in a blur. While they sang the long hymns, and Preacher Amos gave the main sermon, and they prayed, Raymond's imagination was taking him to other places with Lizzie by his side. As everyone rose from the benches after the benediction, he warned himself to remain practical—to not encourage Lizzie's wild, childlike abandon by making the slightest suggestion about courtship. She would latch onto him and expect all their romantic dreams to come true immediately—

But what if she laughed in my face and told me to go take a hike? What if she's crazy about every guy she meets? Maybe I'm the flavor of the day because I'm the only guy at Promise Lodge near her age.

Raymond was pulled out of his whirlwind thoughts by the grip of two small, warm hands.

Lizzie stood in front of him. She had the starry-eyed, ecstatic look of a young woman who'd been told by an angel that she was to carry out the most incredible mission in the world.

"Don't you just *love* Bishop Monroe?" she asked in a rush of excitement. "And wouldn't it be *fabulous* to live here at Promise Lodge? I'd join the Amish church in a heartbeat if we could be here together, Raymond. What do you think?"

Raymond was so stunned, he couldn't think. He could barely draw breath as he got caught up in her whirlwind plan for their happily-ever-after. "I—I don't know—"

"Weren't you listening to the bishop's sermon? Where's your *faith,* Raymond?" she challenged him playfully. Yet she wasn't playing.

Before he could reply, Lizzie whispered, "When God calls, will you respond?"

"Well, *jah*, I—but—"

"*Gut.* It's settled, then." She stood on tiptoe to kiss him on the cheek before dashing off to join the other women in the kitchen.

Raymond wasn't sure what had hit him. He sensed, however, that he had a whole lot of thinking to do, and that his life would never be the same.

Chapter 7

"Oh, but it feels *gut* to make cookies again," Lizzie said as her roller flew lightly over the dough on Wednesday evening. "If Maria had let me make the cookies while she baked the breads and pastries, we would've gotten along a lot better. But she told me exactly how I was to decorate the bells and the holly sprigs and the candy canes—and she insisted that all the bells, holly, and the canes look alike! Talk about a control freak!"

The silvery-haired sisters glanced at one another as though they could elaborate on Maria's behavior while she'd lived at Promise Lodge. But they chose not to.

"My word, Lizzie, you're cutting out more cookies in five minutes than Beulah or I put on a cookie sheet in fifteen," Ruby remarked. "You're *quick,* honey."

"No doubt in my mind that we'll have the most beautiful cookies ever this Christmas," Beulah put in kindly. "It's fun to have you working with us, Lizzie. I bet when you first met us, you never figured on becoming our new best friend, ain't so?"

Lizzie laughed. "True enough," she admitted. "I'm grateful that you—and all the other folks here—accept me for the spacy, twitterpated girl I am.

"And clumsy," she added emphatically. "Today, as I was shelving packages of raisin biscuit mix, one of my bags came untied and the mix spilled all over the floor. Talk about a mess!"

"I bet Dale fussed about *that!*" Ruby said with a laugh.

"*Jah,* he's a meticulous storekeeper," Beulah put in.

The three of them carried their filled cookie sheets toward the oven as Lizzie nodded her agreement. "The dry broom wasn't enough. He didn't get off my case until I'd sponge-mopped the floor of that entire aisle and—"

The ringing of the wall phone caught Lizzie by surprise. "How are you able to have an indoor phone instead of a phone shack like the other residents have at their houses?" she asked. "From what Raymond tells me, Bishop Obadiah would *never* allow that!"

As Beulah answered the phone, Ruby explained in a low voice. "We ladies at the lodge run businesses, you know—and several of us share this phone among ourselves. The preachers decided we could keep it, because it's also the only way for folks outside of Promise Lodge to talk to anyone staying in our cabins."

Nodding, Lizzie quickly slid the cookie sheets

onto the racks of two ovens, shut their doors, and set a timer.

Meanwhile, Beulah's expression softened. She lowered her voice as she spoke into the phone. "Hang on and we'll have him here in a Christmas jiffy, Mrs. Overholt." She pressed the receiver to her bosom and looked at Lizzie.

"Raymond's *mamm* wants to talk to him, honey, so please go and fetch him," she said. "I can't say for sure, but they might have an emergency at their place—but don't worry our boy by telling him that part, all right?"

Lizzie jogged past the kitchen counters and between the long wooden tables in the dining room. When she reached the porch, she saw patches of soft light on the snow in front of cabin #2—which told her Raymond was working on his star plaques. She knocked quickly on the door and stepped inside the cabin.

"You've got a call from your *mamm*," she said. "In the lodge kitchen."

Raymond looked up, bewildered. "But my plaster's wet and I'm right in the middle of—"

"You can take up again with your stars, sweetie, but it's probably best not to keep your mother waiting, ain't so?" Lizzie suggested softly. "Who knows what might have prompted her to call you."

Nodding, Raymond carefully set the star he'd been painting on his worktable, along with his

179

can of gold paint. He wiped his smeared hands on a rag as he hurried toward the door.

Lizzie watched him sprint to the lodge, then returned to his table to see what he'd been working on. Four stars had been spackled, and he'd been ready to spray the first, darkest shade of gold paint on them.

To avoid the temptation to work on Raymond's project, she clasped her hands behind her back. After all, she'd watched him make several of his stars, so she knew he sprayed the darkest color from the center out to each tip of the star—

But how would they look if the different shades of gold radiated out from the center? And what if the sparkly little glass pieces and the glitter accentuated the tips?

"I'll only do one," she whispered, grasping a star before she talked herself out of it.

After all, there was nothing rational about art—or love. Ever since she'd declared her wishes to Raymond after church on Sunday, he surely realized that her main goal in life these days—and for the rest of their days—was to make him happy.

With a quick, swirling motion Lizzie squirted the darkest gold in the star's center—and then impulsively did the same to the other three stars. She followed with rings of the next color, and then sprayed the lightest shade on the tips.

Rather than spooning on the glass slivers, as Raymond did, she dipped the first star's tips into the container of chips.

"Ooh, I like that! Lots more sparkle," she whispered as she continued with the other stars. "And the glitter goes in the centers! And now they're done!"

Raymond would be so surprised—and pleased that his spackle hadn't dried before he could continue his work. Because who knew how long he might be on the phone?

Lizzie left the cabin filled with an exuberant sense of accomplishment. When she returned to the lodge kitchen, the Kuhns were taking the first pans of cookies from the ovens—which meant that in less than eight minutes, she'd created a whole new style of stars for Raymond.

He was still talking to his mother, standing at the back wall of the kitchen, when she waved silently at Ruby and Beulah. She chose cutters of a little house, a snowflake, and a pine tree and resumed her baking.

Lizzie didn't mean to eavesdrop, but she couldn't help hearing every word Raymond said.

"*Jah*, I'm really sorry to hear about . . . if—if you need me to come home, Mamm, I—"

Lizzie's heart rose into her throat. The house she'd cut out became a shapeless wad before she realized she'd crumpled it in her hand.

"I guess I could explain to Dale about . . . but

we've been so busy in the store, I'd hate to leave him shorthanded—"

Lizzie swallowed hard. Had Raymond's *dat* had a serious accident? Or was his *mamm* in a bad way and wanted her boy to return to Coldstream? A woman in a wheelchair, even if she got around pretty well inside the house, was dependent upon somebody strong to maneuver her in and out of a buggy if she needed to go into town.

Or if Alma had taken sick, and Raymond had always been the son who looked after her, she would naturally want him to come home—

"No, I don't really *want* to quit my job," he continued plaintively. "For the first time in my life, I feel like I belong. My plaques are selling like hotcakes, but for you, Mamm—"

But what about me? What about us*?*

Tears welled up in Lizzie's eyes as she doggedly kept cutting out cookies she could barely see. For the first time in her life, she felt like *she* belonged, as well, so the thought of losing Raymond just when something wonderful was developing between them nearly ripped her heart to pieces.

If he left, she suspected she'd be too upset and depressed to keep her monotonous job in the bulk store. But that would mean she'd have to return to Maria's bakery in Cloverdale. And Christmas would be ruined. Her whole life would go down the drain.

Raymond was leaning against the wall, clutching the receiver—listening as the minutes ticked by, with an occasional murmur. Lizzie filled the rest of her cookie sheets with pine trees and snowflakes and carried them to the ovens. The Kuhns' expressions reflected their concern over whatever might be happening on the other end of the phone line.

"All right, I can do that," he finally murmured. "I miss you, too, Mamm. And *jah*, I love you to pieces. Bye, now."

The solid *thunk* of the receiver landing in its hook filled the silent kitchen. Lizzie hated to stare at Raymond, yet the Kuhn sisters were gazing at him for an explanation, as well.

When he realized he'd had an audience for his entire call, he smiled tiredly at them. "My *mamm*'s best friend passed on early this morning. She was upset and crying—"

"Understandable," Beulah murmured.

"—and wanting me to come home for a week or so," Raymond continued. He raked his dark hair back with his fingers, studying his three listeners through his red-framed glasses. "Luckily, I talked her off the ledge. She understands that if I leave, it'll cause a lot of problems for Dale at the busiest time of the year."

"I suspect she misses her boy more than she'll ever admit," Ruby remarked softly.

Lizzie leaned against the counter, waiting to see

183

if he had any more unexpected bombs to drop.

"*Jah*," Raymond agreed. He glanced at the cookies cooling on the metal racks, smiling. "Ordinarily, she and I would be starting our Christmas baking—something we've done together since I was a wee boy, because she had no girls to help her in the kitchen."

Beulah smiled kindly. "You're welcome to join us, dear. We can scare up another rolling pin—"

"And we have a lot of dough to bake this evening," Ruby added.

The *ding* of the timer prompted Lizzie to step over to the ovens. It apparently reminded Raymond that he'd left his project in progress, as well.

"I'm glad you made your *mamm* feel better! And I'm glad you're not leaving us!" Lizzie called out as he reached the dining room doorway.

Raymond turned, smiling at her. "You know, maybe I'll finish the stars I've started and come back to help you ladies. I have this sudden urge to work with cookie dough."

As she pulled the cookie sheets from the ovens, Lizzie's heart danced. She would be doing one of her favorite things with her new favorite person—

But what if he gets mad when he sees what I did to his stars? I probably should've left them alone instead of finishing them the way I wanted to—

just like Maria always jumped in to take control of my *projects.*

Lizzie made sure her back was to the dining room doorway as she continued cutting out cookies. If Raymond was upset with her, she wouldn't have to see it on his face right away—and he'd have time to cool off. She noticed that Ruby had found another rolling pin and Beulah was clearing off some countertop space for him—right next to Lizzie. There'd be no escaping Raymond's reaction to the surprise she'd left him.

A few minutes later he came in.

"We've set you up alongside Lizzie," Beulah said with a knowing smile.

"Where I can keep an eye out for any hanky-panky you young folks might try," Ruby teased from across the counter.

Raymond's face remained impossible to read as he slipped a white apron from a hook in the corner. He smiled at the two *maidel* sisters and washed his hands. After he donned the apron, he pinched a large handful of dough from the batch Lizzie was working with, instead of using what Ruby had placed in his spot.

Lizzie stopped herself before she protested. After all, she'd horned in on *his* project, hadn't she?

As he worked, Raymond's movements were fluid from years of practice. Lizzie couldn't help watching the way his rolling pin deftly spread the dough to the right thickness before he chose a cutter shaped like a wreath. Within moments he'd cut out every possible cookie, leaving very few dough scraps on the counter.

When he glanced at her, Lizzie quickly got back to work. Now, in addition to wondering what he'd thought of her stars, she'd become aware that Raymond's cookie-cutting skills were putting hers to shame. After he'd covered another sheet with snowmen, he put them in the oven, along with the cookie sheets the Kuhns had filled.

Lizzie was aware that the sisters were chatting with Raymond, asking about how his *mamm* was doing and how his plaques were coming along. He was responding as though nothing had been left hanging between him and the girl beside him.

He's ignoring me! What does that mean?

Lizzie quickly rerolled her scraps, striving to catch up with Raymond. Once again, he took a large portion of her dough ball, so when she was ready for fresh dough, she grabbed some of his.

No reaction. It was as though she wasn't standing two feet away from him.

This is ridiculous! Is he not speaking to me because I finished those stars?

By the time Lizzie had cut two more sheets of cookies—and Raymond was working on his fourth one—her frustration was nearly choking her. "Aren't you going to say anything about—"

"Huh?" Raymond blinked as though he'd been on another planet. "Oh, sorry, Lizzie. I was thinking about how lonely Mamm sounded. I'll have to pack it all in after Christmas and go back to Coldstream," he murmured forlornly. "I miss her more than I thought I would."

Lizzie's protest lodged in her throat. It seemed he hadn't even noticed the four stars she'd painted—and now he was pulling out of Promise Lodge. And apparently leaving *her* behind, too.

"I can understand that, Raymond," Beulah remarked. "Mamms hold a special spot in our hearts."

"It's best to love them while they're still with us," Ruby put in with a nod, "because some day, before we're ready, they're gone."

Pressing her lips together, Lizzie fought back the tide of emotions that threatened to knock her off-balance.

I thought we'd agreed we'd be together— thought Raymond knew I wanted to marry him, even if I'll have to join the Old Order. I'm not sure I can handle working in Dale's store or living in the lodge anymore if I don't have a future with him.

Somehow, she finished her share of the baking, but her heart wasn't in it. Disappointment smoldered inside her, as though her heart were a campfire Raymond had doused with his remarks. Never mind that he looked incredibly cute in that white apron—a garment most men wouldn't be caught dead in.

He'd cast her aside. Her hopes and dreams meant nothing to him.

By the time they'd washed the dishes and wiped the countertops, Lizzie knew she was destined for a night of crying herself to sleep. It took all her strength to hide her despair until Raymond was saying *gut*-night and heading for the front door of the lodge. With her head hung low, she followed him through the dark dining room on her way to the curved double stairway that filled the rustic lobby with the glimmer of its polished wood.

As Raymond grasped the doorknob, he turned. "*Denki* for finishing those stars for me, Lizzie," he murmured. "I didn't like the way you changed the paint and glass and glitter—"

When he paused, Lizzie wished the floor would open up and swallow her. He was going to end this conversation with a negative comment that would crush what was left of her withering spirit.

"But then I realized that stars are like people. No two are alike—and every one of them shines in its own special way." Raymond's face lit up as he gazed at her. "You're a shining star in my life, Lizzie. Makes me really sorry I'll be going back to Coldstream—"

"So take *me!*" she blurted.

He sighed. "You don't know what you'd be

letting yourself in for, living in my district. Now that you've fallen in love with the progressive folks at Promise Lodge—and you've made such *gut* Mennonite friends here—Coldstream would feel like a cage. And you'd blame me for putting you there."

Before she could protest, he was gone.

It wasn't a good night for getting any sleep.

Chapter 8

On Friday morning, as Raymond filled the blank spots on Dale's front store wall, he realized Lizzie's stars had grown on him. With glitter in the centers and glass on the points, they resembled sunflowers with sparkly petals—and who was to say these four plaques wouldn't sell as fast as his others had? In the two and a half weeks since he'd first displayed his work, he'd sold fifteen of them! It was more than he'd ever anticipated, and he would soon have to replenish his supply of barnboard, spackle, and spray paint.

Rather than painting on Friday evening, however, he joined Lizzie and the Kuhns for a decorating frolic. They'd stashed more than fifteen dozen sugar cookies in the freezer! Ruby and Beulah had stirred up containers of colored buttercream frosting, and as they set out knives, pastry bags, and several containers of Christmas sprinkles and colored sugars, Raymond realized that he was looking forward to creating sweet, edible art rather than plaques that smelled like paint and varnish.

He marveled at the way Lizzie deftly spooned frosting into pastry bags without making a mess— the way he would have. After they all chose the cookies they wanted to decorate first, Raymond gained a whole new respect for her artistic talent: in less than a minute, she'd outlined four little houses and added rounded doors, windows, and little frosting wreaths decorated with green and red jimmies.

"Lizzie, those are the cutest cookies I've ever seen!" Ruby exclaimed as she and her sister picked up the little houses to admire them.

"We now have a new standard to aspire to—and my plain old frosted cookies will never measure up," Beulah put in.

Lizzie chose four candy cane cookies. "Phooey on that! Nothing tastes better than a sugar cookie covered with buttercream. For a lot of folks at Maria's bakery, Christmas cookies are all about the frosting."

As Raymond swirled green buttercream on a wreath, he stole glances at the way Lizzie squeezed and released the pastry bag to make the stripes on her canes. She had a technique that came from years of experience—and he knew he'd never master it in one evening. After she'd gently pressed the stripes into red sanding sugar to make them sparkle, the cookies became art.

Her facial expression made him hold his breath. Never had he seen Lizzie so focused, yet so relaxed. She held the cookies gently with her fingertips to smooth the edges of the sugary stripes—not a hint of the klutzy store employee who spilled something almost every day. Her easy smile bespoke a deep joy as she set the completed canes on a rack to dry.

I wish I were a cookie, so she'd look at me *that way.*

It occurred to him that he'd been so busy unloading delivery trucks and running the cash register—and making plaques in cabin #2—that he'd spent very little time talking to Lizzie this week.

Is that why she's barely spoken to me lately? Or is she upset because I'm returning to Coldstream after Christmas? After all, she bared her soul on Sunday, all but saying she loves me. And I've paid zero attention to her—as though her feelings don't matter.

Raymond sighed and finished frosting his wreath. After he'd put on a few round red sprinkles, for holly berries, he cleared his throat. "I—I don't suppose you'd want to add a bow to the top of this wreath," he murmured. "Your pastry bag would make it look a lot better than spreading it on with my knife tip, ain't so?"

Lizzie added a scarf and the finishing details to a snowman that wore a hat. "Let's give it a shot," she said. As she squeezed out a red wreath with a few quick movements, his mouth dropped open.

"How'd you do that?" he whispered.

"Magic. Christmas magic," she replied with a shrug. "It's no different from the way you've mastered making your plaques, you know.

Different medium, same mindset—a suspended state of awareness plus muscle memory that enables you to create your art without even thinking about it."

Raymond blinked. Was that *Lizzie* speaking at such a high level about the nature of creating?

When she held his gaze, seated a mere two feet away, he felt himself being sucked in—as though he'd surrendered himself to her, heart and soul. If she knew so much about art from decorating cookies and cakes, what else might Lizzie teach him? He had the sudden urge to spend every waking moment with her—even though they'd have to focus on their separate tasks while working at the store.

"That's a *gut*-looking wreath," she said with a nod. "How about if you swirl the rest of them with green frosting and I'll finish them off?"

"I was just going to ask if you'd dress up the stars I've frosted," Ruby put in.

"You could add some pizzazz to these poinsettias, too," Beulah remarked. "They look like boring pink blobs next to the cookies *you've* done."

"We can be an assembly line!" Lizzie replied. "I used to fuss at Maria for doing all the stars alike and all the snowflakes the same—but with this many cookies to decorate, it really would go faster if we handled them that way. Don't tell her I said that, though!"

In a twinkling Lizzie organized the remaining cookies into stacks. Raymond sat in awe as the four of them worked so much faster as a team than they had separately. Even so, it took them until nearly ten o'clock to finish the cookies and clean up afterward.

As they'd worked, he'd rehearsed different ways to invite Lizzie on a date. After a full day in the bulk store, however—with a busy Saturday the next day, when English customers would flock in all day for Christmas items—he opted for a good night's rest instead. Raymond wanted to be at his best when he worked up the nerve to ask Lizzie out.

She walked to the lodge's front door with him, her silence suggesting that she also had things on her mind. As they stepped out into the brisk night air, Lizzie cleared her throat.

"Want to go for a ride on my motor scooter tomorrow after supper? There's no church on Sunday, so we could stay out as late as we want."

Raymond's insides tightened. He'd seen Lizzie's bright pink scooter parked alongside Dale's car, in the carport behind the bulk store. He'd never ridden on such a small, open vehicle—especially not with a girl driving. "You think there's room for both of us on a—"

"If Maria's broad butt fits behind me, there's plenty of room for you," Lizzie teased.

The picture in his mind's eye, of him slipping

his arms around her as they roared down the road, was too delightful to resist. "Are you heading to Cloverdale? I'll spring for supper—"

"No way! Why would I want to see folks I know—which might include my sister—when I could spend my time with *you?*" she put in quickly. "Let's go to Forest Grove. The Kuhns have mentioned a café there, or we can find our own entertainment and food in places they wouldn't think to go. It's a straight shot down the state highway."

Though the next day would be December twelfth—definitely weather for winter coats—butterflies danced in Raymond's stomach. If their relationship moved forward during their date—because Lizzie had beat him to the punch, asking him out—it might affect his decision to return to Coldstream and never return.

"Best idea I've heard in forever," he said happily. "See you tomorrow, Lizzie."

"Not if I see you first!" she teased.

Chapter 9

As Lizzie rolled her scooter out of Dale's carport Saturday evening, her head was spinning. Should she go through with the surprise she'd been planning all day, or stick to the Forest Grove suggestion she and Raymond had discussed? He was smiling at her, driving her crazy with anticipation, and she wanted their first time out together to be perfect and unforgettable.

But I've been known to go over the top, acting on impulsive ideas that get me in trouble.

"You—you look really cute in those tie-dye overalls, Lizzie," Raymond murmured. "I was wondering how you'd manage your dress while we buzzed down the road."

As she gazed at the sweet, shy devotion on his face, Lizzie thought Raymond deserved a treat that would make a lot of people happy—or at least that's how she was imagining their little adventure. As she'd pondered the possibilities during the busy day working in Dale's store, she'd slipped out during her lunch break. She'd tucked a little bundle into the compartment of the scooter, just in case she went through with her surprise—

We're going. No time like the present—and no present like the time I'll be giving him.

"Here's a helmet for you, Raymond. Sorry it's hot pink—it's Maria's." Lizzie grinned at him, her mind made up as she strapped on her own pink helmet. "Hop on behind me and lean with the turns. I probably won't be able to understand much you say above the roar of the motor and the whistle of the wind—and it's not a *gut* idea to distract me while I'm focused on the road."

Raymond studied the girlie headgear for a moment before he put it on. "It's dark, so it's not like anybody'll see me," he reasoned. "We'll do our talking after we're settled at a table with something to eat."

As Lizzie swung her leg over the seat, she smiled furtively. Raymond had *no clue* about the visions that had danced in her head this afternoon as she'd been filling bags with Christmas jimmies and sugars.

Maybe I should've asked him about this idea . . . maybe it's me who has no clue about what I'm getting us into.

But her mind was made up.

As Raymond slipped his arms gently around her midsection, Lizzie closed her eyes in pleasure at the nearness of his body—and then forced herself to focus on driving. It was cold. The county highway was blacktop, and as the evening's temperatures dropped, the surface could become slick. It was *not* part of her happy plan for them to spin out because she'd lost control of the scooter.

As the motor roared to life and settled into a loud rumble, Lizzie prayed that they'd arrive safely at their destination. Her heart rose into her throat as she steered into the bulk store's back lot and around the building. She gripped the handlebars as they reached the road, pausing to check for traffic. As they rolled forward again, she turned right instead of left.

Raymond's body tensed. He rode silently for several moments before speaking near her ear. "Lizzie, you turned—Forest Grove is in the other direction!"

She nodded, turning her head slightly. "*Jah*, I know," she said above the rising whine of her engine. "Hang on, Raymond!"

Raymond's thoughts raced. What was Lizzie up to? Had she taken a notion to do something wild and crazy without warning him? Or was she showing off before making a wide loop at the next intersection to turn back toward their original destination?

Raymond was overjoyed to be holding Lizzie so close, roaring down the road as the trees and hills flashed by in a blur on either side of them. Yet he was also terrified. Lizzie was in total control, and he could say or do nothing to alter whatever impetuous ideas she had about their evening's entertainment. This wasn't how he'd envisioned their first romantic evening together.

As the minutes and miles sped by, he tried to think about the other towns—or even cafés—along the county highway, but he came up blank. This section of the Missouri countryside was mostly pasture and cropland, interspersed with acres of trees. Bare branches stretched up into the night sky, silhouetted against the magical pale blue of dusk—one of his favorite wintertime sights.

Coldstream.

Raymond exhaled with the sudden realization that the next town of any consequence in these parts was the very place he'd escaped so recently.

His body tingled with joy and surprise—yet Raymond desperately longed to grab the handlebars and turn the scooter around. Coldstream's little diner would be packed on this Saturday night so close to Christmas, and he wasn't any keener about being seen by folks he knew than Lizzie had been when she'd refused to go to Cloverdale. There was no chance of seeing his family there, of course, because suppers in a restaurant were as rare as hen's teeth—

What if she pulls in at the farm? There'll be no way to go anywhere else once our headlights shine through the kitchen window—no way to answer all the questions when Dat, Mamm, and Ezra see Lizzie's tie-dye overalls and my pink helmet.

"Lizzie, you're not—we're not going to Coldstream, are we?" Raymond demanded near her ear.

Beneath her heavy jacket, Lizzie's body was quaking with mirth. Her laughter rang out even as the wind blew it behind them.

Coldstream.

Raymond groaned, closing his eyes. Would it do any good to reason with her?

"Lizzie, the diner there will be really busy tonight—"

Her immediate shrug suggested she'd had something else in mind all along. They were now passing the farms on the outskirts of town, and Lizzie was gearing down to turn off the highway. As she steered onto the road that ran past his home place, Raymond still had no answers for all the questions his parents and Ezra would ask.

Without any apparent hesitation, Lizzie drove the scooter up the lane and stopped near the back door of the house where he'd lived all his life. Light spilled gently from the kitchen windows onto the snow-covered lawn. The aroma of fried meat greeted them.

"How'd you know where I live?" Raymond asked, yanking off the helmet.

Lizzie grinned at him as they got off the scooter. "I um, saw the return address on a letter you got from your *mamm*," she confessed as they dismounted. "I put it into my cell phone to find the driving directions, and—"

"Raymond!" Ezra called out as he opened the mudroom door. "We were just talking about you, and here you are—like magic. With a *friend.*"

Raymond pushed his hair back. The rise in his brother's voice warned him that he was in for some questions. "So I guess you'd better stop jawing about it and set a couple more places at the table, ain't so, Ezra?"

"Not here two minutes and you've resumed your place as the son who gets his way about everything. Sheesh."

When Ezra went back inside, Raymond gazed at Lizzie in the darkness. Her hair was mussed from wearing a helmet. Her circular bun cover, colorful overalls, and scooter announced loud and clear that she was a Mennonite who hadn't yet joined the church. Not the kind of girl his family wanted him to associate with.

"Are you ready for the inquisition? And the way they'll gawk at you?" he asked her.

Lizzie shrugged and started towards the door. "I've been gawked at all my life. Why should this evening be any different?"

Chapter 10

As Lizzie walked through the small mudroom, peering ahead into the Overholts' kitchen, reality hit her like a brick. It was one thing to show up at Raymond's home expecting to be welcomed with dinner—because any Plain family would make room at the table for a son and his friend.

It was another thing altogether, however, to face the curious folks seated in the kitchen. Their gazes held her like high-beam headlights, and she suddenly knew that coming here unannounced had *not* been one of her better ideas.

"God is *gut!*" Raymond's mother cried out as her fork clattered onto her plate. Her arms shot up into the air as she beamed at her son. "Raymond's home!"

Raymond hurried to his mother's wheelchair, parked to the left of his *dat*, and wrapped her in an embrace every bit as urgent as her cry had sounded. This left Lizzie standing on her own, with nothing to shield her from Mr. Overholt's intense scrutiny. Ezra, probably a couple of years older than Raymond, plunked two more plates on the table. He was studying her with a speculative smile, no doubt forming some interesting opinions about her.

"And who might *you* be?" Mr. Overholt asked. "This is surely the Lizzie that Raymond's told us about in his letters," Mrs. Overholt replied without missing a beat. "Have a seat, honey, and eat your supper while it's hot. I'm Alma, and this is my husband, Ervin, and that's Raymond's brother, Ezra. What a *wunderbar* surprise!"

Lizzie flashed Alma a grateful smile as she took the seat beside her, across from Raymond and his brother. "Nice to meet you folks," she said shyly.

"I've never known a girl who drove a motorcycle," Ezra said, passing her the platter of hamburger steaks smothered in fried onions.

"It's a scooter," Lizzie corrected softly. "I got it when I was traveling back and forth to help my disabled sister upstate."

"And you were driving it on the highway on a December night? On asphalt roads that turn slick in a heartbeat?" Ervin asked sternly. His deep-set eyes, framed by bushy graying brows and a U-shaped beard, flashed his disapproval. "We should thank the *gut* Lord we didn't receive a call that you two got hit and were smeared all over the—"

"But that didn't happen," Alma pointed out, shaking her fork at her husband. "And they can stay the night and drive back to Promise tomorrow afternoon, in broad daylight. What a joy, to see the two of you!"

Raymond helped himself to fried potatoes. "Lizzie surprised me," he admitted, winking at her. "I thought we were going to Forest Grove, and she drove here instead—without even asking me for directions."

"I could tell you were missing your family," Lizzie said softly. She looked at Alma then, hoping her words came out right. "And I'm sorry you've lost your best friend, too. Raymond was very concerned about you when he heard your news."

Alma blinked back sudden tears. "That was a tough day, and her funeral was this morning," she murmured in a thin voice. With a tremulous smile, she squeezed Lizzie's forearm. "Mighty thoughtful of you to bring my boy home for a visit. I appreciate it more than you know."

A respectful silence filled the kitchen, but only for a moment.

"It's time for Raymond to face reality and come home for *gut*," Ervin muttered, gazing purposefully at his youngest son. "Everyone knows he won't make a living at painting—"

"Have you sold any of your signs with the sparkly stars?" Ezra butted in. "They *are* kinda cool."

Raymond's glum expression brightened at his brother's question. "As of today, seventeen of them!" he replied. "And thanks to Lizzie's idea about adding a calendar hanger and key

204

holders—to make them *useful*—several Amish folks at Promise Lodge have purchased them."

"Sounds like you've also been getting valuable experience at running a store," Alma pointed out with a proud nod. "I'm sure Mr. Kraybill's glad to have you working there during the busy holiday season. Truth be told, our bulk store might be losing some business to the one in Promise, because folks around Coldstream are saying it's easier to find what they want there."

Ervin's face furrowed. "Who'd want to travel all that way to shop?"

"Several ladies have gone two or three together and hired a driver to take them," Alma replied. "They say the Kraybill store stocks a bigger variety of food—and Christmas items—and that everything appears so much fresher. Depending on what you want at Ralph Raber's store, you might have to dust off the package to see the expiration date."

Raymond's *dat* shrugged, focusing on his food again. "The newness will wear off after the holidays, no doubt. Especially when the roads get icy."

Lizzie kept quiet. It was best not to get caught in the middle of a conversation that see-sawed between defending Raymond and trying to set his father straight. In the end, she sensed Ervin Overholt, as the head of the family, would have his say.

Were all fathers so harsh? How had Raymond endured such criticism all his life?

Lizzie's own *dat* had passed when she was so young, she barely remembered him. Growing up in Malinda and Maria's care had been vastly different from having parents to set the rules and establish their expectations. She realized she might not want to answer to a man.

Raymond was right. If he and I were to marry, I'm not sure I could get along with his father. I would never measure up to his expectations, that's for sure.

After the meal, Lizzie and Raymond did the dishes while Ezra and Ervin went to the barn for the evening's round of livestock chores—which took a while, considering they had a dairy herd to feed and water. Alma insisted on drying, because the drainer sat on a section of countertop which had been lowered for her use.

"Son, you'll need to clear off the bed in the guest room," she said as she added a dried plate to her stack. "And Lizzie, if you need a nightgown, you could get by with one of my poor old things for one night."

"I brought one along, *denki*—as well as a dress for tomorrow," she added. "I'm pretty sure your husband doesn't like these colorful overalls."

"But they're cute!" Alma insisted with a chuckle. "And what woman in her right mind would drive down the road on a motor scooter in a dress? You're a Mennonite, am I right, dear?"

Lizzie was chuckling at Raymond's expression. He appeared amazed that she'd packed to stay overnight. "I grew up going to the Mennonite church in Cloverdale, *jah*. But I haven't taken my vows to join yet," she added with a sigh. "Sometimes I question if that's the path God intends for me to walk, even though my sister says it's high time I committed to *something*."

"That's a promise you shouldn't make until you're sure you can keep it." Alma gazed fondly from Lizzie to her son. "It's understandable that Raymond hasn't been in a rush to join the Old Order, either—a district's leadership determines the impression young people have of the church as a whole."

"*Jah*, Bishop Monroe in Promise Lodge is so much nicer than Obadiah Chupp," Raymond said with a shake of his head. "I'd have no trouble at all taking my instruction and joining there—but that implies that I'd be moving away from *you*, Mamm. I—I'm not sure that would be wise, for a lot of reasons."

"Who's to say you *couldn't* take your instruction and be baptized at Promise Lodge?" Alma countered with a shrug. "That wouldn't mean you had to live there."

Raymond let out a short laugh. "Can you imagine the grief Bishop Obadiah would give us if I did that? He's already upset that so many

Coldstream families have moved away to join that district."

"True enough." Alma's face glowed with love for her son. "Time will tell, kids. We'll be patient and listen for the Lord's voice," she murmured. "If I've learned anything from living in a wheelchair, it's *patience*—and that life works out the way it's supposed to if we don't try to do everything on our own."

By bedtime, Lizzie had grown very fond of Alma Overholt—maybe because she hadn't had a mother for so long. Once she said her good nights, she shook out her dress and climbed into bed with a head full of conflicting ideas. She was suddenly very tired, probably from focusing so intently on the road before she dealt with the various personalities in Raymond's family.

But sleep wouldn't come.

What if Raymond did take his vows in the Promise Lodge district? His mother has it right: I've dragged my feet about joining the church because of the minister in Cloverdale. My sister would be really mad if I joined the Old Order instead . . . and maybe my feelings for Raymond are the wrong reasons to become Amish.

And even if I become Amish, I doubt Ervin will ever think I'm the right wife for his son.

Lizzie sighed. Raymond's *dat* hadn't said a word to her after he and Ezra had come in from doing the chores. He probably suspected that she, with her tie-dye overalls and pink motor scooter, was a bad influence—determined to lead his son astray. And if he kept picking on his youngest boy, Lizzie wasn't sure she could keep her protests to herself.

But this worry is all a waste of time and sleep, ain't so? Now that I've met his family—and they've seen me—I doubt Raymond will want me as anything more than a friend. He'll come back to Coldstream after Christmas, and that'll be the end of it. I'll be alone anyway.

After a long, quiet chat with his *mamm* that had lasted into the wee hours, Raymond rose early to help his *dat* and brothers do the milking. His brothers took turns helping, and this morning Elmer and Earl were already in the barn when he arrived.

Years of practice hadn't made the chore any more agreeable to him. With each udder he disinfected before attaching the milking apparatus—and each smelly tail that slapped him in the face—he realized how eager he was to return to his morning routine at Dale's store.

"That girl Lizzie has some growing up to do," Dat remarked as he stood beside Raymond. Elmer and Earl listened with great interest from across the barn. "I can't believe you rode all the way to Coldstream on that pink deathtrap she drives, either."

What was I supposed to do—tell her to pull over and leave me on the roadside?

Something inside Raymond snapped. "So you'll be glad to hear that Mamm's calling Dick Mercer to drive us back to Promise this morning," he retorted. "That way, we'll not be riding the scooter on the slick blacktop."

He didn't need to see his father's raised eyebrow to know that his tone had crossed the line into disrespectful territory.

"I'm sorry," Raymond added quickly. "Considering the way you've insisted I should come home, I thought you'd at least act pleased to see me last night."

"You're leaving this morning?" Dat countered. "Can't you stay long enough to share Sunday dinner with us and spend more time with your mother? She pines for *you* far more than she's grieving for her friend Sarah."

"The early ride home was Mamm's idea." Raymond sighed. Why was every conversation with his *dat* so fraught with tension these days?

"*Jah*, and she suggested that you could take your vows at Promise Lodge, too," his father put in tautly. "But if you do that—and then end up staying there because that bishop is *nice*—you'll break her heart, Raymond. Do you want that on your conscience?

"And do you believe everything in life's going to be the way you daydream about it—*easy?*"

his father continued when Raymond turned to unhook the milking machine from the nearest cows. "Taking your instruction from Bishop Obadiah and the preachers here will be a frolic, compared to making a living with that painting you like to do. Not that you'll be allowed to continue with artwork after you join the Old Order."

With his jaw clenched to keep from sassing his *dat* again, Raymond nodded. It wasn't the first time he'd heard such a statement, after all.

As they released the cows' heads from their stanchions to prepare for the next group to be milked, the odor of bovine bodies and gasses enveloped him in a fog of resentment. He suddenly couldn't wait to get out of the barn and on the road. He was grateful when his brothers returned to their homes rather than going in for breakfast with them.

The sight of Lizzie in her deep green dress and fresh apron, setting the table as she chatted with Mamm, did Raymond's heart good, however. He realized that his mother had been very lonely in his absence—just as he knew, deep down, that his father was right about his need to find an acceptable occupation.

He would *not* be a dairy farmer. And he did *not* want to subject Lizzie to Dat's constant criticism. So what options did that leave him?

"Would you look at these beautiful cookies

Lizzie brought for us?" Mamm crowed as Dat and Ezra followed Raymond into the kitchen. "A little taste of Christmas!"

His brother went immediately to the plate and snatched a wreath. "Mmm—and they taste as *gut* as they look, too," he remarked with his mouth full.

Raymond smiled gratefully at Lizzie, realizing that this little gift had been part of last night's surprise.

Lizzie might be impulsive and scatterbrained, but she has the best intentions. And she's done these special favors for me as much as for my family.

Aromas of bacon, coffee, and cinnamon rolls soothed his tattered nerves. He was grateful that the conversation remained light during the meal. But he was also glad to see Dick Mercer's van pulling into the lane as he and Lizzie finished helping Mamm with the dishes. He went outside to load the motor scooter into the back of the vehicle, feeling an occasional snowflake on his face.

"It's a good thing I'm taking you kids to Promise now," Dick remarked as they closed the hatchback. "The snow forecasted for this afternoon has decided to arrive earlier than the weatherman predicted."

"We'll be right out," Raymond said quickly.

Once inside, he said a quick farewell to Dat and

Ezra in the front room. When he leaned down to hug his *mamm* in the kitchen, she held him tightly for several moments. Her smile seemed conspiratorial as she closed his fingers around a small envelope.

"Your fare, plus a little something to have fun on," she murmured. She turned to Lizzie then, her expression brightening as she opened her arms. "It was so *gut* to meet you, dear, and I look forward to spending more time with you whenever you can come."

A lump rose into Raymond's throat as he watched his mother and Lizzie share a warm embrace. At least *something* about this surprise visit had gone well.

Once they were settled into the van's back seat, his thoughts whirled in tighter circles. Raymond had so much to say—so many frustrations to get off his chest—yet he didn't feel right discussing personal matters while their English driver was listening. When Lizzie clasped his hand, however, he clung to it for the entire twenty-minute ride.

By the time Dick pulled up beside the lodge building, the snow was falling faster and the overcast sky suggested it might continue for hours.

"*Gut* thing we weren't riding the scooter," Lizzie admitted as they stepped outside.

Raymond nodded. "*Denki* for getting us here

213

safely—and be careful once you're back on the road," he said as he and Dick unloaded the pink vehicle.

When he paid their driver, his eyes widened at the number of ten- and twenty-dollar bills his mother had folded so tightly together. Mamm's suggestion about *fun* seemed extremely generous, and he suspected she'd emptied her can of egg money.

"I'll park the scooter in Dale's carport," Lizzie said. She focused on him with those pale green eyes, as somber as he'd ever seen her. "Then we need to talk, Raymond."

Chapter 11

Lizzie walked slowly back to the lodge as thick, fat snowflakes swirled around her. How could she share her concerns with Raymond without sounding doubtful about his father, their faiths—and their future together? Their trip to Coldstream might not have been the finest idea she'd ever had, but she now had an inkling of the uphill battle that awaited her if she married Raymond.

Then again, maybe he'd never ask her. Maybe his *dat* would forbid the marriage.

And maybe, if Coldstream's bishop is so unpleasant, joining the Old Order to be with Raymond is the last thing I need. I could stay at Promise Lodge and be happier without struggling to accept a different religion and a difficult dat.

When she gazed at Raymond, who was waiting on the porch, however, Lizzie knew she'd never be happy without him. She might be a spur-of-the-moment girl who leaped first and looked later, but never in her life had she been so sure of anything.

The guy with the lopsided smile, wearing houndstooth checked pants and a red sweater, had stolen her heart.

As Raymond speared his fingers into the dark hair that swooped a little too far over the red frames of his glasses, he looked even more nervous than she felt. "Lizzie, if you don't want to be with me anymore, I'll—"

"No!" she cried, racing up the porch steps. "I mean, *yes,* I want to be with you, Raymond! I *love* you! But so many things can come between us, like—"

"If we let them." He swallowed hard, grasping her hands. "We can do this, Lizzie. We can make a life for ourselves if we believe we can."

Lizzie's mouth snapped shut. Where had such confidence come from? Raymond suddenly sounded so decisive. So determined to make it work. And she had declared her love without a moment's hesitation.

"Shall we go in where it's warm? Maybe talk in the room where we have church?" Raymond asked as he opened the lodge's door. "Ruby and Beulah won't think it's proper if I go up to your apartment—"

"You can't. Men aren't allowed upstairs."

"—and if we sit in my cabin, I—I don't trust myself to remain proper at all."

Lizzie blinked. Raymond was blushing. His Adam's apple bobbed as he swallowed, gazing at her as though he couldn't stop.

"I love you, too, Lizzie," he whispered. "You're the brightest star in my life, and if you don't want

216

me, I—I don't know how I'll go on. *Please* say we can work things out."

Her heart thundered. For a guy who'd barely talked to her while they were in Coldstream, Raymond had said a lot in the past few moments. And before she realized what was happening, he'd closed the door and pulled her into his arms, and she got lost in the unexpected exhilarating thrill of—

His kiss.

Oh, but Raymond could kiss! Lizzie wrapped her arms around his neck as he leaned down to hold her closer. His lips searched hers as he clung to her breathlessly, as though he'd never get enough. And she was responding as though she'd been born for this moment. This man.

Behind them, someone cleared his throat loudly. "And what does this mean?" a familiar voice asked.

With a gasp Lizzie let go of Raymond so she could face Dale Kraybill. The storekeeper appeared to be fighting a smile, yet there was no mistaking the stern tone of his question as he stood in the doorway.

"It means I'll be asking Bishop Monroe to start my instruction so I can join the Amish church, sir," Raymond replied firmly. "And it means I'm in love with Lizzie. And I promise you'll never see us doing this in the store."

"And—and it means I'll be taking my instruction, too," Lizzie chimed in. Her heart was hammering even harder as she heard those words coming out of her mouth—because mere moments ago, she'd been talking herself out of a relationship with Raymond.

Dale's raised eyebrow expressed the doubts that had been circling like wary dogs in Lizzie's own mind.

"Are you sure about this, Lizzie?" he asked quietly. "Becoming Amish means more than giving up your motor scooter and playful print dresses, and trading in your bun cover for a pleated white *kapp*. You'll be taking on a faith that will *shun* you—isolate you completely—if you break the rules—"

"Which means I'd better get used to following rules, *jah*?" Lizzie interrupted boldly. "After all these years of being footloose, going my own way, living my life with more structure and purpose sounds like a fine idea, ain't so?"

Dale's eyes widened with surprise. "Good answer," he murmured. "I hope you've thought this through. Use the time during your instruction to be sure you're making a promise to God you can keep without regrets."

Lizzie stepped aside and took Raymond with her. "Guess we're blocking the door. I, um, lost all track of time and place."

"Beulah and Ruby have invited me for Sunday

218

dinner," Dale explained. "Shall I tell them you'll be in shortly?"

"*Jah*! They'll want to know we've made it back from Coldstream," Lizzie replied. She flashed Raymond a grin. "I told the Kuhns where I was taking you, and that we'd be gone overnight, so they wouldn't be worried about us. It seemed like the responsible thing to do."

Raymond's laughter rang out in the lobby. "All of a sudden we're both sounding a lot more responsible, *jah*? We'd better be ready to answer every little question those two will ask us, as well."

"And after dinner we'll go see Bishop Monroe," Lizzie said.

"We will. Because it's the responsible thing to do," he quipped.

For Raymond, the next five days flew by in a euphoric whirlwind. He and Lizzie were taking their instruction with Bishop Monroe and Preacher Amos—who, as a lifelong family friend, was especially pleased to help them along their journey of faith. Life felt more incredibly fulfilling than he'd ever dared to imagine.

Could there be anyone cuter—or more loving—than Lizzie? Who else would set aside her more lenient religion, as well as her reservations about his faith and his father, to prepare for life as Mrs. Raymond Overholt? Raymond knew just how he'd ask that all-important question, but he'd been giving her time to change her mind, as Dale had suggested.

Her kisses told him she was falling even more deeply in love with him, however.

As he stood at the cash register checking out a line of customers—because Dale had encouraged him to take on more of the storekeeping—he couldn't wait for six o'clock. It was December nineteenth, the Saturday afternoon before Christmas. He and Lizzie planned to enjoy the carol sing-along, spiced cider and goodies, and other festivities the Kuhns and the Bender sisters had planned for everyone at the lodge this evening. Gently falling snow covered the hillsides, and he hoped a moonlight walk would provide the perfect time to propose.

As Raymond handed his customer her receipt, however, he froze. Just inside the entryway, Bishop Obadiah Chupp stood gazing around the busy store with a critical eye. Beside him, Dat wore the same doubtful expression as he studied the remaining Star of Wonder plaques. Although their black coats and broad-brimmed black hats were normal winter attire for Amish men, they reminded him of buzzards. Their scowls told Raymond they'd come here as messengers of doom.

Never mind why they're here. Breathe. Wait on the next customer.

Focusing on the elderly English couple who'd placed their items on the counter, Raymond smiled. "Did you find everything you wanted, folks?"

The white-haired woman laughed. "Never fails! I come in here with a list and leave with at least ten items that weren't on it."

"Really puts us in the Christmas spirit to shop here," her husband remarked. He held up the star plaque he'd taken off the wall. "And *this* piece will have a place of honor on the mantel. What a message!"

"I can't wait to watch this star sparkle when it's reflecting the lights from our Christmas tree," the woman said with a gentle smile. "I'll probably sing 'We Three Kings' each time I see it!"

Raymond's heart swelled. "I'm glad you like it," he murmured. "I make those plaques myself, and we've sold all but the few that are left on the wall."

"*You* made this wonderful piece?" she exclaimed excitedly. "Well, I love it even more now that I've met its creator!"

As his cheeks went hot, Raymond wondered if his *dat* and Bishop Obadiah had overheard the compliments his artwork had just received. He focused on checking and bagging, however, rather than looking around to see where his unexpected guests had gone. Dale was outside plowing the parking lot, so it was up to Raymond to keep the checkout line moving smoothly.

"Thanks for your patience, folks! This has to be our busiest day ever!" Marlene said as she joined Raymond behind the counter. "What if you check and I'll bag for you. It'll speed things along now that we're so busy."

The twitch in her smile told Raymond that she, too, had spotted the visitors from Coldstream. "That'll be a big help, Marlene. And did you find everything you wanted today, ma'am?" he asked cheerfully as he began checking the next lady's items.

"I'm so glad you folks opened this store!" she remarked as she unloaded her cart. "You have the best selection of baking supplies and decorations anywhere around. I also got several bars of this goat milk soap to use as stocking stuffers, as well as this locally made cheese for my party trays."

Raymond nodded. "I'll tell Rosetta and the Kuhn sisters how much you enjoyed finding their products—which are made right here at Promise Lodge," he added.

Beside him, Marlene was quickly packing the items into plastic sacks. After he'd totaled the bill, she murmured, "Stay calm, Raymond. We'll handle this like the competent employees we are."

When he looked up, his father and the bishop were standing side by side, blocking Raymond's view of anything else. Their identical stern expressions warned him that spreading Christmas joy was the last thing on their minds. Before he could open his mouth to greet them, Bishop Obadiah started in.

"We've come to take you home, Raymond," he said in his reedy preaching voice. "When I discovered—just yesterday—that you'd begun working here and selling your art, I was sorely disappointed. It's my mission to snatch you back from the devil's own lair and put you on the path to salvation again."

"As you can see, Bishop," Marlene chimed in immediately, "Raymond is running the store and can't leave the cash register while all of these customers are waiting to check out. Why don't you men make yourselves comfortable over at the lodge? Raymond will be there after the store closes at six."

"Your *mamm*'s expecting you home in time for supper," Dat stated, gazing steadily at Raymond. "After the bishop talked to us about this situation, we realized we were wrong to allow you to come to Promise Lodge. If we start now, we'll make it back by dark."

Raymond's throat got so tight, he couldn't swallow. Deep down, he didn't believe his mother agreed with what his *dat* and the bishop were saying—but he knew better than to challenge them. It was an argument he couldn't win.

He kept his voice low, aware that strangers were listening. "But with Dale outside plowing, I can't just up and leave—"

"What's more important, Raymond? Honoring your parents' wishes—following your faith—or working here among English, where temptation lurks?" Bishop Obadiah demanded.

Raymond broke a sweat. How was he supposed to answer such an absurd question? The customers in line, as well as several others in the store, were gazing toward the checkout counter as though they couldn't believe what they were hearing—and some of them appeared ready to lay aside their items and leave. When Dale strode in through the front door, brushing snow from his coat, Raymond prayed hard for a quick resolution to this difficult, embarrassing situation.

"What can I do for you fellows?" the storekeeper asked the bishop and Dat. "If there's a problem, can we possibly shift it into the warehouse? I can take over here if you need me to, Raymond," he added gently.

"Maybe you'd better," Raymond murmured. "I'm sorry, Mr. Kraybill."

The storekeeper's sympathetic smile told Raymond that someone must've warned him about the disruption at the cash register. When he led his two guests into the warehouse to continue their discussion, Lizzie looked up from the worktable, where she was filling bags with old-fashioned ribbon candies. Was it Raymond's imagination, or did her smile conceal a secret?

"*Gut* afternoon, Ervin," she called out. "Nice to see you again."

Dat nodded but said nothing. Raymond was frantically trying to think of a way to stall the difficult discussion he anticipated—but as Bishop Obadiah was opening his mouth to speak, the back door of the warehouse opened to admit Preacher Amos. Bishop Monroe was behind him, closing the door against a gust of snow.

"Bishop Monroe, I believe you've met Bishop Obadiah Chupp from the Coldstream district," Preacher Amos said as the two men approached. "And this other fellow is Ervin Overholt, Raymond's *dat*."

"Pleased to see you fellows," Bishop Monroe said as he shook their hands. "It's *gut* you got off the highway when you did. As we walked over here, police cars and an ambulance were fishtailing on the slick blacktop, probably on their way to an accident."

"Did a driver bring you?" Amos asked quickly. "We'll be happy to fix you all up with a place to spend the night."

Raymond caught a mischievous grin on Lizzie's face as she kept on bagging candy. Had she been the one to fetch Dale, and then call Amos and Bishop Monroe?

"Alma's expecting us back for supper," Dat insisted. "We'd best be pointing the buggy in that direction if we're to—"

"You drove a rig on a day like this?" Amos asked incredulously. "Why in God's *gut* name would you risk life and limb—not to mention your horse—in this snowstorm? You might have made it here in about three hours when the weather was clear, but this snow will make the trip back a lot longer."

"Way too dangerous," Bishop Monroe added with a frown. "The visibility out there is about nil right now. A car could plow into you without even seeing you."

"God will look after us," Bishop Obadiah countered, "because we came on His mission, to fetch Raymond back home."

Raymond was relieved to see that his father was apparently having second thoughts—which meant it was Dat's rig and horse they were risking rather than Chupp's.

As Dat sighed, his body seemed to deflate. "Maybe staying overnight is the better idea," he admitted. "God might be looking after *us,* but that's no guarantee those English drivers can keep their cars under control."

"And if something happened to us on the road," Raymond put in softly, "think about the crisis that would create for Mamm. How about if I call her, right now? Tell her we're staying here until the roads are safer?" he asked, nodding toward the phone on the wall.

Bishop Obadiah bristled like a rooster with its feathers ruffled. "I want nothing to do with staying here overnight—"

"We could call a driver for you, Obadiah," Preacher Amos challenged, "but I wouldn't put Dick Mercer or anyone else in danger just because you have a bee in your bonnet. We're having a carol sing-along and refreshments tonight at the lodge—and a little Christmas spirit would be *gut* for both of you fellows. Shall we head on over and set you up in cabins?"

Chapter 12

As the lodge's big meeting room rang with dozens of voices singing "Angels We Have Heard on High," Lizzie slipped into a back corner with Raymond. She'd sensed that eavesdropping on the intense conversation Bishop Obadiah and Ervin were having with her beleaguered, beloved Raymond wasn't a good idea, but now she hoped to hear what was really going on.

Raymond shook his head forlornly. "Once the road's clear, I don't see any way to stay here—even to finish out my last three days before Dale closes the store for Christmas Eve," he murmured. "Please don't get any ideas about going with me, Lizzie. It's not a *gut* idea to cross Obadiah Chupp."

"Why is he so *mean?* And so determined that you're damning your eternal soul by being here?" Lizzie asked beneath the music. "Surely Bishop Monroe's told him we're taking our instruction, so—"

"That's a sore point, too. He thinks I should be doing that in Coldstream."

Lizzie frowned. She understood now why so many families had left Bishop Obadiah's district to live at Promise Lodge . . . and she wasn't sure she should take on the Amish faith to live in Coldstream. But she didn't express her doubts. That would only make Raymond feel even worse.

"*Denki* for calling Dale into the store, and for phoning Preacher Amos and Bishop Monroe," Raymond said, his eyes alight with gratitude. "I truly believe that Chupp would've expected Dat to drive us home in the snowstorm if those men hadn't interceded for me."

Lizzie sighed. By the time the store had closed at six, seven inches of fresh snow had blanketed the area—and it showed no sign of letting up. She didn't want to think about all the horrible things that could've happened to the Overholt rig in such dicey weather.

"We'll figure it out, Raymond," she insisted, grasping his hand.

He held her gaze as though he had things on his mind he was hoping to say—but he clammed up when Bishop Obadiah broke away from the crowd to speak with them.

"And who have we here, Raymond?" he asked, glaring at their interlocked fingers.

"This is Lizzie Zehr," Raymond replied, refusing to release her hand. "She's also taking instruction to join the Old Order—"

"You'd better consider that *very* carefully, young lady," the bishop said sternly. "We Old Order Amish hold ourselves to higher standards than you Mennonites are accustomed to. We have different ideas about sin and its consequences. And the most unforgiveable sin of all is changing your mind—jumping the fence after you've taken your vows."

As Lizzie held his gaze, she saw no compassion in the eyes that resembled hard black beads. "*Jah*, I understand," she murmured. "Bishop Monroe and Preacher Amos have talked to us on that subject, and—"

"The church here has *no* concept of God's true expectations," Chupp cut in. "If you think—"

"I believe the Bible verse in John that says God loved the world so much that He gave us Jesus so we'd have eternal life," Lizzie stated firmly. "And in this season of celebrating Jesus's birth, I'm even more convinced that God is about love rather than damnation."

Her heart was pounding hard as she countered Coldstream's bishop, but she'd spoken straight from her soul. Christians everywhere believed in John 3:16, a bedrock verse of the Bible. Didn't they?

"That's the trouble with being young," Bishop Obadiah muttered. "You don't know what you don't know."

As he turned to leave them, Raymond sighed. "I'm sorry he's such a negative man, Lizzie. I hope you won't hold that against me as you think about our future together."

Lizzie sighed, too. "You can't control another

man's attitude, sweetie. We'll just have to keep believing things will work out."

But how long can I hold on to that possibility? What if I'm getting myself into a situation I'll be sorry about someday?

By Sunday morning the snow had stopped and the roads were clear. Raymond had heard the plows at work during most of his sleepless night, but he felt relieved when Dat and Bishop Obadiah insisted on staying for church at Promise Lodge rather than rushing home. It allowed him the slim, shimmering hope that Bishop Monroe and Preacher Amos might prevail in the spirit of Christmas as they preached the morning's sermons.

Preacher Amos spoke about how love came down at Christmas, in the form of a helpless baby completely dependent upon His parents—just as humans were beholden to God for everything in their lives.

Raymond nodded at the preacher's points. A couple of pew benches in front of him, Bishop Obadiah sat alongside Dat, but he couldn't see their faces or gauge their reactions to this message about Christmas love.

He sat up straighter when the preacher picked up the star plaque that decorated the fireplace mantel.

" 'Star of wonder, star of night . . . guide us

231

to Thy holy light,' " Amos read in his resonant voice. "This Christmas, what if we allow ourselves to feel *wonder?* To be as amazed about the miracle of Jesus's birth as a child again?"

After letting his challenge settle in the congregation's minds, Preacher Amos continued.

"When I look at our star plaque at home, where our calendar now hangs, and the morning sunlight makes it sparkle and shine, I let myself forget that it's barn board and paint," he said in a hushed voice. "Instead, I let the star awaken in me that sense of mystery and awe the wise men must've felt when they realized God was fulfilling Isaiah's Old Testament prophesy about a star coming out of Jacob—the promised Messiah—and that *they* were to be a part of it!"

Raymond couldn't recall ever seeing a preacher's face so alight with happiness or hearing a sermon that rang with such quiet conviction. Who knew his plaque would inspire such a stirring Sunday message?

"And *we* are fulfilling God's mission as well, my friends!" Amos continued. "As we enter into this final leg of our journey to Bethlehem, let our hearts be filled with the glory of the Lord and the wonder and joy of our Savior's birth! And let us spread that wonder and joy to others, wherever we go!"

Raymond's whole body thrummed. How could

his father and Bishop Obadiah possibly harbor ill will or negativity after such a sermon?

Later, after prayers and another hymn, Bishop Monroe stood up to deliver the second, longer sermon. He smiled confidently at everyone in the lodge's meeting room.

"You've probably heard the old joke about how different Jesus's birth would've been had the three wise men been women," he began jovially. "Instead of gold, frankincense, and myrrh, they would've arrived with practical gifts like a casserole, diapers, and baby powder."

Chuckles came from both the women's and men's side of the room.

"It's a humorous story," the bishop continued, "but between the lines it reminds us that in Bible times—and today—men have been the church's leaders, but the women have always done the real work of keeping faith and family together. Think about your mother, and the other women you've admired in your lives, and you'll know this to be true."

Raymond's eyes widened. He already knew how Bishop Obadiah would react to Monroe's thoughts about females and their place. And from things he'd gleaned from the local women's conversations, Raymond sensed Monroe Burkholder was going down this conversational path on purpose, to provoke the Coldstream bishop while he sat among the folks of Promise Lodge.

The tall, broad-shouldered bishop paused to look directly at Bishop Obadiah before he continued. "One of the messages Christmas brings us is the need to respect our wives and mothers, and to encourage our young men to show love for women rather than assuming they have the right, as sons and husbands, to dominate them," he insisted. "This is borne out in the very first chapter of Genesis, verse twenty-seven, which says God created the male *and* the female in His own image.

"Let us also remember," Bishop Monroe continued earnestly, "that God could have saved His ancient people from their sins by any means He wanted, yet He decided His Son should be born in human form. And he chose young Mary to bear the baby that would become our salvation."

Raymond noted that both women and men were nodding at these words. Bishop Obadiah began to shift on the pew bench, however, his tension mounting visibly during the rest of the service. The final words of the benediction had barely left Bishop Monroe's mouth when Chupp jumped to his feet.

"You people preach nothing but heresy!" he cried out. He was so agitated that his untrimmed U-shaped beard rippled as he hurried to the front to address the congregation. "Not only has Amos Troyer admired *artwork* to the point of worshipping a graven image, but Burkholder has totally ignored the true creation story in Genesis—and all the rest of the Bible's teaching about how women are to remain silent and submit to their men!"

"Ah, but there are two creation stories in Genesis," Bishop Monroe countered.

"This is all the more reason for me to return young Raymond to Coldstream," Chupp continued, totally ignoring what Monroe had said. "He can take his instruction in a district that follows the *true* Amish faith—"

"He's already preparing to join the church *here*," Preacher Amos put in.

"Which is a direct route to damnation!" Bishop Obadiah ranted. "And as for what Raymond should learn about respecting women—"

"Stop right there!" Amos's wife—who'd been Mattie Schwartz when she lived in Coldstream—stood up with the fire of conviction in her eyes. "Why should any of us listen to a bishop who allowed my first husband to mistreat me to the point that he *broke my nose?*"

"And what about all those barn fires?" her sister Christine demanded as she, too, stood up to accuse Chupp. "Not only did we lose our barn in one of the blazes we suspect your son Isaac started, but my husband died trying to put it out. Meanwhile, you looked the other way, Obadiah."

"You looked the other way when Isaac and his friends were caught drinking in *our* barn, too,"

Rosetta put in as she joined her older sisters. "And then it caught fire—"

"And Isaac threw my daughter in a ditch, trying to compromise her after she reported the Bender fire to the sheriff," Preacher Eli Peterscheim said as he rose from the preachers' bench. "Is it any wonder our families have come to Promise Lodge? We want nothing more to do with your version of salvation, Chupp!"

Raymond's eyes felt ready to pop. He'd heard whisperings about the events the Bender sisters and Preacher Eli had mentioned, but no one had ever openly challenged Bishop Obadiah in Coldstream. As someone else stood up on the women's side, Raymond's breath caught in his throat.

It was Lizzie. And she appeared so fired-up— yet fearful—that he loved her even more.

"I'm taking my instruction to join the Amish church, as well, Bishop Obadiah, but—but I could *never* live in your district!" she declared with a hitch in her voice. "Instead of encouraging us to love one another, all you seem to do is condemn people. Every time you open your mouth, a cloud of black smoke comes out."

As the room rang with condemnatory silence, Raymond's heart sank. Lizzie had just announced, in front of God and everyone else, that he would have to choose between her and his family. If she still agreed to marry him, she wanted no part of living where he could be with his dear, needy mother.

"I don't have to listen to this," Bishop Obadiah muttered. He found Raymond on the men's side and pointed at him. "It's not proper to travel on the Sabbath, so we'll be heading home before first light tomorrow, Raymond. Be ready."

Chapter 13

That night in his cabin, Obadiah was so wound up about the waywardness of the Promise Lodge district, he anticipated a restless night. The full moon beamed through his window, yet its serene beauty was lost on him as he fumed about folks who refused to see that his way of faith was the *right* way.

When he finally fell asleep, he continued to toss and turn until he was overcome by a strange dream. He saw approaching him the three mystical kings who'd come from afar to worship the newborn Jesus. As they crossed the sand on their camels, Obadiah heard the tinkle of harness bells on the warm desert wind . . . saw the sparkle of magnificent, jeweled robes and inhaled the pungent aroma of incense as they approached him. He dreamed so vividly that he felt enveloped by the majestic presence of these ancient sages who'd followed a star to Bethlehem—and who were dismounting from their camels to speak with him.

Who am I that these wise, powerful men have chosen to see me?

He watched in awe as the first king approached him at a ceremonial pace. His robe was a deep blue like the night sky, spangled with golden stars that shimmered as he walked. A crown of gold sat atop his head, with sapphires set into its peaks, and his face was covered with a gossamer veil shot through with gold threads. Obadiah was too enthralled to speak, ready to fall to his knees in such a powerful potentate's presence—

But when the king detached the veil, it was Rosetta Bender who stood staring at him. Her eyes could look directly into his soul, and she was clearly disgusted with what she saw.

Obadiah suspected he was dreaming—he'd consumed too many cookies with coffee before bedtime—but he couldn't wake up. When he tried to tell Rosetta to leave, he couldn't utter a sound. He nearly jumped out of his skin when a loud male voice filled the cabin.

"Obadiah!" the invisible presence called out. "You recall that Rosetta remained at home to care for her aging parents until they passed on—but do you remember how you constantly badgered her to find a husband? And belittled her because she'd passed the age of thirty without attracting a man? Is it any wonder she and her sisters sold their farms to leave your district? And *then* you declared they were going to hell because they started the Promise Lodge community without your permission!"

As Rosetta's gaze continued to bore into him, Obadiah struggled in vain to protest the voice's accusations. What had come over him? Why was he unable to move or speak?

"And let's not forget the way you disgraced Deborah Peterscheim for notifying the police about the Bender barn fire instead of holding your son Isaac and his friends accountable for setting it—and for attacking her," the ominous voice continued. "That's despicable, Obadiah."

When Obadiah tried to defend himself, nothing came out. At long last Rosetta stepped aside, but he felt no relief. He was being held hostage— and two more of the mysterious robed figures remained on the horizon.

Obadiah swallowed hard. He was the one who'd always called the shots, and it was a nasty shock to have his control taken away from him.

As the second regal figure approached, Obadiah tried desperately to escape—or to wake up, for he was surely having a nightmare. Unconcerned about his anxiety, the next king advanced at a stately pace and stopped in front of him. This visitor's deep green robes were trimmed in gold, and emeralds glimmered in his crown. The face was hidden behind a veil made of miniscule golden pipes that tinkled frenetically in the rising, hot wind. Above the tiny chimes, the eyes of this visitor revealed themselves to be female—and filled with tears—as they watched him relentlessly.

Fear rose up Obadiah's throat. Why did he feel

so powerless—unable to look away from this distressing visitor? The overwhelming aroma of incense suddenly choked him as the king's heavy robes parted in the center, like curtains opening on a stage.

Beneath the regal clothing, a fire raged, engulfing a white barn. The deafening, pathetic cries of dairy cattle escaping the flames filled the cabin, along with clouds of thick, black smoke. Obadiah began coughing uncontrollably. When a man rushed inside the burning structure, he tried to call out a warning, but some inexplicable force still muted him. As the barn's roof collapsed with an ominous creak, a single cry of agony pierced the night sky.

"Obadiah!" the powerful male voice boomed around him again. "It was Isaac who also set the Hershbergers' barn on fire after he and his friends had been drinking there. Willis lost his life that night, leaving Christine and her daughters to fend for themselves as they struggled to maintain their dairy. Instead of holding your son accountable, you hounded Christine about getting married again, totally ignoring her loss and grief."

When the wind drove the smoke from the cabin and the second apparition went to stand beside her sister, Obadiah tried again to awaken from this terrifying nightmare. His arms and legs felt paralyzed, however, as the third king approached him. He began sweating profusely, terror rising within him because he knew whom to expect this time—and she was far more outraged and outspoken than her younger sisters. Golden threads glimmered on her rich robes of purple and scarlet, which billowed in the gale-force wind. The gossamer veil attached to her ornate, ruby-encrusted crown shimmered as she held his gaze with her silent accusations.

Slowly and purposefully, Mattie Schwartz pulled her veil aside to reveal a face so bruised and battered that he barely recognized her. Her nose sat at an unnatural angle as blood splattered onto her gown.

"Obadiah!" the deafening voice said again. "This is what Marvin Schwartz did to Mattie on one of the several occasions he lost control of his temper. Yet you turned away from her suffering and supported her husband's right to *discipline* her. If it hadn't been for Marvin's unchecked diabetes, Mattie surely would've died before he did."

Obadiah shook uncontrollably. He tried to look away from Mattie's ghastly face, yet he couldn't move his neck or close his eyes. He struggled for breath, wondering if the three angry apparitions would now attack him while he was at their mercy.

Instead, they raised their arms to point at him.

"How does it feel to be defenseless and alone, Obadiah?" Rosetta demanded. "Before long, everyone in Coldstream will get fed up with your lack of compassion. Young people—like Raymond and Lizzie—won't want to remain there. You'll soon have no one left to preach to."

"It's about time you confessed and begged for forgiveness—for your heinous behavior and heartless lack of compassion!" Christine declared.

Mattie came to lean over Obadiah as he lay in the bed unable to move. Blood plopped onto the sheets as she shifted her shattered nose into place to set the bones, grimacing in pain.

"This is your day of reckoning, Obadiah," she said in a ghastly voice. "Are you prepared to meet your Maker? To stand before God as He confronts you with the sins you've committed against the women in your district? Unless you change your ways in a hurry, it would be better for you if you'd never been born."

Obadiah began to cry, struggling against the invisible bonds that still held him fast in the bed. For a moment all three of the Bender sisters hovered above him—

Until the air got sucked from the cabin. The terrifying vision went with it.

Obadiah went limp all over. What on earth had just happened to him?

Very carefully he sat up in bed. He felt weak, as though he'd been bedridden with a devastating disease. The moonlight showed him that the cabin was unchanged—and he was grateful that he saw no blood on the bed. But his damp sheets attested to the ordeal he'd endured while under a tremendous amount of stress.

He used the bathroom and finally sighed with relief. "Well, at least it's over now," he murmured. "What a nightmare that was—"

No, Obadiah, I'm not finished with you. Don't you dare act as though nothing has happened!

It was that powerful male voice again, only inside his head this time. Maybe he was losing his mind—

Or maybe I'm giving you a chance to start again—after you've apologized to the people here that you've treated so shabbily.

Obadiah blinked. He was filled with the overwhelming sense that this was God Himself talking, and that he'd better do more than just listen. It was one thing to brush aside a nightmare starring the Bender sisters, but it was folly indeed to ignore a visitation from the Lord.

But what were his options? It was two in the morning—not a good time to knock on doors and apologize. Nightmare or not, Obadiah still intended to start back to Coldstream in a few hours, because—among other reasons—Alma Overholt needed to have her youngest son home for Christmas.

Something made him look in the drawer of the nightstand. A tablet and a pen were there, as though they'd been placed for his specific use—

yet another detail that convinced him a higher power was at work.

Obadiah sat down at the cabin's small table and turned on the battery lamp. He bowed his head, because he was completely out of practice at apologizing.

I need your help, God, because without it, I'm going to write this letter all wrong—just as I've done so many other hurtful things over the years. Maybe I've been a bit arrogant—

There was the sound of a throat clearing.

Obadiah sighed. *All right, so I've been extremely arrogant, always insisting on doing things my own way. Show me how You'd have me live, Lord. Help me follow Your star to worship and serve You and Your Son. Please.*

He wrote, and he wrote some more. He addressed each of the Bender sisters' situations. He apologized to Amos Troyer and to the entire Peterscheim family—especially daughter Deborah. He included Marlene Fisher and her brother, the most recent folks to leave Coldstream. He even complimented Monroe on a thought-provoking sermon. And finally, he thanked young Lizzie for reminding him that love was the reason for the season—and for everything else pertaining to God's creatures, great and small.

When Obadiah recopied the letter in his best handwriting, it was six pages long. As he was folding it to leave it on the table for his hosts, someone knocked on the cabin door.

Raymond stood there, holding his suitcase. "Dat's got the rig hitched up. We're ready to go."

Obadiah smiled at him. Raymond's red pants and oversize glasses made him stand out as an artistic type, but he was a good kid, trying to find his way in the world. And as his bishop, Obadiah now realized that he was supposed to offer encouragement and guidance rather than judgment and condemnation.

"Let's hit the road, Raymond. We have a long way to go and a lot to talk about."

Chapter 14

"Lizzie, look at this letter! Bishop Obadiah has undergone a miraculous change of heart, and he's thanking you for being a part of it."

As she accepted the pages Rosetta handed her before supper Monday evening, Lizzie sighed. From her room, she'd watched the Overholt rig depart in the predawn darkness. She'd spent the day in the store with a huge hole in her heart because Raymond hadn't been there.

She understood why he had to go. But his departure felt so final.

She'd meant what she said in church, about refusing to live in Coldstream because Bishop Obadiah was so critical and unloving. But where did that leave her?

Alone, mostly. Probably for the rest of my life. Why would Raymond choose me over his family?

As Lizzie sank into a kitchen chair, the Kuhns and the Bender sisters went on about their cooking. She began to read, convinced that nothing Obadiah Chupp said would measure up to Rosetta's mention of a change of heart. After all, that cranky old man wouldn't know a smile if it smacked him in the face.

Yet the bishop was apologizing—mentioning

specific things he was sorry for and asking the folks who'd left Coldstream to forgive him.

> And, Lizzie, you were right to remind me that God is love, and that I need to reflect His love in my dealings with you and Raymond and everyone I meet. You have a sparkle as bright as that star the Sunday sermons were about, and I wish you well as you take your instruction to join the Amish church. Our faith needs enthusiastic, spontaneous young women like you to keep it fresh and alive.

Lizzie blinked. She had to read Obadiah's words about her two more times to let them sink in.

"Um, how do we know Obadiah wrote this letter?" she asked cautiously.

Rosetta, Mattie, and Christine burst out laughing.

"We've all said that same thing," Mattie admitted. "But Amos recognizes Obadiah's handwriting. He thinks we should give the bishop a chance to suit his actions to his words—especially during this season of love and light."

"Monroe believes that because all things are possible with God, we should offer Obadiah the forgiveness he seeks, in *gut* faith that his letter is sincere," Christine put in. "He's calling it a Christmas miracle!"

"And it came about because Raymond brought his star plaques to sell at Dale's store," Rosetta pointed out with a big smile. "You never can tell which little things we do and say will lead somebody to follow God's star."

As the Kuhns put in their remarks, Lizzie rose to help with the final supper preparations. She wanted to believe Bishop Obadiah had turned over a shiny new leaf. But she also needed to know how his change of mindset might affect the plans she and Raymond had made about joining the Old Order . . . and getting married.

"I've only just met him, so I'll go with what you ladies say," Lizzie remarked as she took dinner plates from the cabinet.

While she set the table, she pondered the bishop's letter again. She was arranging the silverware when the phone rang in the kitchen. Mattie answered it, and then said, "Alma Overholt! Merry Christmas to you, dear!"

Lizzie's pulse picked up. Surely Raymond and his *dat* had arrived home hours ago, so why would his mother be calling Promise Lodge?

"Lizzie?" Mattie called out. "Somebody special wants to speak with you!"

Lizzie's heart thumped like a drum. What if Ervin had run into trouble on the road? What if Raymond's *mamm* was calling to break the news about a bad accident—or something awful Bishop Obadiah had said during the long drive?

She tried to set aside these worrisome thoughts as she took the receiver from Mattie.

"*Jah*, hello?"

"Lizzie, it's a joy to hear your voice, dear," Alma said. She sounded cheerful and upbeat, as though she had something wonderful on her mind. "I wanted you to know about Coldstream's news today—because although we don't rejoice in the misfortune of others, it sometimes brings us a new opportunity."

"*Jah*? And what would that be?" she asked breathlessly. Alma was in fine fettle, obviously unconcerned about traffic accidents.

"Early this morning, Ralph Raber, who owns Coldstream's bulk store, had a massive stroke," Raymond's *mamm* replied in a more subdued voice. "He made it to the hospital, thank the *gut* Lord. But this being such a busy week, his wife was beside herself because she can't be with Ralph and also keep the store open. Would you believe Bishop Obadiah told her that Raymond, with his experience at the Promise Lodge store, would be the perfect man to take the place over?"

Lizzie's mouth dropped open. Maybe there was something to Obadiah's change of heart, after all.

"Raymond's at the store now, looking the place over before he opens for business tomorrow," his mother continued. "We all expect him to be running the place for quite a long time, even after Ralph recovers, because Ralph is no spring chicken."

Lizzie sucked in her breath. Did she dare believe this job at the store could become Raymond's full-time employment?

"Raymond asked me to call you, sweetie, because he—and the entire family—would love to have you here with us for Christmas," Alma said earnestly. "He's crazy for you, Lizzie. He believes this opening at the store might be the answer to his prayers—employment that gets him out of milking cows for the rest of his life.

"And we all have a different opinion of Bishop Obadiah now, too," she added happily. "We're hoping this Christmas spirit that's overtaken him will last long after the holidays are behind us. So will you come?"

"*Jah*! *Jah*, I'll be there!" Lizzie blurted out. "I'm so glad you called. And I—I'll find a better way to get there than driving my scooter, too!"

When she hung up, Lizzie gazed at the phone in a euphoric daze. Why did she sense that this single phone call might've changed her entire life?

"Somebody looks mighty happy," Ruby teased behind her.

As the other ladies chuckled, Lizzie turned to smile at them. "Raymond's going to manage the Coldstream bulk store, because Ralph Raber had a bad stroke early this morning. And I'm going to the Overholts' for Christmas—but I'll have to find a ride—"

"No, you won't," Rosetta interrupted. "Truman and I will be happy to drive you there in the pickup."

"And we can send casseroles and Christmas goodies for the Raber family when you go," Mattie put in. "This is such *gut* news for you, Lizzie!"

"*Jah*, I'm happy that your chin's not dragging on the floor anymore," Beulah said with a chuckle.

Christine sighed. "Well, it sounds like you and Raymond won't be staying at Promise Lodge," she said ruefully. "But we all want the best for you. You'll have a wonderful-*gut* time visiting the Overhholts. They're a fine family."

"There's nobody nicer than Alma, and she's always hoped something—and somebody—special would come along for her Raymond," Mattie said with a nod. "I believe she'll be getting exactly what she wants for Christmas this year."

Chapter 15

On Thursday afternoon—Christmas Eve—Raymond watched Lizzie step out of a big pickup. His heart rose into his throat. It was nothing short of a miracle that she'd agreed to spend the Christmas holidays with his family! She'd sounded so critical of Bishop Obadiah's mindset at church, he'd believed he might never see her again once he left Promise Lodge.

But here she was, hurrying along the snow-packed path toward the house. Rosetta and her husband were following, but Raymond had eyes only for the young blonde with the glimmering green eyes. She looked too cute for words in her red and green plaid dress. Her coordinating green flip-flops sported silk poinsettia blooms that almost covered her bare toes.

Lizzie would be quite an eyeful for his conservative Old Order family. But Raymond suspected she had a few comebacks ready if anyone made critical remarks about her attire—or the Mennonite faith she'd grown up in.

When he opened the door to await her on the front porch, Lizzie rushed into his arms.

Raymond held her as though he couldn't let her go. The Wickeys were watching, and a few family members might be peering through the window, but he kissed Lizzie anyway. And she responded. Oh, but this exuberant young woman could kiss!

"Lizzie, it's so *gut* to see you—"

"When your *mamm* called, I couldn't stay away—"

"And we have so much to talk about!"

"Because Bishop Obadiah wrote us *quite* a letter before he left Promise Lodge," she continued in a rush. "But I didn't come here to talk about *him!* What's the Coldstream bulk store like? Do you really get to take it over? Will it be a full-time job for you—something you can count on for a long time, or—"

Laughing, Raymond hugged her close again. As Rosetta and Truman came up onto the porch, he smiled at them. "*Denki* for giving Lizzie a ride. Come in and see everyone! Stay for coffee and cookies, or even join us for supper!"

A knowing smile lit Rosetta's face as she focused intently on him and Lizzie. "We'll stay for a bit, but we've brought food and Christmas goodies for the Raber family. Then we want to get home for the scholars' Christmas Eve program at the lodge."

"*Jah*, we have some scholars in our family still rehearsing their pieces for tonight," Raymond said as they stepped into the front room. "Now that I no longer have to memorize holiday poems or lines from Luke's Christmas story, I enjoy

254

watching the kids suffer the way I did at their age. My favorite part of the school program was always the refreshments afterward!"

The loud laughter and conversation spilling out of the kitchen made Lizzie hesitate—probably because she'd met only his parents and Ezra on her previous visit. He took her hand.

"Don't be nervous, sweetie. They all want to meet you," he assured her. "Mamm's been telling them what a special girl you are—and my mother never lies, you know."

When they entered the kitchen, where his parents, his brothers and their families were gathered around the fully extended table, the room went quiet. Raymond cleared his throat. Lizzie was the only girl he'd ever brought home, so his siblings were understandably curious about her.

"I'd like you to meet Lizzie Zehr," he said, savoring the feel of her small, damp hand in his. When she gazed up at him, Raymond felt eight feet tall. "Let's introduce everyone, starting with the oldest—"

"And there'll be a quiz, to see whose names you remember!" Ezra teased. "Hey there, Lizzie! You came back. Raymond was in a real sweat about whether we'd scared you off last time."

Lizzie's laughter helped Raymond relax. He introduced Enos and his wife, Barbara, and their five kids. After that came Earl and Maggie, with their four kids and newborn baby. Elmer and Lovina also had four kids, with a baby on the way. Along with his parents and Ezra, that made twenty-three pairs of eyes focused on him and Lizzie. It was a daunting moment for him, so he could only imagine how overwhelmed Lizzie might feel.

"Hey there," she said. "This is a lot different from my house, where it's just me and my sister. But I *will* learn your names!"

"And for those of you who didn't make it to our wedding," Rosetta put in, "this is my husband, Truman Wickey. It's so *gut* to see you Overholts again!"

The conversations all started up at once as Rosetta and Truman took the chairs Elmer had brought to the table for them. Raymond was steering Lizzie toward the two empty seats on one side of the table—except she made a beeline toward his mother at the far end.

The sight of Lizzie reaching for Mamm, and Mamm grabbing her in an eager hug, made Raymond's heart go still. Surely this holiday— and their life beyond it—would be blessed indeed because his mother already accepted Lizzie for who she was. Flip-flops, plaid, and all.

Even Dat was smiling at the girl he'd been so critical of before. Raymond chalked it up to another Christmas miracle, akin to the one that had altered Bishop Obadiah's entire mindset on

Sunday night at Promise Lodge. The long ride home in the rig had proven that Coldstream's leader had become so much kinder and gentler that Raymond wondered if he'd gotten a personality transplant.

His heart swelled with happiness and gratitude to God. Just a month ago, when Dale Kraybill had hired him, Raymond had had no idea of the wonderful things to come. When Lizzie looked at him, still holding his mother's hand, he could dare to believe that his life would work out. At long last, he'd found his place in the world—right beside Lizzie.

After an afternoon in a kitchen that rang with voices, followed by an evening of hearing the Christmas story retold by the scholars of Coldstream's school, Lizzie finally got to be alone with Raymond. As she walked across the pasture beside him—wearing boots Alma had loaned her—she inhaled the frosty night air. In the moonlight, the rolling landscape took on the mystical, hushed glow of the pristine snow.

The stillness refreshed her. Her heart was so full, she didn't know where to begin.

"It was quite a shock tonight when Bishop Obadiah announced that Ralph had passed on," Raymond murmured.

"Not a happy way to end the Christmas Eve program," Lizzie agreed. "And not a fine time of year to deal with such a tragedy, either. His family's Christmas holidays will have a cloud over them for years to come."

"But maybe God didn't want him to struggle through the long recovery time they were anticipating," Raymond put in. "After having two more strokes early this morning, he might not have survived to come home."

Was it improper to find a silver lining in such a sorrowful cloud? Lizzie tried not to sound too excited about what Ralph's passing might mean for their future.

"So, what's the store like?" she asked. "I'm guessing there's no electricity—"

"And no rhyme or reason to the way it's arranged," Raymond said, shaking his head. "We've been spoiled, working in Dale's business with its bright lighting and fresh merchandise and clean, white walls."

Raymond sighed. "The store here looks tired, Lizzie. I doubt it's been painted in years. I also suspect the shelves need to be cleared of items that've gone beyond their expiration dates."

He slipped his arm around her shoulders as they continued to walk. "And if the bookkeeping and ordering system are anything like the rest of the place, I anticipate some headaches while I get them organized properly."

Lizzie listened, hoping she didn't appear as concerned as she felt. The things Raymond had mentioned sounded like a lot of work. Vastly different from what they'd become accustomed to with Dale, who was a meticulous storekeeper.

"On the bright side, there's an apartment upstairs," Raymond said in a more hopeful tone. "And the four employees who've worked there for years assured me they'd do whatever it took to keep the store going while Ralph was laid up."

"They'll be a big help as you start your reorganizing efforts," she agreed. "Especially now that Ralph won't be around."

As Raymond drew a breath and exhaled, a wreath of vapor wafted around him. He stopped walking to lightly rest his hands on her shoulders.

Lizzie sensed he was working himself up to say something important. Her stomach filled with butterflies. Ever since she'd watched him leave on Monday morning, she'd been telling herself to think carefully—to stand by her own future wishes and goals, in case a moment like this one actually came about. Her life had been on hold for a few days—with the possibility that she might not connect with Raymond again if his parents or his bishop forbade him to court and marry a girl who'd been raised Mennonite.

"What about you, Lizzie?" Raymond whispered. "Will *you* help me? You could still be baptized into the Old Order at Promise Lodge and then, if—if you'd marry me—we'd have an apartment, and full-time work together, and—"

"Yes," she whispered. Her throat was so tight, however, the sound barely came out.

"And my life would feel complete," Raymond continued urgently, "because my family's crazy about you—Mamm just loves you to pieces—"

"Yes, Raymond." Overwhelmed as she was with delight, he probably had to read her lips to get her answer.

"And after the way Bishop Obadiah praised you all the way from Promise Lodge to Coldstream," he continued, "even Dat has admitted that you and I are well matched, so—"

"Yes, we are!" Lizzie cried out. "And yes, Raymond! My answer is *yes!*"

As her voice rang out over the snow-covered pasture, Raymond's mouth clapped shut. He gaped at her. "Oh, my stars, it is? You'll be my wife?"

Laughing with uncontrollable joy, Lizzie threw her arms around him, pulling him down for a kiss. Raymond's lips held hers captive for several long, lovely moments before he grabbed her up to spin her around.

Her spirits—her soul—were flying even higher than the rest of her as their laughter carried lightly through the crisp, wintry air. When Raymond kissed her again, Lizzie felt all the disconnected pieces of her life falling into place.

"Lizzie, you've given me so much to look forward to!" he murmured.

"And you're giving me a new life with a big, happy family!" she put in ecstatically. "And I'll have a *mamm* again, Raymond! That gift alone means so much to me."

Raymond closed his eyes, appearing very gratified by her remark. "Mamm was telling me earlier this week that my Star of Wonder plaques led me to you, Lizzie, and gave my life a whole new purpose," he whispered with a hitch in his voice. "She said my time at Promise Lodge was well spent, learning a new trade, and she was willing to let us live there if that's where we'd be truly happy."

"I'd intended to stay there, too, with you or without you," she murmured solemnly. "But somehow God softened Obadiah's heart and freed him from his judgmental, negative ways. So your *mamm* gets to keep her youngest son— and now I get to keep him, too."

With a contented sigh, Raymond grasped her hand. "Let's go back to the house and tell everybody our news. We've just given the Overholt family a whole new reason to celebrate Christmas, ain't so?"

Starlight Everlasting

Rosalind Lauer

For Carly and Hanna,
two shining stars

Chapter 1

R achel Coblentz extracted herself from the festive chatter in the Christmas shop to approach the front window, where she pushed aside one of the dangling silver ornaments and looked beyond the glow of white light to Main Street.

Where was Luke?

It was nearly seven o'clock, and the chill air of the November night seeped through the glass of the display window. If Luke and his father had worked the Saturday-morning shift at the factory as planned, their hired van should have arrived back in Joyful River an hour ago.

Most of the town's shops were closed, and the restaurants were winding down for the night. A few shoppers made their way through the brisk wind, returning to their cars with shopping bags or popping into the general store for one last box of fudge or jar of homemade jam. Cars whooshed past, along with an occasional gray buggy rolling slowly behind its horse. But no Luke. Not yet.

With Christmas lights and garland decorating many of the storefronts, the town looked festive and peaceful; sleepy, but not yet asleep. Blessed with a lovely winter's peace. Rachel knew her heart would be graced with that same contentment, just as soon as her husband arrived back in town. Not just peace, but happiness and joy, too. The expectation made her jittery and giddy. She was a grown woman of twenty-one years—a married woman, at that—and yet she went through this anticipation every week or so. She couldn't help it. After spending days and weeks apart from Luke, each time he returned felt like a holiday.

Have patience, she reminded herself. It was not one of her strong points, though she'd had to practice it a lot lately as she spent each week waiting for her husband to return from his job up north. The separation was hard on both Luke and her. It was not the way she'd imagined her life as his wife, living hours away from her husband, but with local work drying up, the factories up north offered the only way that many Amish men from this area could make a living.

Despite the hardship of missing Luke, Rachel was grateful for her loving family and the shop she'd been chosen to manage in Joyful River. Aunt Madge had hired her to breathe a bit of life into the place, and Rachel had jumped at the chance to make a few inexpensive renovations to spruce up the shop and bring its focus back to the meaning of the holiday. Gone were the shelves of boxed ornaments and displays of fake snow turned gray from dust. Instead, the shop now contained a meandering white picket fence that provided ample space to hang ornaments and lights.

And that night, after the shop had closed, a handful of Amish carpenters had begun their work on phase two of the update: the transformation of an old chicken coop from Aunt Madge's yard to a replica of the manger where the Christ child was born.

Rachel was sorry Luke wasn't there to see the shop in full motion. Christmas was in the air! Sounds of laughter, hammering, and cheerful voices filled the space. Some of her younger brothers and sisters were singing carols as they added ribbon to ornaments or strung them up on the white picket fence. By the time they were through, the store would resemble a Christmas wonderland!

Glancing over at the carpenters, Rachel smiled as her father took charge. Her dat, Roy Fisher, had a subtle manner of pointing at something and challenging others to step up. As Rachel watched, her father held a level along the roofline of the miniature hut and motioned to the younger men.

"This end needs to come up," he said, pointing to the back of the roof.

In response, one young man ran a tape measure along the rear support, while another scratched the hair behind his ear and considered how to make the adjustment. So much work for a store display, but Rachel was grateful for the precision craft of the builders. The picket fence path they'd installed a few weeks earlier had already been a hit with customers.

She was also glad to see her father in the thick of things, as he'd been laying low since Mem's death, leaving the house only for church or work at the Amish furniture factory. The loss of Dara Fisher had left holes in so many hearts, but Dat, despite the love of his seven children, seemed to feel his new loneliness and isolation most acutely.

Over at the sales counter, Rachel's youngest siblings sat or kneeled on chairs so that they could easily reach the flat surface usually reserved for wrapping purchases. Since the entire Fisher family was present for the project, Rachel and Julie had decided to put everyone to work, which meant the young ones got to decorate ornaments.

"That's a very pretty heart, Polly," eighteen-year-old Julie told their youngest sister. "Do you want to dip it in red glitter?"

Polly nodded, her gaze trained on the twinkling decorations.

"I'll pour a little bit out for you." Julie tipped the vial, and sparkles streamed onto a paper plate. "Just be careful not to spill them. And don't get them in your eyes." As one of the Amish teachers at the schoolhouse, Julie knew how to handle children of all ages, and she had a way of engaging them in projects and tasks that kept them busy and happy.

"Do we have more wibbon?" asked six-year-old Willie.

"That's ribbon, with an *r. Rrrr,*" Julie said in an even tone.

"R-r-ribbon," Willie repeated. "Is there any left?"

"We have white and green. Which would you like?"

"White!"

Julie handed over the ribbon.

Watching the little group, Rachel admired her sister's way with the children. Such patience! Rachel loved each and every one of her six siblings, but since their mother's death a year ago, she'd earned an unwanted reputation as the bossy sister. It was frustrating, but could she help it if the little ones needed constant prodding to keep the day running smoothly? As the oldest child, Rachel saw it as her job to keep the household moving along.

"I'm hungry," said eight-year-old Eli as he placed a dot of glue on a shiny blue orb. "Are we getting supper soon?"

"You ate before we left," Julie said. "Remember the soup and sandwiches?"

"But I'm so hungry," he whined.

"I'm hungry, too," Truman called from one of

the displays, where he was hanging ornaments with sister Bethany.

"You boys are always hungry. Bottomless pits!" Julie shook her head, then glanced over at Rachel. "Do you have any snacks stashed in the back?"

"Aunt Madge is bringing some fried chicken," Rachel offered. The treat from the family restaurant was meant to be a gesture of thank-you for the men who were working through the evening to help out, but Rachel knew there'd be more than enough for everyone to eat. "She'll be here any minute now."

"See? Supper's coming," Julie said encouragingly. "You are very fortunate boys."

"Mmm. Chicken!" Willie brightened.

"The best fried chicken in all of Joyful River," Eli said. "I hope she gets here soon." He returned to his task, carefully gluing gold sequin stars to sapphire-blue glass balls. The contrast of gold and dark blue was quite striking on the ornaments—sure to be a hit with customers, who swooped up the hand-decorated ornaments for their Christmas trees, wreaths, and garland.

Knowing Julie had the little ones under control, Rachel went over to the display where the older siblings kept busy.

"Look how pretty!" Bethany's face glowed with wonder as she hung a shiny red glass ball on the network of lights crisscrossing the whitewashed picket fence that had been installed last week. At age twelve, the towheaded girl was quite fond of pretty things, as evidenced by the makeup that Rachel had discovered stashed in her school bag.

"I wish we could put these lights up on our fence at home," Bethany added.

"They wouldn't work without electricity," Rachel reminded her sister, "and we all know that Amish homes don't plug into the power grid."

Amish homes operated off the grid, using other power sources like propane, coal, kerosene lamps, and LED lights, though their district deemed it acceptable to use electricity and phones in rented shops and businesses.

"I know, but they're so sparkly," Bethany said longingly. "I wish we could have Christmas lights at home."

"If you want to see things sparkle, look up at the stars in the sky," replied nine-year-old Truman. A collector of trivia and facts, Truman had developed a fascination with the night sky that had led him to read books and articles about astronomy. "Gott gives us shining stars every night."

"Stars are nice," Bethany agreed, "but these little lights make my heart happy. Look at the way the new picket fence lights up the shop."

Turning to take it all in, Rachel realized her sister had a point. Now that lights and ornaments covered most of the white picket fencing that zigzagged through the store, the little fence truly glowed, emanating soft light in a welcoming path.

"You're right," Rachel told her sister. "It does warm the heart." She couldn't wait to share it with Luke, who spent his days in a dreary factory, working a machine that folded wrappers over candy bars.

"It's not a hard job," Luke had explained. "It's just boring. Metal machines whirring, the same thing, every hour and every day." The dull factory was a stark contrast to the heavenly light of the shop.

"Luke is going to love this."

"He is," Bethany agreed. "Where is Luke, anyway? He's usually home by now."

"Running late, I guess," Rachel said, not wanting to admit that she was beginning to worry about him.

"He's never going to believe how beautiful you made a worn, old picket fence. You have good ideas for decorating, Rachel."

Rachel gave her sister's shoulder a squeeze. "Denki for your help. And you, too, Truman. It's because of you that I got the idea for the Christmas star display over the manger."

Truman's grin was barely visible, as he didn't look up from the task at hand. "That's silly, when you already knew the story of the Christmas star that led the three wise men to find the baby Jesus."

"Yah, I knew the story." Rachel was used to her brother's very literal view of the world. "But your love for stars reminded me how the Christmas star was an important part of the birth of the Christ child."

"I guess that was a good reminder." Truman nodded to himself as he hung another ornament. "Then, you're welcome."

She patted Bethany's shoulder again, but refrained from touching Truman, who didn't always take well to physical contact. "Good work, you two." She glanced back toward the shop entrance. "I'm going to see if I can find out what's keeping Luke."

Turning her back on the noise and chatter, Rachel went to the door and slipped out into the cold night. The CLOSED sign rattled a bit as she pulled the shop door behind her, and the music from the art gallery's speakers two doors down filled the night. She recognized the Christmas carol "It Came Upon the Midnight Clear." The song prompted her to glance up at the scattering of stars that dotted the indigo sky.

"It is a midnight clear," she observed. Well, not midnight, but such a wide, clear sky tonight. Rubbing her arms for warmth, she breathed in the starry expanse above, knowing that Gott's creations had the power to soothe her soul.

But tonight, the real excitement and joy would be Luke's arrival. She looked up and down the street, focusing hard, as if wishing could make him appear. As the clip-clop of horse's hooves diverted her attention, she folded her arms across her chest to brace against the cold. Was that the Coblentz buggy? She squinted into the darkness but soon realized it was drawn by a horse—not the sturdy mule that had served the Coblentz family for years.

Oh, what was keeping him?

Glancing back at the shop, she was struck by the simple beauty of the window display—three oversize silver ornaments hanging from fishing line and surrounded by white lights and pine branches interlaced with silver garland. The center ornament was shaped like a star, and it had inspired a new name for the shop—Star of Wonder—a change Rachel planned to make, as long as the store owner, Madge Lambright, approved. So far Aunt Madge had been supportive of Rachel's plans for the store, including the redecoration now underway.

Just then the flash of a dark figure at the end of the street, near the diner, caught her eye. Was that Luke, hurrying her way on foot?

A wide-brimmed hat, dark winter coat, and a dark muffler . . . it could have been any Amish man. But the way he moved, his long legs swallowing the sidewalk in huge strides while he seemed to hover over Gott's earth . . .

It was Luke.

Joy swelled in her heart as she gave a wave and headed his way. After nearly a week of being apart from him, there was so much for them to pack into their hours together. Not even two days of joy and contentment before they had to start another long, sparse lonely week all over again.

When she was close enough to see his features in the light of the streetlamps, she paused to savor the sight of him—broad shoulders, lean body, and tall stature. He was a head taller than her, which made her feel girlish instead of gawky around him. It was too dim to feel the warmth from his chocolate-brown eyes, but she knew that look—that flash of equal amounts humor and concern—when he drew closer.

"Rach?"

The sound of his voice lifted her heart and filled her with a flurry of joy.

"Is that you, or has Gott put a Christmas angel in my path?"

"I think your eyes must be failing, my dear husband. I'm no angel."

"Well, after a long week, you are a heavenly sight, for sure."

Laughter rumbled in her throat as she ran the rest of the way and jumped into his arms.

Laughing along with her, Luke caught her with both arms, and kept her suspended above the ground as he swept her around in a twirling embrace. Rachel held tight to his shoulders, loving the warmth of him, the mixed scent of mint soap and warm wool, the bristly feel of his coat against her cheek. When they stopped twirling, she closed her eyes and cuddled close to him. All was right with the world when she was in Luke's arms.

She felt him take a few steps and opened her eyes to find that he'd carried her to the shadowed vestibule of the bakery, which was closed for the day. The nook allowed them a bit of privacy, but there was still enough light for her to see his face, his perfectly curved lips, his smoky dark eyes, and the short hair of a beard that he had started growing on their wedding day.

"I missed you so much." She pressed her lips to his, taking comfort from the brief kiss. "Where have you been?"

"Off in a factory, watching chocolate bars find their wrappers," he said. "Someone has to bring home the bacon."

"Oh, you!" She patted his shoulder playfully as he eased her feet to the ground but held her in his embrace. "I meant, why are you so late?"

"An accident on the main highway. By the time we reached the scene there only a cleanup crew sweeping glass, but we prayed that everyone was all right. It must have been quite a wreck, as we sat for half an hour and then crept along for longer."

"I was so worried."

"I knew you would be. Worried and impatient."

"You know me well. But here you are, at last."

"Back to you, my love," he said. "I always come home to you."

"I long for the day when we both come home to each other at the end of each day," she said. "Think of it, Luke. How wonderful would that be?"

His lips went taut, his face strained in a frown for a moment. "I'm sorry I can't be here with you all the time, Rach."

"I'm sorry, too, but I'm also grateful to be married to a man who sacrifices to provide for his family. That's what we're working toward, isn't it?"

They kissed again, and this time the fire of his lips warmed her from head to toe. She longed to be alone with him, just the two of them in the privacy of their room. But that special time was still hours away. And despite the darkness and the cover of the bakery vestibule, public displays of affection were frowned upon in their Amish community.

They ended the kiss, and she reached up to trace the line of his jaw and chin. "Your beard is growing in well, Mr. Coblentz," she teased. Following Amish tradition, Luke had kept his face shaved until they had married two months ago.

"Denki for noticing, Mrs. Coblentz."

279

She smiled up at him, trailing her fingertips from his jaw down to the warmth of his neck, dipping beneath the collar of his jacket.

"Ach! Icicle hands!" He quickly clasped both of her hands together, breathed some warmth onto them, and began rubbing them. "We need to get you inside. You don't even have a coat on."

"Because I ran out in a bit of a fright, searching for my husband," she admitted.

"I once was lost, but now I'm found," he said, echoing a line from a hymn they both loved. "Here, take my coat."

"No need. We'll be back inside in a jiffy," she said as they headed back to the shop, but he was already tucking the wool garment over her shoulders so that his warmth encircled her.

"I can't let my new bride catch cold," he said.

Although they'd been married for two months, Luke still called her his new bride, and Rachel loved hearing the nickname.

"So tell me," Luke went on, "are the carpenters doing a good job for you in the shop?"

"I'll show you, and you can see for yourself," Rachel said as she opened the door and led him inside. The blast of warm air took the chill off her skin as she and Luke stepped over the threshold and paused. "We're just about finished decorating the fence, and so far, customers seem to love it."

Luke stared, wide-eyed. "Rach, it's beautiful.

Hard to believe this started as an old picket fence."

"And a run-down chicken coop. We haven't decorated that yet, but we'll get on it as soon as the men finish up." She nodded as some of the men looked over and waved a greeting at Luke. "The manger will have plenty of stars overhead. It's sort of my way of bringing the true meaning of Christmas into the shop. I talked to Bishop Aaron about it, and he liked the idea." She looked up at her husband, so glad to be by his side again. "So? What do you think?"

"I think it's wonderful," he said, a smile lighting his face. "The best Christmas shop Joyful River has ever seen."

Chapter 2

For a moment, Miriam Lapp had thought her eyes were playing tricks on her.

It wasn't every day one saw an Amish couple embrace beneath the festive holiday lights of Main Street. Such a sweeping sight! The gesture of young love had tugged on her heartstrings.

At first glance, she didn't know the identity of the mystery couple. But after they'd emerged from the bakery doorway and headed to the Christmas shop, she'd recognized them. Newly-weds Luke and Rachel Coblentz.

Miriam had almost pointed the sweet couple out to Madge Lambright, who walked alongside her on that November night, but then Madge had been in the middle of explaining a pie recipe. Miriam didn't want to interrupt, and perhaps she'd wanted to savor the moment on her own. She'd always been a matchmaker, and there were few things quite as satisfying as bringing folks together. In her view, love was the one gift from Gott that could fix all of life's problems.

While she wished she could take credit for getting this particular couple together, she knew Luke and Rachel had been loyal to each other since grade school, when Luke had defended the unusually tall girl from a few testy youngies who'd teased her about her height. From that moment, Rachel had looked up at the Coblentz boy with thanks and admiration, an attachment that had eventually turned to love.

How Miriam enjoyed a good love story! She knew Rachel and Luke's tale well because Rachel's mother, Dara Fisher, had been a close friend, allowing Miriam a bird's-eye view of the developing romance. Rachel and Luke had hoped to marry more than a year ago and were in the planning stages just before wedding season when Dara was diagnosed with cancer. The couple had postponed their wedding, determined to wait until Dara felt better—good enough to attend the event. Sadly, that day had never come.

Since her friend's passing, Miriam had tried to mother Dara's children as much as she could, while tending to seven of her own. Yah, it was hard to keep up with all of them, but Gott had blessed her with plenty of love and nurturing to go around. When Rachel and Luke married this past September, Miriam and Alvin had been happy to host the event at their dairy farm. It had warmed Miriam's heart to know how happy Dara would have been to have her oldest daughter marrying the love of her life.

Unfortunately, the newlyweds had been rocked by Dara's medical bills and a financial downturn in the area, forcing Luke to head out of town each week for a factory job. Miriam had racked her brain for ways to help. Without farming skills, Luke had been at a loss for local employment. But one summer day when Miriam had passed by Lambright's Christmas shop, she'd caught a whiff of an idea. The dusty old place had been long neglected, and Madge's niece Tilly had lost interest in running the place after the birth of her third child. Knowing that Rachel had been trying to find work, Miriam had approached Madge, the shop owner, with her idea. Madge had been happy to hire Rachel to manage the shop, and everyone seemed pleased with the new arrangement.

And that night, with a renovation well underway, Miriam was helping Madge deliver fried chicken for the volunteers. A brisk wind rocked the lights and ornaments strung high across the street. It was a cold clear night, the sort of weather that nipped at nose and toes, though Miriam and Madge were able to keep warm from the heat of the aluminum trays in their arms— food from the diner.

"So good of you to provide dinner for Rachel's work crew," Miriam said, glad for the warmth of the bins beneath her gloves.

"It's the least I could do," responded Madge. As owner of the popular diner in town, which she ran with her husband, Emery, Madge frequently contributed food to friends, families in need, and charity events. "I told Rachel I would pay the carpenters, but the men offered to work for chicken."

Miriam chuckled. "That speaks to how much folks love your fried chicken, Madge."

"It's never a problem to throw a few extra meals in the fryers, and I'm anxious to see the final outcome. I'm a little worried at the idea of a chicken coop in the center of the shop, but I have to trust Rachel on this one."

"The girl has some good ideas, Madge. I popped in this week to say hello, and I was bowled over by what she did with that picket fence." Miriam had been pleasantly surprised to see how clean and bright the shop had been. Gone was the fake snow that had captured its fair share of dust. Now ornaments were removed from their boring boxes and strung up on the fencing alongside glittering white lights. "Everything was bright and clean. I think your shop's shaping up beautifully."

"I reckon that must be true, based on the recent sales," Madge said. "Business was so slow last year that I thought about ending my lease and closing up shop. But since Rachel did a quick cleanup and restocked ornaments in July, we've been doing well. She kept the shop open during the renovations, which isn't an easy thing to do. Now we're turning a good profit."

"I'm glad to hear it. Rachel needed a job, and I think it does her good to get out of the house a bit. Ever since Dara passed, so much of the care of those children has fallen on the two older girls."

Madge nodded sagely. "Julie and Rachel are such a big help to Roy. They're good girls. But I do worry about the younger children. Five young ones growing up without their mother. It's a very sad thing."

This truth stabbed at Miriam. "You're so right, Madge. Your brother Roy Fisher is a good man and a caring father, but children that young need a woman's care." She shook her head. "I'd take them all in, given the chance, though I know they'd miss their home."

"And wouldn't Alvin be surprised to see seven new faces popping up at your dinner table," Madge teased. "With the seven children you already have, that would be quite a brood."

"I don't think my husband would even flinch," Miriam said. "Alvin knows the importance of family, and he'd be glad to take more little ones under his wings. But Roy is doing his best, isn't he? And he has the older girls to help."

"Indeed. And with Julie being a schoolteacher, we know she's had plenty of experience with the young ones."

"That's a blessing," Miriam agreed, though she knew those young ones still missed their mother. No amount of casseroles and baked goods, which she frequently bestowed on Dara's family, could stop the longing for a mother's love. But she would keep letting them know they were loved.

"Here we are," Madge said, pausing before the shop to peer at the simple display of three dangling ornaments in the window. "Well. So far so good."

Miriam hurried to open the door with her free hand. "After you!"

Miriam watched from behind as Madge trudged in, paused with her armful of warm aluminum trays, and took in the shop. Although the Amish didn't fuss with much decoration for Christmas, Miriam always loved the lights and decorations that she saw throughout the rest of the town. The lights and festive garlands were a bright reminder of the joy and excitement of the season of Christ's birth. And this scene, with tiny white pin-dots of light everywhere, reflected on the surface of shiny ornaments, certainly captured the peace of Christmas.

"What is all this?" Madge called out, garnering the attention of Rachel and the volunteers. "I thought I was on Main Street, but I seem to have stepped onto a starry path to Bethlehem!"

For a moment a curious silence filled the shop, and then there was laughter as faces broke into smiles and the women were greeted and welcomed. Of course Madge liked the new decorations. Who wouldn't?

Rachel emerged from around the side of the crèche and hurried over to her aunt. "That's exactly what I was going for, Aunt Madge. The Christmas star! I'm so glad you recognized our theme."

"Couldn't miss it," Madge said. "You've done a wonderful job with the place, Rachel. But, tell me, before my arms cramp, where should we lay out all this food?"

"You can put it over here, Aunt Madge!" Will called, drumming his hands on the countertop. "We cleared it off for you."

"Perfect," Madge said, lowering the stacked trays to the counter. She squinted at Will, whose spot on the stool made him level with her eyes. "And it looks like you have a front-row seat to supper."

"Yup!" he said, his eyes bright with interest as Madge opened the lid on a steaming tray of mashed potatoes.

Suddenly Will was joined by his siblings, who waited patiently as Miriam and Madge set up the food. "We have fried chicken, mashed potatoes, mac and cheese, and mixed veggies," Madge announced. "And if you want something a bit heartier, there's a tray of sliced roast beef in gravy."

"And cookies for dessert," Miriam added, handing out utensils and paper plates to the children and encouraging them to dig in. She went over to wrangle the group of carpenters, which included her son-in-law Harlan, and encouraged them to grab some supper before it got cold. Then she located Rachel's stash of paper cups and made sure everyone got water to go with their meals.

As Miriam made the rounds, she visited with Dara and Roy's children. She got an earful from Eli and Will about the upcoming Christmas presentation at the Amish school. Bethany asked about Miriam's daughter Lizzie, who was around the same age, and Miriam promised to set up a time when the girls could be together at the farm. Truman kept his gaze down, but he answered her questions politely and told her some exciting star facts. A marked improvement for the boy, who struggled when he was around so many people.

Four-year-old Polly explained that she was Rachel's special helper here in the shop. The little girl dragged Miriam to the small back room, where one corner was set up with a rolled-up mat and a crocheted blanket—no doubt one of Dara's creations.

"Here's where we take breaks. And naps, too." Polly unfurled one of the mats and collapsed on it, her thin little legs curling up under her blue dress as she sighed and pretended to sleep.

"A room to nap in," Miriam said, smoothing down the throw blanket over the back of a chair. "What a cozy place for you and Rachel to have."

Polly nodded. "We like it," she said firmly.

As Miriam followed the little girl back to the

gathering, it occurred to her that Rachel had a rather full plate for a newlywed Amish wife. Here she was, managing a shop, bringing her youngest sibling to work with her most days. Well, that made sense, as Roy had his job at the furniture factory, and he could hardly tote little Polly to work with him.

Then, after school hours, Rachel and Julie shared the duties of tending to the other siblings, the housekeeping chores of laundry, cooking, and cleaning. Such a heavy load for two young women with full-time jobs outside the home. She glanced over at Julie, who was organizing the children as a cleanup crew after the meal. For a young woman of eighteen, she handled more than her share of responsibilities, teaching at the schoolhouse and helping to care for her siblings.

Just then Miriam's musings were interrupted by a bit of commotion.

"Oh, no you don't!" Rachel called over to the group of men, who had reassembled to complete their work. "Don't let Luke near our little manger scene."

Miriam glanced over at the men, who stood back, laughing as Luke made a show of swinging a hammer clear through the air.

"It's a running joke for us," Rachel said, touching Miriam's arm as they both watched the men. "Luke is notorious for his lack of carpentry skills. My dat teases him that he needs to stay far away from tools and lumber."

As they watched, the men moved aside as Luke took a hammer and nail and took a wild swing. When the hammer struck the wood, he jerked his arm back, pretending that it had struck his fingers instead of the nail. The clownish move evoked much laughter as he gripped his hand and danced around in mock pain. The smallest children rushed forward, pretending to console him.

"I can see that this isn't the first time he's pulled this stunt," Miriam said.

"Nay, and I hope it won't be the last," Rachel said with a happy sigh. There was no missing the spark of love in her blue eyes as she watched her husband. "There's something wonderful about a man who doesn't take himself too seriously."

"Indeed, there is," agreed Miriam.

"Watching him, you would think that his lack of skills didn't bother him in the least," Rachel said quietly. "But I know that's not true. Luke feels bad that he's not a good fit for most of the jobs in Amish country. Farming, carpentry, buggy repair . . . he's tried them all."

"I know he has," Miriam said. "And he's a hard worker. He just hasn't found the right fit, I reckon."

"They appreciate him at the factory in Maple Run. It's not the most satisfying work, but he'd do it gladly if it didn't take him away for most of the week."

"It's got to be hard on the two of you," Miriam said. "Married couples are supposed to be together."

"Every week is like climbing a hill. Moments like this when he's home are such a joy. But then, come Monday when he has to head back, I feel like I'm falling off a cliff all over again." Tears shone in Rachel's eyes when she turned to Miriam. "I'm sorry. I don't mean to complain."

"Poor dear, it can't be easy." Miriam patted Rachel's back gently. It was times like this when a newlywed girl needed her mem. "You know you can always come to me for help or just to blow off steam."

Rachel nodded and sniffed. "I know that."

"I'll pray that Luke finds a local job soon." Miriam had faith in the power of prayer. "In the meantime, you're doing good work here. Little Polly showed me her nap area at the back of the store. She seems very happy to be a part of the shop."

"She's a joy to have around. Our brothers are a bit more challenging, but boys will be boys."

Miriam laughed. "They keep us on our toes."

"They sure do," Rachel agreed.

"Well, you know, if you ever need help with the children, I'm happy to oblige. There's always room for more in our home."

"I appreciate your offer, but it's a blessing to have a place to stay with my younger siblings. At least I have a purpose to fulfill while I'm waiting for Luke."

"Rachel!" Truman called. "Come, see the nativity scene. The men have finished working."

"Be right there," Rachel said, then confided in Miriam. "In the nick of time. I can finish decorating on Monday, but right now we need to get the children home before they fall asleep in the manger."

"Yah, and I'll be nodding off right beside them," Miriam said, stifling a yawn before returning to her task of cleanup. The shop would remain closed the next day, as the Amish didn't work or transact business on Sundays. But when Rachel opened on Monday, Miriam wanted the place to be spic and span.

Miriam wiped down the sales counter and sent two boys out back with the sack of trash. As she tidied up, her conversation with Rachel kept reverberating in her thoughts. The young couple's dilemma appealed to the "fixer" inside Miriam. It was an instinct engrained far deeper than the desire to be a matchmaker, a hobby that had caused her husband much consternation but always, always was worth it in the end.

What could be more important than bringing together two people in love? Miriam knew love had the power to bring together couples, families, even entire communities. Throughout her life she'd been privileged to witness Gott's hand in unifying his people. And tonight, listening to Rachel, she'd glimpsed the painful loneliness of separation. Such a problem for Rachel and Luke!

But Miriam-the-fixer was on the case.

She loved Dara's children dearly, and she would not rest soundly until she knew they were all right. Alvie would tell her to let them be, let them work it out, but the mother inside her knew she had to help these young folks.

For what was love if she didn't share it?

Chapter 3

A s Goliath's hooves clip-clopped along the pavement, Luke let himself savor this one moment. Everyone had been full of good food, Christmas spirit, and the satisfaction of a job well done when they'd left the shop. Now he drove one of the Fisher buggies with Rachel by his side and three of her siblings in the back—the picture of Amish life. This was how Gott meant their lives to be, and he imagined a future in which he and Rachel had children of their own—a buggy full of Amish children with happy faces and kindness.

Luke took his eyes off the road for a second to glance at his beautiful bride, who shared a warm glow beneath the lap blanket that she'd neatly tucked around their legs.

A blush of pink dotted her cheeks, maybe from the cold. The stray hairs that sprung out beneath her prayer kapp appeared silver in the occasional flash of oncoming car lights. And her eyes, blue as a summer sky, and just as soothing. In Rachel's eyes, he saw hope and love and faith in Gott. When their eyes met, he felt the promise between them, the commitment to love each other always and forever, husband and wife.

More than anything in the world, he wanted to fill her life with love and happiness.

But lately, he sensed that he was falling short of his promise, being away from home so much. One rainy night when Luke had felt cooped up in the tidy Mennonite boardinghouse where they stayed in Maple Run, he had told his father that he worried he was doing the wrong thing, living apart from his wife.

Levi Coblentz had looked up from his Amish newspaper and frowned. "A man must provide for his family," Luke's father had said. "When our people were farmers, we could be a stone's throw away all day, never far from home. But shrinking farmland has forced some of us to work at other occupations. I don't like leaving home each week any more than you do, son, but right now we must support our family."

Support the family. The duties of an Amish husband were deeply engrained in Luke. It was his joy to take care of Rachel, her siblings, and any children that, Gott willing, came along. But in the work world of Amish life, he didn't know where he belonged. Although he was a hard worker, he hadn't been born into a family of farmers or carpenters or buggy makers who learned their occupation as they grew up. Consequently, when Amish folks in Joyful River were hiring help, Luke usually was at the bottom of their list.

Not good enough, not skilled enough, not experienced enough.

He was a grown man of twenty-three without an occupation.

"I'm a hard worker, but I wasn't born to an occupation. I wish my father was a farrier," Luke once told Rachel. "Or a wheelwright. Or a dairy farmer. I like cows. And cheese."

"Cheese is delicious," she'd agreed, "but wishing won't make it so. Gott made you to be the man you are, the man I fell in love with."

He was grateful for her love but maybe not so worthy. In an Amish family, the man was the head of the household, the one responsible for providing for his family. His dat used to repeat a phrase popular among Amish fathers, saying, "I like to have my feet under the table." It was a throwback to when most Amish men were farmers who could sit at the family table each day for breakfast, lunch, and dinner. Men worked the land they lived on, and home and family were the center of their lives.

Luke longed to know such a life. Right now most of his days focused on the factory. Most nights, he even dreamed of it; restless dreams in which leagues of chocolate bars moved through the cue of the machinery, smooth and ready to be wrapped. In his worst nightmares the machine ran out of paper, and he couldn't manage to stop the mechanism to reload, and bare chocolate bars went flying down the conveyor belt toward the boxing area.

And then a supervisor would appear, wagging a finger and warning that they'd take the money for damages out of Luke's pay.

When that dream raged on until its end, Luke usually woke up in a sweat, his heart racing as he reminded himself that it wasn't real. In fact, he handled the big equipment well. His supervisor had said he might be in line for a raise after the holidays. Good news, though it was hard to appreciate with a job that pulled him away from home.

A life spent mostly without Rachel was full of bleak, long days. And now, with the holidays coming, the weeks of separation were wearing his spirits even thinner. Next week was Thanksgiving, and before Luke had left the factory, his supervisor had warned him about taking time off for the holidays.

"You're the new man on the factory line," Mitch had told him. "I'd like to give you the time you want, but my hands are tied. Company policy dictates that, as a new hire, you fill in for shifts that more senior workers want off. That means working Thanksgiving and Christmas Day."

The news had hit him harder than a kicking mule. Working on Christmas? When Luke and his father had taken the factory jobs, they'd assumed they would be able to take time off to return to their families for an extended holiday celebration.

"Time off for holidays and harvest wasn't a problem when we worked at the Plumdale factory," Dat had said when they discussed the matter during their van ride. "I have to admit, son, I'm getting worn down by this job. You, you're young and energetic, but I'm getting on. I could make do with a simpler job in Joyful River, even a job that doesn't pay much."

Luke had studied his father, struck by his weariness. He'd noticed Dat slowing a bit, but he'd never heard him sound so defeated. "We both need jobs closer to home," Luke had said. "Jobs that allow us to be with our family on Christmas, and every other day of the year."

"True." Pushing back his hat, Dat had scratched his head, a look of concern in his eyes. "This isn't going to go over well with your mother."

"Mem's not the only one who'll be upset," Luke had said. He knew the news was going to bring disappointment to their entire family, and with Thanksgiving less than a week away, Luke would have to break it to Rachel soon.

"Hey, you," Rachel said, touching his arm and turning to him so that her knees pressed against him on the front bench of the buggy. "You look so serious. What's on your mind?"

One look at the hope flickering in her blue eyes told him this was not the time to break bad news.

"This and that. Thinking about the holidays."

"I can't wait for the holidays," she said, squeezing his arm. "Finally, we'll have some time to be together. It's our first Christmas as a married couple, Luke. I so want it to be special."

"Every day with you is a special one," he said.

"I pray for the time when we can be together, day and night. I know it's going to happen for us. One day, soon, you're going to find a job here in Joyful River."

He nodded. "Dat and I are going to ask around after church tomorrow, see if anyone needs help."

"That's a good idea. You never know. With the cold weather here, folks might need help chopping wood or winterizing their house."

He forced a smile but kept his eyes on the partially lit road ahead. They both knew that small projects would not be enough to keep him employed here in Joyful River, but he didn't want to dampen her enthusiasm.

"You never know," he said. "Sometimes things happen out of the blue. Like when your aunt asked you to take on the Christmas shop, right? That was a surprise."

"A welcome surprise," she agreed. "And it's been going well. Aunt Madge told me that sales are up. We're getting more customers than ever."

"Who can resist that winter wonderland you created? Looks to me like you're selling more than just ornaments. Folks that come in get to have a Christmas experience."

"You know, that's exactly what I was trying for." She leaned closer and kissed his cheek. "I just needed you to put it into words."

He smiled, savoring the nearness of her. "I especially like your focus on the Christmas star and the nativity scene. It seems right to bring folks around to the meaning of Christmas."

"That was inspired by Truman," Rachel said, glancing to the back of the buggy to see if her brother was listening. "He keeps telling me how special the Christmas star is this year."

"Are you talking about me?" Truman piped up, interrupting his sister Bethany, who had been telling a story. "I heard my name."

"You heard right," Luke said. He had a special connection with Truman, a nine-year-old who didn't favor the activities of typical boys and didn't have many friends his age. Most Amish boys didn't have the patience to comb through library books on astronomy—which Truman seemed to memorize—or to carefully draw the configurations of heavenly constellations, or to stare at the night sky for hours, identifying planets and constellations.

Luke found it all fascinating, though he understood how other children found it hard to relate to Truman.

"Our Truman puts off the other boys at school,"

Rachel had confided in him. "It's just his habits, not looking people in the eyes and not wanting to be touched and things like that. He's odd, I'll admit that, but the boy has a good heart."

"A heart of gold," Luke had agreed. Having lost an older sister to a rare disease that had limited her life to barely a year, Luke understood the love a person felt for a family member who didn't fit the mold. In an Amish family, love ran deep for a special child, Gott's singular blessing.

Now Truman's interest was piqued. "What are you saying about me? Good things, I hope."

Luke laughed. "When it comes to you, my friend, I have only good things to say. We were talking about the star theme for the Christmas shop."

"I gave Rachel the idea," Truman said.

"You did," Rachel agreed. "And tonight, when I asked Aunt Madge about renaming the shop Star of Wonder, she thought it was a great idea. I'll get to work on hanging the sign Monday morning."

"Wait, wait!" Truman said. "Today is Saturday, isn't it? The Saturday before Thanksgiving?" His voice boomed with excitement. "How could I forget? The star's first appearance." He tapped Luke's shoulder from behind. "Stop the buggy. Stop, Luke. I have to get out, now!"

"What?" Rachel turned around to engage the

boy. "Truman, what's wrong? Tell me what's wrong?"

"What's wrong is that I forgot tonight is the first night. And it's a clear night, too. It'll be perfect. How could I forget? Stupid, stupid."

"Now take it easy there, buddy," Luke said, keeping his eyes on the road. He knew that the best way to respond to an outburst from Truman was with calm. "Why do you need to get out of the buggy?"

"To see the stars! The Christmas stars!"

"The stars you've been telling me about," Rachel said. "That's right. You told me they were going to start appearing in the night sky."

"Tonight." Truman was tapping on the back of the buggy bench. "Stop the buggy. I need to get out."

"I want to see them, too," Eli said. "Can I get out?"

"We can't stop here," Rachel said. "It's too dangerous to get out on the dark road."

"We're almost home," Luke offered. "We can all try to spot them when we get back to the house."

"I don't want to wait," Truman complained. "What if I miss them?"

"Take some deep breaths," Rachel said. "You need to calm down, and remember what you told me? They're Christmas stars. They'll be around for a few weeks."

Bethany pressed her face to the dark buggy window. "I can't see anything from here. But, Truman, how did you know the stars were coming out tonight?"

"I read it in a science magazine. Grace got it for me from the library."

Grace Sullivan was an Englisch girl who helped out in the Christmas shop. Having recognized Truman's special interest, Grace had brought him astronomy books and articles from the school library.

"I should have remembered," Truman said.

"Your timing is perfect," Luke insisted. "We're almost home, and since you remembered, we can all do some stargazing together."

"I don't understand why the Christmas stars are coming out tonight for the first time," said Bethany. "Where were they before?"

"In outer space, of course," Truman explained. "Tonight's the first night they're supposed to be visible to the naked eye, which is all I really have, since I don't have a telescope. I do have binoculars, but I left them at home."

"We'll have you home soon," Luke promised. "And then you can run inside and fetch your binoculars. That'll give you a very good view."

"But I don't think I can wait," Truman said plaintively.

"Of course you can," Rachel said. "Now, take a deep breath and count to ten. Then let it out very slowly, counting to eight." She spoke slowly, guiding her brother through the routine they used to help him calm down. "That's it. Let's do it one more time."

Listening to his wife take charge of the situation, Luke thanked Gott for Rachel's backbone. She knew how to handle her brothers and sisters with just the right combination of firmness, calm, and sympathy. What a fine mother she'd make if one day Gott blessed them with children.

For now, with Rachel and him spending most nights apart, those plans would have to be on hold.

When Luke turned into the Fishers' driveway, Eli and Bethany let out a cheer.

"We're home, Truman," Bethany said. "Aren't you excited?"

"I need to get my binoculars," he said.

The minute Luke brought the buggy to a halt, Truman opened the door, climbed out, and scrambled into the house.

Rachel sighed. "That one has a one-track mind, but I do enjoy his enthusiasm."

"Can we stay up and search for the Christmas star?" asked Bethany.

"Maybe for a little bit," Rachel said as she folded a lap blanket and climbed out of the buggy.

When Luke climbed out of the opposite side,

Eli came over and tugged on Luke's coat. "Why is this star so special?"

"Every star is special, in Truman's eyes," Luke said with a grin. "But we'll have to ask him to explain again."

"I hope we can find it," Eli said. "I want Truman to be happy."

"We all want that." Luke clapped a hand on the boy's shoulder and hustled him over to where Rachel and Bethany stood staring up at the sky.

Their mouths hung open in little "O's" and their eyes were round and dreamy.

"You two young misses look like you've spotted an angel," Luke teased.

"Nay," Rachel said, "but we found a glorious star. The brightest in the sky."

"I think it's the Christmas star," Bethany said. "It must be."

Luke and Eli followed their gaze up to a star that couldn't be missed. Brighter than most, it seemed to have a flaming center that glistened like a twirling gem. "Praise be to Gott," Luke said. "His creations are magnificent."

Rachel came to his side and took his hand, and he felt her joy and contentment in that simple squeeze of her fingers. They might be lonely hearts most days of the week, but that night they were together, man and wife.

The peaceful silence was broken when the door of the house blew open and Truman emerged, struggling to run with his binoculars dangling around his neck and his fat astronomy volume under one arm.

"Easy there, buddy," Luke said.

"Truman! Come, quick!" Bethany cried. "We think we found your star!"

Chapter 4

Rachel leaned into her husband's warm embrace as Truman raced over to join them, his binoculars jostling awkwardly. Within two steps he'd lost his grip on the large book, which fell to the ground. It landed on its spine and flopped open on the gravel driveway.

"My book!"

"Let me hold it for you." Although reluctant to leave Luke's side, Rachel had to break away to stoop down and pick up the book.

Luke stepped forward and put a hand on Truman's shoulder. "Look up, buddy. Is that the star you were talking about?"

Truman's head tilted up as he scanned the sky. "That's it!" he gasped. "That's the Christmas star!"

Rachel felt herself relax with relief. When Truman was happy, everything went more smoothly.

"It's very beautiful," Rachel said. "The brightest star in the sky."

"That's what the article said." Truman spoke without looking away from the shining object. "I read that it would be the brightest star in the early night sky. Some astronomers think it's similar to the star that the wise men followed to find the baby Jesus."

"You mean the three kings in the Bible story?" asked Bethany.

"That's right," Truman said.

"What Bible story?" asked Eli. "Tell me the story."

"It's about when Christ was born," Rachel said, crossing to the side porch to place Truman's book in a safe spot. "There were wise men who heard that a savior was born, but they didn't know how to find him. So Gott put a very bright star in the sky, lighting the way for them to find baby Jesus and bring him gifts."

"Gold, frankincense, and myrrh. That's what they brought," Bethany said. "I remember because we did a skit about them in the school program a few Christmases back."

"That's good that you remember," said Rachel. "And now look what Gott has sent us—a star that might be as bright as the original Christmas star."

"I wonder why it shines like that," Eli said.

"It's extra bright because it's two stars," Truman explained without lowering his binoculars. "It's actually two stars moving really close to each other. So close that they're joining together in a big explosion called a nova. I read all about it."

"A nova." Luke slipped an arm around Rachel's waist and pulled her close once again as they stared up at the lovely sky. She leaned back against him, loving the glow of security and peace she felt in his arms. "Two stars together? That sounds like us, Rachel."

Savoring his warmth, Rachel smiled at the romantic notion. "Our own Christmas stars," she said. "And every night when we're apart, we can look up and know that we're waiting under the same sky, under our Christmas stars."

"A star can't belong to you or me," Truman pointed out. "Gott made the stars for everyone on earth."

"You're right," Luke agreed, his mouth so close Rachel could feel his warm breath on her cheek. "You're right, and I'm willing to share."

Rachel laughed softly and let herself relax in this moment, gathered with family and gazing up at the vast indigo heavens scattered with countless stars. "Gott's night sky is a good reminder to us that we're all together under the stars." She squeezed Luke's arm, adding, "Even when we live in different towns."

The kiss he placed on her cheek made her melt a little inside, though the romantic moment was interrupted when Julie came striding up the driveway.

"Dat's waiting in the buggy barn to help you with the buggy, and Goliath needs to be put out." Julie looked at the little group curiously. "What's the holdup here? And why aren't you children getting ready for bed?"

"We're watching the Christmas star!" Eli

responded, his squeaky voice full of so much enthusiasm that Rachel and Luke both chuckled.

"I'll bring the buggy to the barn," said Luke. "It was good of your dat to wait, but I can take care of it."

"Are the little ones already asleep?" Rachel asked. Julie and their father had left the shop ahead of them, hoping to get Polly and Willie to bed.

"I tucked them in a few minutes ago. Polly fell asleep on the way home."

"Denki for looking after them," Rachel told her sister before turning to the children. "And thank you all for your help with the shop. It's been a late night, but we got the work done ahead of the sabbath."

"It has been a late night," Julie said in the firm voice of a schoolteacher. "Time for everyone to get to bed."

"Can we stay up a little bit more to watch the sky?" Eli asked.

"If Truman gives us a turn with the binoculars, we might get so see some shooting stars," said Bethany.

"We have church in the morning," Rachel reminded them. It had been a good day, but a long one, and right now she wanted nothing more than to ease into her warm bed and snuggle with her husband.

"Please, please, please just a few minutes?"

Truman asked. "The sky is so clear, I can see many constellations. I'll point them out to everyone. And I'll share the binoculars."

Julie cast a look at Rachel, folded her arms across her chest and sighed. "All right. Ten more minutes. But I do hope you get some of this star business out of your system, Truman. Because you can't be talking about it at school."

"I know, I know," Truman said. "Rules are rules. I can talk about the stars and planets at home, but in the classroom, we stick to lessons."

"Right," Julie said. "And don't lecture the other children on what you know, 'cause sometimes the boys resent that."

Rachel felt a twinge of sympathy as Truman gave a deep nod of agreement. Poor guy. He was big for his age and incredibly single-minded, which often didn't sit well with his peers. He had no friends at school, and sometimes he was bullied by a few of the older boys. She imagined it made things a bit harder on Truman because one of his teachers was his sister. Although Julie and her coworker emphasized strong Christian principles like love for one another and kindness, there were always a few mischievous children in the schoolhouse.

When the children finally were ushered inside, Rachel kissed them all good night, adding a special hug for her sister Julie, who was her partner in mothering since Mem had passed.

"What would I do without you?" Rachel asked, patting Julie's back.

"The same housework and nose-wiping," Julie said as she headed up the stairs, "only twice as much."

Glancing out the kitchen window, Rachel saw the white beam of an LED lantern in the buggy barn that told her Dat and Luke were still out there. She left the lamp over the kitchen table lit and took a small battery lantern into the bedroom with her.

Although she and Luke had been married only two months, she felt very much at home in their little bedroom behind the kitchen. Years ago, when her grandparents lived in the house, Dawdi had used the room for an office when he sold furniture. After her grandfather had retired, Mem had used it as a sewing room, where she'd stitched together dresses and pants on the old treadle sewing machine.

Now, it was the place where Rachel and Luke lived. The room was barely big enough for a bed, a nightstand, and a few hooks on the wall, but when the chores were done and the lanterns were extinguished, this room was all the world the two of them needed.

She popped into the small first-floor bathroom and then back to their little nest. Her dress, apron, and prayer kapp were hung on a hook, and she pulled a flannel nightgown over her head. Thinking of her husband, she huddled on the bed with a crocheted blanket over her lap and began to unplait her hair. Most nights she left it in a braid, but Luke liked it wild and free, and she loved to please him. Marriage had taught her that her husband was the one person in the world with whom she could share her true self— the woman inside her. Much had been revealed on their wedding night, but surprisingly, that had been only the beginning. Over the weeks and months, they continued to learn new things about each other in intimate ways. Hearts and bodies, fears and dreams. How she looked forward to the time when they could be together, always!

But for now, she was grateful to have two nights with him in their little abode. Even before Luke had gotten his job up in Maple Run, they had decided to live here for a while. It was not only a way to save for their own place but it also allowed Rachel close proximity to her father and siblings so that she could help keep the household running with ease. When Luke had gotten the factory job, Rachel had seen it as a blessing to be here, living each day with family while she waited for Luke's employment circumstances to change.

She climbed under the quilt and felt the immediate release of the burdens of the day. The shop, the children, the waiting for Luke . . . all the weight of her worries slid away as she moved her bare feet over the smooth bedsheet, curled up onto her side, and closed her eyes. The soft sheets were heavenly!

She allowed her mind to wander to the week ahead—a shortened workweek, because of Thanksgiving. Would Luke stay for the entire weekend? How wonderful that would be. The holiday dinner was going to be hosted by Aunt Madge and Uncle Emery, who were the true cooks of the family. Rachel and Julie had promised to bring some pies, which reminded Rachel that she needed to get her grocery list together and get baking soon.

The door opened and Luke leaned in. "At last! A moment alone with my wife!"

"You're a good sport." She giggled. "Surrounded by Dat and my six siblings."

"The little ones, they bring me joy, even when they act like children," he teased, sitting on the bed to unbutton his blue shirt. "You know what they say. You don't marry the woman. You marry the family."

"That's certainly true with my family. The young ones love you, Luke, and they truly need us now more than ever."

"I know that. Spending time with them is second to my greatest joy in life." He leaned down and kissed her lips, luring her to full wakefulness. "Being with you."

She reached up and ran the palm of her hand down over the contours of his chest. "Come to bed."

"You don't have to ask twice," he said, squeezing her hand before quickly changing into his pajamas.

"Dat had your ear for a while in the buggy barn," she said.

"Yah. He was going over possible jobs for me here in Joyful River."

"Really?" Her eyes opened wide. If Luke could get a local job, that would make everything so much better. "Does he have some prospects?"

"Nothing definite, but he mentioned a few men I should talk with tomorrow after church."

"Amish business owners who are in need of a reliable, upbeat man with a big personality?"

"Most folks like reliable," he said. "Big personality, not so much."

Both Rachel and Luke were aware that Amish culture didn't encourage drawing too much attention to one's self. Sometimes it was a drawback for Luke, who wasn't struck by vanity, though he enjoyed drawing folks out and making them laugh. And with his height and big, booming voice, well, Luke was definitely a big personality, and Rachel loved every aspect of that.

Luke sighed with satisfaction as he went to his side of the bed. "There's nothing like being home in your own bed."

She felt the mattress sink with Luke's weight, and the room went dark as he extinguished the lantern. "Now, then." The touch of his fingertips running down her back made her draw in a quick breath. "How sleepy are you?" he whispered.

She rolled over to face him, and he scooped her close. "Never too tired for you." It was such a thrill to be received in his strong arms. He was always there to catch her when she needed saving.

Chapter 5

When the sun glowed pink and orange over the hills Sunday morning, Luke was out of bed and full of energy. It felt good to be home! Just waking up beside Rachel set his heart aright for the day. Then the added bonus of having her father and siblings in the house gave him dozens of small tasks to juggle and endless opportunities to make them smile.

Since it was a church day, the management of breakfast, feeding chickens, and foisting the small ones into their church clothes was nothing short of chaotic. Sometimes the hectic morning irritated Rachel, but Luke loved it. Rachel was the main boss, a natural leader, and Luke tried to support her and make work fun at every turn.

"My church pants are too small!" Truman complained, calling from the top of the stairs where he stood, trying to yank a small pair of dark trousers over his underwear.

Luke went to the bottom of the stairs and paused. "You're right on that. Those pants don't fit."

"They fit two weeks ago," Rachel called from the kitchen.

"But they don't fit now," Truman insisted, tugging on the waistband.

318

"That's because they're *my* pants," shouted Willie from somewhere upstairs.

"No, these are mine," Truman insisted. "I know because I put them in the closet, and that's where they were."

"They're mine," Willie said, shuffling down the hall in a sea of black fabric. "These must be yours."

"But I got these from the closet, and—" Truman's mouth dropped open when he saw his brother swimming in the large pair of trousers. "Oh. These must be yours."

"Another problem solved." Luke laughed from his position at the bottom of the stairs. "It's going to be a wonderful day."

Breakfast was oatmeal and sausage, a serve-yourself day, as there was no time to waste. Once Luke hitched up the large buggy, he posted himself in the kitchen to cajole the younger ones to eat something, knowing they'd be cranky soon if they went without food. He had to cut Truman off after five sausage links, and Polly refused to eat anything at all until he sprinkled a handful of chocolate chips onto her oatmeal.

"Chocolate?" she said, her eyes opening wide in wonder.

"Shh," he warned her, handing her a spoon. "Let it be our little secret."

Although they could have taken two buggies, they preferred to pile all nine souls in together, which wasn't so bad with the little ones squeezed in and sitting on laps. They had lap blankets and Julie had made sure to fill two hot-water bottles, but they really didn't need them with all the body heat. "An Amish heating system," some folks called it.

When they turned up the road to the home of Jerry and Netta Kraybill, Luke tweaked Willie's chin and smiled at Rachel. Although he'd part reluctantly from his wife during most of the church preaching, songs, and social, Luke always looked forward to the community gathering. Church brought their community together, giving everyone a chance to show support, praise Gott and enjoy each other's company. It was social time at its best.

They waited their turn to unload and hand their horse and buggy off to hostlers, young men and boys who volunteered for the job. Straightening his jacket and hat, Luke watched Rachel and Julie lead the little ones off, while Bethany joined with two of her friends. Everyone was following the directions on a chalkboard sign that showed different genders and age groups where to meet. Following tradition, married men sat together, married women were in a group toting young children, and various other groups were similarly organized. Truman and Eli followed the chalkboard sign that pointed them to the boys' meeting place in the workshop.

"I wish I didn't have to sit with the boys," Truman said. "They can get rowdy."

Luke nodded sympathetically. "I remember those days well." In truth, he hadn't minded a bit of rowdiness when he was Truman's age. But overall, folks of all ages sat through the church meeting with as much respect as they could muster.

Heading toward the buggy barn, Luke felt a smile warm him from within as he spotted friends along the way and stopped to greet them. Micah Brubaker. Sam Lapp. Jacob Kraybill. Some of the guys pulled him into a bear hug, some were more reserved, but all of them seemed happy to see him.

Joy brimmed over inside him, nearly bringing tears to his eyes.

It felt good to be home.

Over the next few hours, Luke let himself get lost in the hymns and words of the preachers. When the last hymn was sung, Luke joined with his friends to partake of sandwiches and baked goods and catch up on news. The buddy group had plenty of stories to share, but Luke knew that he would have to tear himself away at some point and talk to some of the older, more established men about getting hired. He needed to work toward a time when he could see his friends and family throughout the week, not just on weekends and church days.

Checking out the folks milling around, he spotted Emery Lambright, owner of the successful Country Diner on Joyful River's Main Street.

"Luke Coblentz!" The portly, gray-haired man clapped Luke on the shoulder. "How is it that I never see you around town anymore, young man?"

"It's because I spend most of the week in Maple Run," Luke explained. "Dat and I got jobs at a factory up there after work dried up in Plumdale."

"Ach, that explains it." Emery's gray beard bobbed as he nodded quickly. "How is that going?"

"The job is fine. Pays well, but it's hard for us to be away from home."

"Maple Run? What is that, an hour or two in a van?"

"Closer to two. Far enough that we need to board there during the week and come home for Sundays. Right now, they're demanding that we work Thanksgiving and Christmas."

"Christmas Day?" Emery winced. "What sort of place is open and operating during the most important holiday of the year?"

"I know. Crazy, right?" Luke shook his head. "I'm trying to find something closer to home. Do you know of anything? Or maybe you need a dishwasher or a cook in the restaurant?"

"The diner is Madge's business. As you can see," he said, patting his ample belly, "I eat away enough of the profits without spending all day in the restaurant. Mind you, I raise the chickens and do the bookkeeping, but my wife, she runs the operation. Getting in her way would be like walking in front of a tornado."

"That dangerous?" Luke asked with a grin. "She's a woman who knows her mind."

Emery looked around, as if to make sure no one was listening, then answered, "The best kind. But feel free to ask her."

"I will," said Luke. "Right now, I'll take any job if it means spending Christmas with my new wife."

"A man wants to have his feet under the table," Emery said. "Let me ask around for you. Say, Paul." He caught the attention of a man passing by with a plate of food in hand. Luke recognized Paul Graber, the farrier who cared for Amish horses in Joyful River. "Do you have a minute? Luke here is looking for work. Are you taking on any new hands?"

Luke held his breath, hopeful for the answer.

"Tell me, Luke, do you have experience trimming and balancing a horse's hooves?" asked Paul.

"Can't say that I do," Luke admitted, "but I'm willing to learn. I get on well with horses, and they seem to like me."

Paul grinned. "I reckon they do. I'm still breaking in two nephews who're trying to learn the business, and we've been busy trimming hooves, getting ready for winter weather. Talk to me in the spring if you're still interested, and we'll see what we can do."

Luke couldn't bear to think about working up north until spring, but he thanked Paul, and the man moved on. When Luke and Emery made their way to the food table, Emery inquired about work at the bakery and the outdoor market, but no one could think of anyone who was hiring. Luke thanked everyone, adding that he would keep looking. "Though I've got a good job up in Maple Run, my heart and my family are here in Joyful River."

"Home is where the heart is," said Delilah Esh, owner of the bakery. "It may sound corny, but you'll rest easier once you find work back here."

Luke knew she was right. He would keep looking, but for now, he was grateful to Emery for helping him get the word out.

The afternoon allowed time for plenty of conversation and visiting with friends. As was the custom, men and women congregated in their own groups. Teens and Rumspringa youth tended to mix more, gathering around a bonfire and playing pickup games of soccer or kickball.

Luke occasionally looked over to Rachel, who sat in a cluster of married women, many of them getting up from their seats to chase or corral their young children. Polly sat with Rachel for a bit, but then she was folded into a group with her older siblings, who were playing a game beyond the Kraybills' nearly frozen garden plot.

As the afternoon gathering was drawing to a close, the church members thinned out. In a few hours, the Rumspringa youth would return to this space for a singing, a session of lively songs, conversation, and snacks. Glad that his courtship days were done, Luke ventured over to a group of older women and found his mother, Sabina, in a gaggle of women listening to old Millie Stevick talk about a miracle cream she'd found advertised in an Amish magazine. Luke tried not to listen, but who could miss the woman's announcement that her bunions had been cured?

"Mem." Luke kept his voice low, trying not to siphon off Millie's attention. "I have a question."

With a nod, Sabina Coblentz extracted herself from the group and came over to join him. "Good to see you, son," she said as they strolled toward a quiet part of the barn. "And I'm grateful to be spared from that conversation. I've heard enough of warts, moles, and bunions to last me a lifetime."

They chuckled together, and Luke smiled down on his mother. Although Luke had towered over his mother since age sixteen, Sabina Coblentz had always kept him in check. When it came to her children, she was a small powerhouse.

"I wanted to say a brief hello," Luke said, "since Dat and I have to leave tomorrow. Our time at home is always too short."

"Indeed," Sabina said, reaching up to cup his cheek affectionately. "That's why I'm so relieved that he's going to be giving up that factory job."

"He . . ." Were his ears playing tricks on him? "He's giving up on work?"

"Oh, not completely. He's found a job in the Hostetlers' harness shop, here in town. Didn't he tell you?"

"I didn't know." Luke glanced over toward the cluster of older men, a waning group with the late afternoon hour. There was his Dat, still sitting with Len Hostetler. Well, it was no wonder, as the two men had been talking up a storm all afternoon. "That's good news, then."

"What's that?" Rachel's voice was unmistakable. "You know that good news needs to be shared, don't you?"

Luke turned to take in his wife, whose sparkling blue eyes and sweet smile calmed him. Her presence eased the sting of the news a bit. It wasn't that Luke didn't wish a new job for his father; it was the prospect of continuing his exodus up north alone each week that left him feeling chilled.

"Rachel, dear girl, it's so good to see you."

Sabina went up on tiptoes to kiss her cheek. "I've been meaning to stop into the shop, but I don't get into town much these days."

"She's turned the place around," Luke reported, putting one arm over Rachel's shoulders. "You need to see the new decorations, Mem. It will get you in the Christmas spirit."

"I'll stop in soon, I promise," Sabina said. "I'll have more opportunity to get a ride into town once Levi is back." She turned to Rachel, adding, "That's my good news. Levi found a job here in town, so he's only got a few more days' work at the factory."

"That's wonderful news!" Rachel said.

"Yah," Luke's mother agreed, "and it came in the nick of time, what with the foreman telling our men that they had to work on the holidays."

Luke stiffened as the words flew out of his mother's mouth. He hadn't told Rachel yet, but Mem couldn't have known that. Had Rachel picked up on it?

"I'm happy for Dat," Luke said, trying to plow through before Rachel noticed. "He's been right tuckered out with the long factory hours and the travel up north."

"Wait a minute." Rachel leaned to the right so that his arm slipped off her shoulders. Her eyes were stormy with confusion. "The holidays? What do you mean?"

"Thanksgiving and Christmas," Sabina said.

"Since our husbands are the more recent hires, they're expected to work both holidays."

Rachel's mouth dropped open as she turned to Luke, a pained look of betrayal on her face, as if he'd just stabbed her in the back. That look—her disappointment—it filled him with shame.

"But now it looks like Dat's found a way out of that," Luke said, trying to steer around the painful topic. "So Len offered him a job at the harness shop? What does Dat know about buggy collars and hames?"

"As much as any other Amish man, I suppose." Mem gave him a wry smile. "I think it's more a matter of Len and Linda wanting to spend some time away from the shop, and they know Levi is a reliable man who'll learn the trade and tend to the customers."

"I reckon you're right," Luke said. "Good for him."

Mem nodded, pleased, as she looked over toward Dat.

It was the sort of break old Dat needed. But that was no help to Luke and Rachel.

Luke glanced back at his wife and was immediately overcome by a sinking feeling. Rachel was upset; he could see it in her glassy blue eyes and tightly pursed lips. She looked as if she were about to cry.

He knew that it was all his fault, but he didn't know how to begin to remedy the situation.

Chapter 6

Rachel's heart raced in her chest, thundering as if she'd just run the back acres of the Lapp Dairy Farm.

Luke would be working on Christmas Day?

Their first Christmas together, and they would be hours apart. And this week—Thanksgiving—would he be here? All her treasured plans of chatting with relatives, enjoying delicious pies and socializing with her husband at the Lambright home were about to blow away like a fast-moving cloud.

The unfairness of it all nipped at her composure, and the fact that Luke had kept this from her made the ache in her heart even worse. She swallowed hard, trying to contain herself and tamp down the rumbling feelings of betrayal and hurt and embarrassment as Luke finished the conversation with his mem. She didn't want her mother-in-law to see her turmoil; this was a personal matter, between Luke and her, a matter a husband and wife needed to work through on their own.

Fortunately, Luke's mother was so chipper about Levi's new job offer that she didn't pick up on the underpinning of the conversation. "I'd best get going," Sabina said, looking over toward the dwindling group of older men. "Looks like your dat is ready to head home."

Rachel forced a smile as they said their good-byes and Sabina moved away. It was embarrassing—mortifying—to be stuck here, in the Kraybills' buggy barns, with this simmering emotion about to boil over inside her.

"I'm sorry," Luke said as soon as his mother was out of hearing range. "I just got word from the factory foreman, and I knew I had to tell you, but . . ."

"Why didn't you?" she whispered.

"I didn't want to ruin our short time together."

"Don't you understand?" She shook her head. "We need to be truthful with each other. Always. A bit of bad news won't ruin our love. Sad things will happen. Accidents, tragedies. We hope and pray for the best. But, Luke, we need to weather these things together, to help each other through the hard times."

"I know that," Luke said. When she lifted her chin to meet his eyes, he seemed so contrite, so worried. "I'm sorry. I thought I could protect you, shield you. I hoped that I'd find some kind of job today, like Dat, so that I wouldn't have to even think about spending the next few weeks away from you."

"And how did that go?" she asked, restraining all emotion.

"I wasn't as lucky as Dat. I got the word out,

but no work." He looked down. "So it's back to Maple Run for me."

Seeing his disappointment, she softened. "I'm sorry, Luke. I know how much you wanted to find something close to home."

"I do. And I will." When he looked up at her, she saw determination in his eyes. "We'll get past this, Rach." He reached out and touched her arm. "Are you still mad?"

How could she stay mad at him when he felt so bad? And none of this was his fault. She hated this separation, this obstacle, but they would only make it through the difficult times if they supported each other. "I think I'm over it," she said. "But no more secrets, Luke. Do you hear me?"

"No secrets," he promised.

It wasn't until their buggy was rolling down the road behind their trotting horse that all the consequences sank in. Rachel was going to be alone for the holidays. Sure, she'd be with her family, and she could probably survive Thanksgiving without Luke. But the thought of spending Christmas away from her husband made her a little sick inside. She bit her lips together and turned toward the window. It wouldn't do to upset the children.

The buggy pulled up in front of the house, and Rachel and Julie hustled the children out. Rachel watched as Dat and Luke took the buggy on to the garage, where Goliath would be set free to roam the small pasture they shared with a few Amish neighbors.

"The temperature's dropped," Julie observed. "I'll build us a fire."

"I don't mind the cold," said Eli.

"Me neither," Willie agreed. "Cold is good for football."

"I want to play!" Truman said.

"First change out of your church clothes," Rachel said. "Then you can play until dark."

"And once the sun goes down, we can stargaze," Truman said.

"After a long day, I think you'll be wanting bed by then," Rachel said.

"Please, please, please?" Truman begged.

It was hard to say no to a boy who had one earnest desire. "We'll see," Rachel said. She changed out of her church clothes and then bundled up in a sweater, coat, scarf, and big black bonnet. She and Luke needed to talk, and with a houseful of family, they needed the privacy that the miles of surrounding farmland afforded.

She met him in the mudroom, where he switched his jacket for a thick coat, his shoes for a heavy pair of boots. He stepped out the door, and she followed him with a long woolen scarf, which she wrapped around his neck.

"I don't need that," he insisted.

"I don't want you to catch cold."

"All right," he said. "Only because I understand you having the desire to wring me around the neck."

Smiling, she linked her arm through his and they set off into the brisk, cool air. "It's not your fault that the boss is making you work on holidays."

"But I've let you down. A good husband would have a job in town. A good husband stays with his family."

"I disagree. You're a good husband because you're sacrificing those things to take care of us."

"Mmm." He groaned a little. "It's a terrible choice."

"I know." As they approached the laurel hedge of the Dienners' adjoining farm, Rachel tried to have a realistic view of the future. "I know you need that job, but as I look ahead, I just can't imagine it, Luke. Thanksgiving is going to be so sad without you. And Christmas . . . it just feels so wrong."

"I know. This is our first Christmas as husband and wife. We need to be together." He squeezed her arm, helping her over a mucky rut in the mostly frozen road. "I don't know how to make that happen, but I'm not spending Christmas without you."

She turned to him. "What if you don't work Christmas? What will they do?"

He shrugged. "Probably fire me."

"We can't have that," she said. "Or can we? Could we get by without your pay come December? At least for a while? A month or two?"

"We made a promise to your dat," he reminded her. "He's relying on us to help pay off those medical expenses. We can't back out now."

"I know that. I just thought we might be able to make do for a few months." She sighed at the reminder of those hospital bills—Mem's treatment. The procedures had bought her a little time, but in the end, Gott had chosen her time. And here they were, a year later, boxed into a difficult situation to earn enough to pay that debt.

"What about the money I'm making at the shop?" she asked. "I could ask for a raise."

"It helps," he said. "It helps a lot, Rach. But if we want to keep paying as we promised, I need to keep the job in Maple Run."

She let out a huff of breath, which formed a white puff in the air. "I hate that place."

"Maple Run?" He grinned. "But you've never been there."

"I know, but it's the town that's pulling you away from me, and I don't like that at all."

"All right, here's an idea. I know it's last-minute, but maybe you can come up and stay with me in Maple Run this weekend for Thanksgiving. I'll have to work the holiday, but we'll be able to spend some time together. I could show you the town."

Rachel shook her head. "I've never spent a single night away from Joyful River, let alone Thanksgiving."

There was amusement in Luke's eyes. "You make it sound as if you'll shrivel up into a rag doll when you reach the county road."

She smiled. "Was I that dramatic? It's just strange to think of making a trip like that. I promised to bake pies for Thanksgiving, and the children will miss me."

"You can bake your pies before you go, and the children will have one another, and Julie, and your dat. And countless cousins, aunts and uncles at the Lambrights' Thanksgiving dinner. I'm sorry to miss that, but it will make it easier to bear if you're with me." Luke released her arm and jumped onto the top of a low stone wall bordering the Dienner property. "Think of it, Rach. We'll be together, and you'll have a chance to see a bit of Gott's creation. We used to talk about traveling a bit. Going to see the ocean, maybe a trip to Florida. Well, this is a start."

Watching him preach from the short wall, she recognized how hard he was trying to set things right. "Listen to you, comparing the ocean to a factory town north of Lancaster. You really should find a job in sales, Luke. You could charm me into buying the moon."

"Is it working?" he asked. "Are my sunny Amish charms persuading you?"

She took his hand, stepped up onto the wall beside him, and leaned up so close she could feel his warm breath on her cheek. "I'll buy that moon. Can you wrap it in a box for me?"

"With a big bow," he promised, taking her into his arms.

Their lips met, a soft touch of warmth in the nippy cold. For a moment, Rachel let wondrous sensations wash over her as she savored the thrill of Luke's embrace. These sweet times for them were so rare. The notion of spending some time in Maple Run, just the two of them, made her heart soar! After all that Luke had sacrificed for Rachel and her family, she could certainly give up a holiday with her family. For now, she would have to push away her worry about leaving the children for the holiday and open her heart to a new experience with her husband.

As they were kissing, she shifted her foot and felt her boot slip on the wall.

"Oof!" she cried, as she lost her balance and teetered toward the ground.

"I gotcha." Luke held on tight, managing to right her and pull her onto steady footing.

"You're always here to catch me when I fall," she said, loving the spark of love in his eyes.

"Always." He took her hand and, together, they jumped to the ground. "So. I'll talk to the van driver about bringing you out Wednesday. Can you have your pies baked by then?"

"I reckon. And I'll be sure to bring pie for us. Do I need to bring enough for everyone in the bunkhouse?" she asked. "Wait. Do they have a room for women there?"

"It's men only, and I wouldn't put you through that. I have a few cousins in the area who might put us up. I'll find us a place to stay."

"I'll need to talk to Aunt Madge about the shop. We're closed on Thanksgiving Day, but I'll have to find someone to cover for me Wednesday and Friday."

"You have Grace. She knows the store well."

"She's scheduled to work, but she might need help. It's a busy time for us." Rachel mulled over the possibilities. "Maybe one of her sisters will want to do it. Or maybe Julie would pitch in over the weekend. Either way, I'll work it out. We're going to make this happen," she said, her spirits lifting at the newly hatched idea. "Oh, Luke. You've managed to turn this awful thing into an exciting adventure for the two of us."

"See how that works, Rach? When we're together, we can climb any mountain."

Her wonderful husband was right. And with that problem solved, they still had nearly twenty-four hours until he had to leave her side. Determined to make the most of it, she held fast to his hand as they walked into the winter twilight, watching the deepening sky for the first sign of their Christmas star.

When Rachel awoke Monday morning, she let her waking moment be a prayer of thanks for the man sleeping beside her. The sound of his breathing, the rise and fall of his chest, the peaceful look that graced his handsome face . . . Luke's very presence had a calming effect on her.

She moved out of bed quietly and cracked the shade so that she could peer out at the sunrise. The sky was still dark above, but the nearby hills and rooftops were golden, and the orange and lavender swirls on the horizon filled her with hope. Maybe this would be the week that Luke found a job here in town.

She had mentioned this in her prayers before, but it worried her that she was asking for something so small. And was it too petty? It also worried her that the prayer hadn't been answered, and she knew Gott had a purpose in everything. Was she supposed to learn patience? Courage? Or maybe Gott's answer was her trip to Maple Run. Could there be a solution in her adventure with Luke?

She had to keep faith. Trust Him. Be patient.

Oh, that patience thing was such a problem for her.

She dressed quickly, went down the hall to the bathroom and then to the kitchen to begin her tasks: Coffee, bacon, eggs, and lunches for the schoolchildren. So much to do before the school bell rang!

Within minutes Luke and Dat came in, grateful for coffee. Julie followed, and they talked about their plans for the day. Most of the shop decoration had been completed before they left Saturday night. Today, Luke and Rachel planned to hang the new sign out front and tidy up for the rush of customers expected later in the week, after Thanksgiving.

When the clock came up on half past seven, Luke went upstairs to roust the children from bed with a few verses of "Down to the River," his voice booming, " 'Oh, brothers, let's go down, down to the river to pray!' " His rollicking rendition of the song made Rachel laugh out loud as she spread peanut butter and marshmallow onto bread for the children's lunches.

"Luke sure is happy today," Julie said as she popped an apple into her own lunch cooler.

"Today and every day," Rachel said. "He's a man who wakes up happy each morning."

"Truly a blessing," Dat said, as he gathered up his own lunch pail and headed out to the road, where Harlan Yoder would pick him up so they could ride together to the furniture factory.

Within the hour the four children were ready for school and loaded into the buggy. "We're off for another exciting day!" Julie called before climbing into the front seat to take the reins.

Waving to them from the side door, Rachel marveled at her sister's cheerful everyday attitude. Julie was a dutiful sister to the younger ones, and a wonderful teacher who truly enjoyed her work with the lower-grade students.

Once Luke coaxed Polly to finish her breakfast, the three of them climbed into the smaller buggy and headed into town. "What a blessing it is to have you here," Rachel told Luke. "You spare me the morning cold, harnessing the horses and hitching up the buggies. Julie offers to take a turn, but she has a long day at school. I try to spare her."

He smiled. "I'm happy to do it. I wish I were around more to ease your load."

"I know." She was determined to keep asking around for work here, but in the meantime, a trip to Maple Run this week would be a good diversion.

As they rode down Main Street and Rachel looked ahead toward the shop, she noticed quite a few folks milling around on the street. "Looks like something's going on," she said. There was often a short line in front of the bakery, but these folks were farther down, closer to the front of the Christmas shop.

Luke gave a curious shrug as they rolled ahead, pulled along by Caspar. "Let's see." He brought the mule to a stop in front of the shop so that Rachel and Polly could climb down and weave into the group. As Rachel pulled Polly around two ladies and stepped onto the sidewalk, she could see that the crowd was actually more organized than she realized. The Englisch folk—mostly women, some pushing walkers— were actually lined up in a queue that began at the door of the Christmas shop.

"Good morning," Rachel said, nodding at the cheerful ladies. "What's going on here?"

A tall woman with a cloud of silver hair stepped up from the front of the line. "Guten morgen," she said brightly. "We've heard about your store, and we know you're not open just yet, but we wanted to be first in line. We saw the pictures on social media—that little lit path through the shop. It looks adorable. Like a Christmas wonderland."

"You just follow the picket fences," a woman in a purple felt hat with a sparkly jewel said. "I saw photos online. Sparkly white fences covered with ornaments, like little gems. Is this the right store?"

Rachel was so taken aback by the lovely description, so surprised to see the line of shoppers, she could only nod.

"Folks, you've come to the right place," Luke said, moving past a couple who wore red Santa caps. Rachel realized he had pulled into an empty spot down the street and tethered the buggy to a hitching post.

"We drove all the way here from Maryland," someone said. "What time do you open up?"

"Usually not until ten," Rachel said, sliding the key into the lock.

"But we'll make an exception today, seeing as you've come so far," Luke announced. "Just give us a chance to set up inside. Who else is from out of town? Everyone?"

As Rachel opened the door and ushered Polly inside, she heard her husband chatting with the ladies in line, answering their questions and joking around with them in that amusing way Luke had. She switched on the many display lights and the twinkly white Christmas lights that covered the pathways of picket fences. In the dim shadows of the shop, the sparkly Christmas wonderland came to life.

"Christmas is still here," Polly said, smiling over the glimmering scene.

Rachel chuckled as she moved toward the back of the shop. "Want to help me check the nativity scene? That's the thing most important to me now."

"Truman set it up. He did it all, except he let me put the baby in his crib."

"Truman was quite eager to put the statues in place," Rachel said, approaching the little half of a hut built right into the store. Rachel had cleaned and painted the wood from the old chicken coop before moving it here, hoping to brighten it up a bit. But the way the men had constructed it, the single peak of the roof over the simple shack, gave it a raw beauty that tugged at her heart.

"Praise be to Gott," she said quietly, grateful for the way it had come together.

A simple star glowed over the manger. The large figurines, basic depictions of shepherds and sheep, wisemen and Jesus's family, had come from a discount store. They were plain, and yet, they told the story that needed to be told.

"All right," she told Polly. "We're ready to open."

That day began the bustling business of Star of Wonder.

In her wildest dreams Rachel had not expected so many customers to come from far and wide just to visit a little country Christmas shop. But she did understand what they had come to see.

Folks were hungry for a meaningful journey. They were eager to follow the path of the white picket fences, meandering through reminders of Christmas that led them finally to the reason mankind celebrated the season.

That little nativity scene. The birth of the Savior.

On Truman's suggestion, Rachel had dangled star ornaments from the ceiling at turns in the path, giving the feeling that the traveler was following the stars.

"You've created a shop that tells the Christmas story," Aunt Madge said that afternoon, having stopped in to see what all the commotion was about on the street. "Not to mention that you've turned the shop into a right good business. Good job, Rachel."

Rachel nodded at her aunt, but there was no time to chat as she had to return to the sales counter, where Luke needed some assistance with transactions. She spent much of the afternoon working the calculator, while Luke wrapped ornaments and chatted up the customers. He always found the right thing to say, a little joke or a kind word that made folks smile.

By the time Grace came in to work after her classes were done, the line outside had dissolved, but customers still meandered through the shop.

"I hate to say it," Luke said, touching Rachel's shoulder, "but I need to go. The driver is waiting outside."

She let out a deep breath but smiled at him. Saying goodbye was usually so hard—the low point of Rachel's week. But tonight, hope was a beacon. She had gotten clearance to go from Aunt Madge, who asked only that someone fill in for Rachel for the few days that she'd be gone.

As Rachel turned to her husband, she didn't feel the usual sting of saying goodbye. "It's good to know I'll see you in just two days," she said.

"And I've got a lot of pies to bake between now and then."

He chuckled. "I doubt you'll have time to bake with all these customers wanting a taste of Christmas."

"You were wonderful with the customers, Luke. And, look at that!" She smiled up at the new Star of Wonder sign. "You got the sign hung out here." The placard she had painted was clear and readable, helped by a string of white lights that had been configured in a star formation. "You made a star! It's perfect!"

"I'm glad you like it. All the ladies who were coming and going seemed to like it."

"Denki for all your help. The day went by so quickly with you by my side."

"We were a great team." He leaned down to kiss her cheek. "Two days?"

"Two days," she agreed, watching as he went to the door. She watched him step outside, then sprang forward. "Luke, wait!" She caught up with him outside the shop and pulled him away from the overhang of the building. "Our Christmas star! Do you see it?"

Tipping his head up, he squinted toward the sky. "I don't see any stars. I think it's too overcast."

"I don't see it, either, but we know it's there."

He nodded. "Some of the things that really matter can't be seen. We just have to have faith."

"Faith," she repeated, holding his gaze as he backed away toward the waiting van. When he reached the door, he took one step inside, and, hunched down, he turned back to wink at her.

Chapter 7

Julie Fisher couldn't help but smile as she placed the stack of papers on her desk and turned to face the class in the one-room Amish schoolhouse. It was time for the Christmas announcement, and for Julie, anything related to Christmas was reason for joy.

The milky sunlight of winter illuminated the children's faces so that they looked somewhat angelic. Julie grinned, knowing that was just an illusion. After two years of teaching, she knew that these students were little works in progress. Hence the many wall decorations that instructed them on good manners, keeping clean, and showing others kindness and love. She liked to think those lessons made Amish children different from the Englisch. Yah, there were maps on the wall as well as numbers and the letters of the alphabet, just like other schools. But here, children were taught to practice faith, love, and kindness above all else.

Four of the children in this one-room schoolhouse were her siblings, and while she loved them dearly, she tried not to show any favoritism. In fact, due to their extended church community, she'd known the other children long enough to love them, too.

With more than thirty children in the entire schoolhouse, there was never a dull moment! She valued each and every little student, many of them eager to learn how to read and write and do arithmetic. As the lower-grade teacher at Joyful River School, she had a full slate with six feisty first graders, four second graders, and six third graders.

"Boys and girls, this afternoon we're starting something that I know you'll enjoy," Julie said, putting a finger to her lips as she strolled down the aisle, prompting her students to pay attention. "Let's have quiet now so that Teacher Lena and I can explain."

From the back of the room, Julie's colleague Lena Schmucker slid the dividing screens aside as she instructed her older charges to do the same. "Pencils down. Eyes up."

"Since we're all excited about Thanksgiving holiday tomorrow, we're going to use this afternoon to get started on our Christmas program." Julie's announcement was greeted by smiles from most of the children, many of the younger ones missing one or two of their front teeth. "Over the next few weeks we're going to make some Christmas decorations for our classroom. The little ones will be coloring winter scenes, and we'll be dipping pine cones in glitter and making paper chains."

That made them happy. She felt the lifted spirits

in the room and noticed bright eyes watching as Lena joined her at the front of the room. A hand went up in the back of the room, and Lena called on thirteen-year-old Violet Graber.

"When will we get our roles for the Christmas program?" Violet asked.

Julie and Lena exchanged a look. In their planning meeting, they had already picked Violet to play the Virgin Mary in their nativity scene. The dark-haired, blue-eyed girl was one of the oldest students in the class, and they hoped her very responsible attitude would help to corral the smaller children in the most complicated part of the Christmas presentation. But Violet didn't know she'd been chosen yet.

"We're going to assign parts today," Lena said. "But first, let's talk about what our presentation will include this year. We'll do the 'Merry Christmas' poem, which is divided into fourteen different speaking parts. Most of those will go to older children, and you don't have to memorize your lines. You can read them from a card."

"But practice is important," Julie said. "We all want to do our best for our family and friends who attend the program. I know your parents are looking forward to it."

Every year the Christmas show was a well-attended event, a source of joy for the students and their families. It was also a wonderful reminder of the meaning of Christmas. As Julie's mem used to say, "Jesus is the reason for the season."

"We'll be singing a few Christmas carols, which we'll practice over the next few weeks," Lena explained. "So far we've decided on 'We Three Kings' and 'O Come, All Ye Faithful.' So if you know those songs, you'd do well to start singing them over the Thanksgiving weekend."

"We'll have a chorus of Christmas songbirds!" Julie added. "The highlight of our program is the nativity scene that tells everyone about the birth of baby Jesus. Teacher Lena and I have carefully chosen parts for everyone in the class."

One of Julie's first graders, Addie Lapp, raised her hand. "Can I pretend to be the baby in the manger?" she asked sweetly. "I'm small, and I won't cry at all."

The sweet girl touched Julie's heart. "I'm sure you'd be very good at it, but—"

"But Jesus is a boy," called Buddy Brubaker.

"Buddy, please don't call out," Lena told him. "In this classroom, we wait our turn."

The fifth grader rolled his eyes in response.

Julie turned back to the little girl. "How would you like to be an angel, Addie? We have some halos and wings in our costume bin."

Addie smiled and gave a happy nod.

Another first grader's hand shot up. "I want wings, too!"

"Let's have patience, boys and girls," Julie said. "If we sit quietly, Teacher Lena will tell you what part you'll be playing."

"All right." Lena held up the cast list they'd compiled and began to read it aloud. "Lizzie Lapp will be our narrator. Tommy Kraybill will be the baby Jesus, and the other first-grade boys will be little lambs. The first-grade girls will be angels. Mary will be played by Violet Graber, and Joseph will be . . ."

As Lena assigned parts, Julie looked over the students, the neat rows of desks, the walls decorated with cheerful messages. How quickly the year had passed when she was in the building.

At home, with the demands of her siblings and the memories of her lost mem, time moved a bit more slowly. Not that Julie minded helping out with the younger ones. It was just hard to be in the house sometimes, especially when Mem's kitchen, her sewing machine, and her washer were a reminder of the wonderful woman who was missing from her life. Since Mem's death, Julie had learned that love took different forms, and hearts broke in so many different ways.

Lena continued reading. "Jamie Schmucker and Peter and Paul Lapp will be shepherds. Ezra Graber, Buddy Brubaker, and Truman Fisher will be the three wise men."

Truman's hand shot up. "Teacher Lena!" He

351

seemed breathless with urgency. "I don't want to be one of the three magi. I want to be the Christmas star."

Julie wanted to groan. She was always concerned when her brother Truman drew attention to himself at school. The boys his age hadn't learned tolerance yet, and they were prone to teasing him for being different. Julie kept her face blank; best to let Lena handle it.

"A star?" Lena frowned. "There's no star part in the show."

"But the star is a very important part of the Christmas story," Truman explained. "It was the very unusual, very bright star that let the wise men know that Gott was sending a savior from heaven."

Lena nodded. "I see your point, though we've never had anyone play the star before."

"I know how to do it," Truman said. "I know all about stars."

"We could include a star." When Lena looked to her for agreement, Julie just shrugged. "All right, then," Lena said. "Truman will be the Christmas star, and Jamie Schmucker will be the third wise man."

When the parts were assigned, they moved on, dividing into older and younger classes to discuss costumes and roles. As Truman was joining the circle of older students, Julie noticed that Buddy Brubaker remained at his desk. When Truman came upon him, Buddy slid his foot out into the aisle, causing Truman to trip.

There was a commotion as Truman lurched forward, knocking into an empty desk chair as he went down.

"Good grief!" Lena said, hurrying over. "Truman, are you all right?"

Julie extended a hand, but her brother shook his head and stiffly pushed himself up from the floor. "I'm okay. I—I tripped."

"Over Buddy's leg." Julie turned to Buddy. "That's no way to treat your classmate."

"I was just stretching my leg out."

Julie didn't believe him. "That was an odd time to stretch out, when you were supposed to be on the other side of the classroom."

When Buddy tried to shrug it off, Lena guided him through an apology, and then everyone moved on. But as Julie was talking to her students about the role of angels, sheep, and cows, she had trouble shaking the incident from her mind. Mostly because Buddy Brubaker's behavior seemed to be getting worse.

The boy clearly didn't understand the golden rule: *to love your neighbor as yourself.*

What would make the boy come around?

She would pray on it and try to puzzle it out. Math was a favorite subject of hers, as there was no problem that couldn't be solved. With Gott's help, she would solve this dilemma.

After the first short rehearsal, the class was given the treat of starting to make decorations for the Christmas program. The older children made paper chains to string round the classroom, and the little ones took turns painting glue onto the tips of pine cones and then dipping them in glitter. It was a joyful way to spend the last afternoon before Thanksgiving.

When the afternoon bell rang, the children bundled up in coats and hats and headed out the schoolhouse door to the waiting family members outside. This time of year, most of the students were picked up by parents in horse and buggies or hired drivers in cars. In the summer months, many of the older children rode to school on their scooters. Only those who lived close to the school walked. Today, two vans were parked outside, waiting alongside seven gray buggies, their horses shifting in the cold parking lot.

Dressed in coats, Julie and Lena monitored the wide front porch of the schoolhouse, greeting parents and chatting with the children as they waited for their ride. Despite the cold the mood was festive, as it was the beginning of a long weekend. Julie remained cheerful, but she wished folks would move along more quickly. She was due in town to help out at the Christmas shop, since Rachel had headed off for her trip today.

"Happy Thanksgiving, Teacher Julie!" Addie

Lapp called as the family buggy pulled away.

"See you Monday!" Julie waved, and then saw the Brubaker buggy approach. Even from here she could see that the driver was Micah Brubaker, Buddy's older brother.

Oh, not today. She'd been expecting that Buddy's mother, Viola, would come for him, giving her a chance to chat about Buddy's attitude. Of course, she could explain the situation to Micah, but things were complicated between them.

Through the past few months of singings, she had sat near him at the table, talking and sharing anecdotes. Mutual friends had told Julie he was interested in her, a bit of news that had made her heart race. But time after time, at the end of the singing when single guys offered to give a girl they liked a ride home, Micah had left alone in his buggy.

Just last Sunday night at the Kraybills' house, they'd had such a lovely conversation and a few good laughs. And then, he'd gotten up from the table and left without even a goodbye.

It would be awkward to speak with him. Best to let Lena see Buddy and his older sister Bridget off.

As Julie stepped back onto the porch, she felt Micah's eyes on her. He was steering the buggy this way. No avoiding him.

She turned around to find the Brubaker children,

and saw Buddy and his friend Ezra pestering Truman, chirping "Twinkle star! Twinkle star!" as Truman tried to walk away from them.

"Boys," she called, but they didn't seem to hear her. She strode down the porch and went to them, holding one arm in front of Truman to stop the taunting. The distress on her brother's face made her heart sink.

"This is not kind behavior," she scolded.

"But he wants to be a star," Buddy said in a cloying sweet voice.

Julie was so upset she no longer felt the bitter cold. "Boys, what is the walking rule in our classroom?"

Buddy didn't budge, but Ezra and Truman spoke in unison: "To understand another person, imagine walking in his shoes."

"Denki," she said, trying to bring the scolding round to something more positive. "It's good that you remembered."

"Are you ready to go?" asked a deep voice. Micah stood beside Julie, smiling down at his brother. "Or are you having such a good time learning from Teacher Julie that you want to stay at school?"

"I'm ready," Buddy said emphatically, scrambling off toward the buggy.

Micah smiled. "Have a good Thanksgiving," he said, then turned away.

"Wait." She hurried to catch up with him. "I

wonder if you could get word to your mother to stop in after the holiday? I'm a little concerned about Buddy's behavior."

"Why? What's he up to?"

She didn't want to tell him. This sort of problem could interfere in their friendship. But she'd opened the door. "He's been teasing others. Being unkind."

"Well, we do have a lot of teasing going on round our house. And boys will be boys."

Julie felt her spine stiffen at the way he dashed it all off. "It's becoming a problem," she said. "I'm only mentioning it because I'm concerned about your brother. Will you tell your mem?"

"I'm not bringing bad news home on the eve of a holiday," he said. "I'll tell her to talk to you."

"You do that," she said. As she watched him go, she wasn't sure what disappointed her more. Was it his lack of respect for her as a teacher? Or his lack of concern for his younger brother?

Either way, the young man who'd once been her heart's desire was proving to be a disappointment.

Chapter 8

"Yah, you've come to the right place. I'm Greta Coblentz. Welcome to Maple Run." The woman who opened the door and ushered Rachel into the small clapboard house didn't spare a smile, but then her arms were taken up by a bundled-up infant, and the wisps of hair sticking out beneath her prayer kapp indicated that she'd had a long day. Greta didn't look much older than Rachel, but with a house and three children, she was so much further along in life.

"Denki for having us," Rachel said. "I hope it's not too much trouble, with the holiday and your little ones. Luke said you have three?

"Two girls and a boy. The girls are asleep for now." Greta pushed the door closed with a grunt. "A sticky door, but I need to close it tight. It's cold out there."

"It is! But it's cozy in here." She put her borrowed suitcase down and went over to warm her hands by the potbelly stove. "You've got such a nice fire going. I'm grateful."

"John claims that this stove eats more than all of us combined," she said. "But in winter months, we can't go without it. You must be chilled to the bone from your travels."

"I'm fine." Rachel felt a bit guilty to have

traveled in the warmth of a heated van, though the draft along the floor had reminded her of the dropping temperatures outside.

"Please, sit down. Our husbands should be off their shift soon. In the meantime, can I get you something hot to drink? Some tea or cocoa?"

"Cocoa would be wonderful," Rachel said, unbuttoning her coat. "But let me help you."

"The kettle's already warm. It's no trouble."

"Please, I'd like to help." Rachel took a step forward. "Can I mind the baby for you?" When Greta shot her a curious look, she added, "I don't want to disturb him, but I'm the oldest of seven, and it would make me feel right at home."

"There's no disturbing this one, as long as he's in someone's arms. All right, then." Greta placed the infant in the crook of Rachel's arms. "Our Johnny likes to be held. My mother says he's spoiled, but John says the baby is soothed by the sound of a heartbeat."

"I like the heartbeat notion." Now that she could see his little face, Rachel was surprised by the alertness in the baby's eyes. "You want a little human connection, do you?" she asked softly.

Greta went off to the kitchen, and Rachel rocked back and forth, cooing softly and taking in the cozy living space. Here she was, miles from home and daring to ask a relative stranger if she could hold her baby!

This was the wonder of travel. She hadn't

realized that venturing away from Joyful River would make her question things so much, but as she'd ridden in the van, passing countless houses, shopping centers, farms and wooded areas, Rachel had begun to wonder about the possibilities for her life.

She felt different here in Maple Run. Had Gott brought her here for a reason?

Greta soon returned with the cocoa, and they chatted easily, the ice now broken between them. A few minutes later when the men arrived, Greta told Luke that his wife was an angel, and she told John he was in trouble for not inviting his cousin to stay earlier.

"Here he is, all alone in Maple Run. A home-cooked meal every now and then would have been nice," Greta said, teasing her husband.

"He'll get a fine meal tomorrow," John said. He explained that after work they would be joining the festivities with Greta's family, and assured them they were quite welcome at the dinner. "I'll be glad to have another Coblentz in the mix," John said.

For a few minutes they sat and talked about life at the factory and the pace of things in Maple Run. Rachel mostly listened, intent on the baby in her arms. His steely-gray eyes seemed to watch her every move. Luke sat beside her, his arm pressed to hers, and she drew strength from his warmth and the rumble of his laughter.

Was this what family life would be like for them?

Rachel had not imagined such peace and contentment. She hoped that Gott was opening her eyes to things that could be.

When Rachel woke the next morning, any thought of peace was torn by a shrill baby's cry mixed with the trill of a child's scream. Luke's side of the makeshift bed of sleeping bags on the floor was empty. Probably already off to work, and it sounded like Greta could use a hand.

Rachel quickly got ready for the day and appeared in the kitchen, adding a pin to her prayer kapp. "Good morning! I'm sorry to sleep so late."

"It's early yet." Greta pointed her to the coffeepot on the stove, and Rachel filled a mug. "These little ones are my roosters," Greta explained, "crowing before the crack of dawn."

One of the little girls, the only one who was out of nightclothes and wearing a dress and apron, came right over to Rachel and pressed into the skirt of her dress.

"Mem, it's a girl!" the child exclaimed. "How did she get here?"

"Rachel is our visitor," Greta explained. "A driver brought her here. This is Penny, our oldest. She's four," she said, putting her hand on the little girl's coppery hair. "And that's Sandra, eating the marshmallow pieces out of her cereal."

"Sweets for the sweet," Rachel said.

Greta moved to swoop the cereal box away, but Sandra let out a shrill peal of objection. Undaunted, Greta closed the box and quickly tucked it away in a cupboard. "Sorry, but someone needs to be the grown up here."

"I know how that is," Rachel said, thinking of how she'd had to extract herself the previous day when Polly had erupted in a fit of tears at her departure. Fortunately, Miriam had been at the shop to smooth things over after the van rolled off.

"What can I do to help?" asked Rachel. The kitchen seemed neat and tidy. "Can I make breakfast for us? I'm pretty good at scrambling eggs."

"That would be a help. Gives me a chance to go through my cards and find the Raber family recipe for apple sugar dumplings."

"Sounds tasty!" Rachel tied on a cooking apron and got to work.

The day went quickly, with a few items to prepare for that night's dinner and the three children to corral. Rachel happily alternated between entertaining the children and helping in the kitchen, all the while carrying on a running conversation with Greta. Rachel quickly learned that they had much in common, both having been raised in rural towns of Pennsylvania Dutch Country, and so they enjoyed sharing stories

362

that made them laugh and memories of family members they loved dearly.

That evening, when Rachel and Luke entered the Raber home where dinner was being hosted, they received a warm welcome from Greta's relatives. Greta's mem, Ida Raber, made a huge fuss over her three grandchildren and shared her regrets that she couldn't spend more time with them. Ida had taken a job at a local Amish-owned sandwich shop, and while she was relieved to have the money to make ends meet, she missed her time with her grandchildren.

"They miss you, too, Mem," Greta said, and the enormous hug between them reminded Rachel of the times she'd been enveloped in her mother's arms. She missed Mem every day, but she had learned how to move ahead, mostly out of necessity. There were still Fisher children back at home who needed some mothering care, and Rachel and Julie were trying their best to fill that gap.

The guests made a fuss over their contributions to the dinner, especially the apple dumplings. "Almost worth laboring over a sizzling pan of oil," Greta told Rachel under her breath. They chuckled together but were interrupted when Greta's sister stuck out a platter of bacon-wrapped dates and insisted they try them.

Rachel had never heard of such a thing, but the treat was delicious.

"Like bacon candy," Luke said. "Two all-time favorites!"

The evening was full of good will and laughter. At one point, Luke and Rachel were introduced to the leader of the local Amish community, Bishop Stan Flaud, a thin man with a sandy-brown beard and warm brown eyes. After a bit of conversation, the bishop asked a question that surprised Rachel.

"Are you thinking of moving here to Maple Run full-time?"

Luke's eyes opened wide as he looked to Rachel and shook his head. "No, sir. I'm just here temporarily for the factory work."

"I can't tell you how many times I've heard that answer," Bishop Flaud said, a twinkle in his eyes. "And then a few months down the road, folks come back to me and ask to join our church. We're a growing community. I'd say around half our church families moved here from somewhere else because of the factories."

"I reckon times are tough all around," Luke said, nodding. "But we'd never leave Joyful River. It's our home."

"Our families are there," Rachel added, thinking of Dat and the children, Aunt Madge and Miriam. Their own bishop, Aaron, who'd led them in their marriage vows. And the many young people they'd grown up with who were now starting families of their own.

"There'd be too many folks to leave behind," she added.

"I understand." The bishop nodded. "Luke, you're here to earn a living for your family. There's no shame in that. But the weekly travel is hard on a family. Down the road, if you decide to make Maple Run your home, rest assured there's an Amish community here to lend support."

They thanked the bishop, and even after he moved on to speak with someone else, his advice stuck in Rachel's mind. Had it been a sign? She hoped not. She was enjoying her time here with Luke, but she was eager to get home to her family, her daily joys. Even the Christmas shop! Visiting a new place had reaffirmed that she was blessed with a good life in Joyful River.

When they returned to the Coblentz home that night, the children were put to bed and Greta brought out a trivia game from the cupboard. "Time to test your knowledge," she said, wiggling her eyebrows.

Rachel teamed up with Greta, girls against boys, and the four of them enjoyed playing the game until well after midnight.

"These gals are wearing me down," John said, rising from his chair, "and I've got the early shift again in the morning."

"I do, too." Luke rubbed his eyes with the backs of his hands. "But it's been a good day. Denki for having us. Because of your generosity,

Rachel and I got to spend the holiday together."

"It's been our pleasure," John said.

"Rachel has been a huge help with the children and the kitchen," Greta said. "She's great to have around."

"I've enjoyed our talks," Rachel agreed. "I admit, I was nervous about coming here, but you've made me feel right at home."

"Wouldn't it be great if you two decided to move to Maple Run?" Greta suggested. "We could be neighbors. There are a few rental houses around the corner, and we could do meals together, and evening games."

"That would be fun," Rachel agreed. Somehow it seemed very grown-up to be spending time with another couple who already had three children.

"We'd love to have you nearby. But look out when we set up Chinese checkers," John said. "Greta wins every time."

Chapter 9

The next day dawned cool and sunny with white winter light filling the front room of the little house. While the men were at the factory, Rachel and Greta took the children for a short walk to get some fresh air. With the help of Greta's baby buggy, they made it to a park on a hilltop that had a sandbox, swings, and a slide for the children. Best of all, it afforded a view of the scattered homes in the area, the extended valley, and the green hills in the distance.

While the girls played, Rachel carried the baby in her arms, marveling at the changes in Johnny's expression as he watched Sandra go down the slide or studied a flaming-red leaf that Penny brought him.

On the walk home, Greta directed Rachel down a different street. "I want to show you something," Greta said as they approached a house with a sign staked into the front lawn. FOR RENT. "This place is for rent, and I think you could get a good deal. The owner is in our church."

Rachel stopped before the yellow ranch house, a little amazed at what Greta was thinking. Much as she'd enjoyed her visit, she had no plans to stay. "It looks neat and clean," she observed.

"And it's a five-minute walk from our house."

"I'll keep that in mind," Rachel said with a smile.

In the late afternoon when the men returned from the factory, Rachel and Greta had their dinner well underway. A Tater Tot casserole was baking in the oven, and the smells of hamburger, melting cheese, and onion made Rachel's mouth water.

The minute Luke walked in, Rachel could tell something was up. She could see the sizzle of tension in his eyes, the careful parse of his movements. Luke wanted to talk. With nearly an hour of baking time ahead, they decided to take a walk.

"Besides, I learned the neighborhood today," she said, wrapping a knit scarf around her neck. "I know a little park situated on the top of the world!"

The sky was turning lavender gray as they set off for their walk. Shadows along the sidewalks lengthened, but there were occasional street-lamps that warded off the night. By the time they got to the little park, night had fallen and they were able to pick out their Christmas star in the sky. From the summit the glimmering stars in the sky seemed to reflect on the landscape below, where lights seemed to be sprinkled in clumps over the little valley. Most prominent were the smokestacks of the factories—four towers in all, with blinking red lights.

"You know, Maple Run isn't much to look at

up close, but from up here, the lights are nice," Luke said.

"It's a pretty view." She took his hand. "And our last night here." In the morning they would get an early ride back to Joyful River, arriving in plenty of time for Rachel to open the shop. Luke had two days off, and she suspected he'd spend the next day helping her in the shop. She wondered how Grace and Miriam and Julie had fared, running the shop during the legendary Black Friday shopping day. "I'm eager to get back home, but I sensed you had something on your mind that couldn't wait."

"You read me so well. I just wanted to get this off my chest. I went to the boss and asked about getting off for Christmas. I figured since I sacrificed and worked Thanksgiving, he might be a little flexible, but I was wrong."

"You have to work Christmas Day?" Although it was old news, the impact still hit hard. This was supposed to be their first Christmas as a married couple.

"That's what they're saying. That's the bad news."

She took a deep breath, trying to ride out the disappointment. "We can't be apart for Christmas, Luke."

"But I can't quit this job. Not yet."

"Then I'll come to you. I'll come back here for Christmas." Rachel knew it would hurt to miss Christmas with her family, but Luke was her husband now, her future was with him. "I'm pretty sure Greta and John would put us up again. We can work around your schedule and make it a wonderful day. But most important, we'll be together."

"You would make that sacrifice for me?"

"You sacrifice for me every day that you're here," she said. "The important thing is that we'll be together for Christmas."

"You're right," Luke said. "It will be a different sort of holiday, but if you're here, I'll be happy."

Sacrifice. Together. Happy. The things that mattered echoed in Rachel's mind as she moved into his arms and pressed her cheek to his chest. They were making difficult choices, but she knew they could meet this challenge.

"That's not all of it," Luke said. "There's more news."

"Is there any good news?"

"My boss at the factory really likes my work, that I've learned a lot about operating the machinery. He says if I stick with it through the New Year, I'll be promoted."

"Oh, Luke." She had to acknowledge his accomplishment. "You're such a hard worker."

"This time he told me what the new salary would be. Almost double what I make now."

Rachel bit her lips together. "That's . . . that's a lot of money."

"If I stay with the job, we'll be able to pay down your family's medical bill in a matter of months instead of years." Luke shrugged. "It really threw me for a loop, you know? I mean, we both want to get back to Joyful River, but then this offer comes along. And the bishop already told us we'd be welcome here. And we do have some family, John and Greta."

"And Greta showed me a cute little house we could rent, just a short walk from here," she said, following his line of logic. "It would be a place where we could be together, not just on weekends. All week long."

"I don't know what to think," Luke said. "What's the right thing to do?"

"I'm not sure, either, but doesn't it feel like Gott is pointing us in a certain direction?" Rachel's mind was already racing ahead with thoughts of moving. They wouldn't have much to pack if they found a furnished house. If not, Luke's dat had a storage shed full of furniture—desks and chairs and beds—that they could haul up here. It would actually be fun to make a little home with Luke, a cozy nest for their future family.

"That look in your eyes," he said, "I can't read it. What are you thinking?"

She drew in a deep breath and met his steely gaze. "I think we should seriously consider moving here to Maple Run."

Chapter 10

After a long day on her feet, Julie was grateful to take a seat at the checkout counter of Star of Wonder and start tallying up the sales. It was Saturday night, Rachel's first day back, and they had finally closed their doors to customers an hour after the scheduled time. Luke and Truman were outside, helping their last customers load up their cars. The rest of the children were scattered through the shop, restocking ornaments in various displays.

"Are you sure you don't mind doing that?" Rachel asked.

"Not at all! I like the math part, even without a calculator, and while you were gone, Grace showed me how to reconcile the day's sales with the cash and checks in the register." She pressed a button on the old cash register to find the day's totals—always a satisfying process.

"Denki for your help," Rachel said. "I couldn't have gone to visit Luke without you. Without all of you!" she said, turning to the children.

"We like being in the shop," Bethany called from the star ornament display. "All the lights make me feel happy inside."

"And the customers have taken kindly to you," Julie said. It had warmed her heart to see the way the children had engaged customers, talking about how they decorated many of the ornaments and relaying the Christmas story involving the manger scene with its lovely star ornaments about it. Even Truman had opened up a bit, explaining things to the Englisch ladies and helping them carry purchases to their cars. The social interaction had been so good for him and the customers had been impressed by the "adorable Amish children" with "such manners!"

Now, as Julie totaled up the checks, she felt someone move close and sling an arm around her shoulders.

"You're a wonderful sister," Rachel said.

Julie chuckled. "If you say any more, I'll lose all touch with humility."

"I know you have to go back to school Monday, but I need to ask for a favor, for down the road a bit." Rachel looked back to make sure they were alone, and then perched on a stool beside her. "The thing is, I'll probably need you to help cover the shop around Christmas. Just a day or two. Luke has to work Christmas, and I'm going back to Maple Run to spend the holiday with him."

"Oh no! That's terrible." Julie pushed the calculator aside to study her sister. "What will we do without you on the most wonderful day of the year?"

"I hate to miss our holiday together, but I'm

sure you'll make do." Rachel folded her hands on the table, almost in prayer position. "It's hard for me, leaving you and the children, but . . . I think it might be Gott's will for us. At least for now. Luke's work is in Maple Run, and they want to promote him. If that's where the work is, it's where we need to be."

"Wait. What are you saying?" Julie felt the floor drop out from under her. "Are you going to stay in Maple Run?"

"We're thinking of moving there. Maybe for a year or so, until we can save some money, to pay for the hospital bills. He's tried to get a job here, but times are hard."

"I don't want you to go, but I understand." Julie covered her sister's hands with hers and squeezed tight. "Whatever you decide, you know I'll be here for you."

"What? Where are you going, Rachel?" Bethany was suddenly behind them, a broken ornament in her hands.

Julie winced as Rachel drew in a breath. "Luke and I might have to move to Maple Run."

"No!" Bethany flung her arms around Rachel. "I don't want you to go!" Bethany said before Julie could shush her.

"Let's keep this quiet," Rachel said. "It's not a definite thing, and we don't want to upset anyone."

"Well, I heard you, and I'm upset," said Eli.

"Me too," said Will.

"Me three," said Polly.

Julie turned around to see all the children staring, their brows fraught with concern. "Good grief."

"Don't tell Truman," Bethany said. "He's not good at handling things like this."

"Tell me what?" Truman asked as he and Luke entered the store on a gust of cold wind.

"All right, Fisher family, gather round," Julie said, looking from her older sister to Luke. "Time for everyone to hear a new Fisher Family Secret."

Over the days since she'd learned of Rachel's plans, Julie had tried to remain cheerful. As she tended to the children at home and channeled her energies into teaching the children at school, she stayed positive. But inside, her heart was aching.

She was afraid of losing her sister to the factory town up north.

When Rachel told Dat the plan, he took the news well and immediately considered hiring someone to help out with the housekeeping. "For a while now I've been thinking that we need a maud. With you girls working at jobs, I see that you're worn thin with all the cooking and cleaning."

Both Rachel and Julie had bristled at the idea of a housekeeper—a stranger—though they had been amenable to the possibility of letting Polly spend her days with Miriam Lapp while the other children were off at school.

With a sigh, Julie pushed those sad possibilities to the back of her mind as she led the children through a rehearsal of the nativity scene on a Wednesday afternoon in December. Julie and Lena had lugged the box of costumes out of the closet and dusted them off, so that the children could try them out.

So far the children seemed delighted with the pieces that Amish mothers had sewn over the years. Looking over the garments, Julie felt a bittersweet twinge as she recalled her own mother sewing them around this time of year. "The school needs another shepherd's tunic," Mem would say, and then she'd happily set to work pinning and cutting the pattern from old fabric.

The angels looked adorable in their long white bibs sewn from bedsheets. On the night of the show, they would pin on little halos that fanned up over their kapps. Mary, Joseph, and the shepherds were slipping on tunics in royal blue, green, and scarlet. The wise men wore different colored bibs, with one in purple, one in emerald green, and one in gold that surely had been made from an old tablecloth.

One look at the wise men gathered around Truman's desk told her that Buddy was back to his old tricks. Truman hated it when they surrounded him.

"What's going on, wise men?" she called over to them.

Ezra and Jamie took a step back as if caught red-handed, but Buddy just smiled at her, a cold smile.

"Truman doesn't have a costume," Buddy said in a taunting voice.

"I don't need one," Truman insisted. "I have to put batteries in this star, and then it will light up. When I push the button."

"We'll get batteries," Julie promised. "And the wise men need to be over there by the black-board."

Julie went over to round up the boys and usher them to the correct spot. "That's where you begin your journey. Remember? That's where you first find the star in the east, and you follow it over till you get to that pillar."

As Julie watched the three wise men, she wondered how she might get through to Buddy Brubaker. She had talked to his mother briefly after Thanksgiving, but Viola had shrugged off her concerns over Buddy's aggression, saying that children grew at their own pace and on Gott's time. Julie had avoided an argument, but she had stressed that hurtful behavior could not be permitted at school.

And then, Julie had thanked the woman for stopping by and handed her an envelope addressed to Micah.

That part she regretted.

What had made her think that it was a good idea, sending a note to a fella she admired when there was a chance he didn't feel the same way?

At the time, the problem had seemed clear as a glass of water. She liked Micah, and he seemed to like her, but he wouldn't act on it. What was keeping him from making the next move? She wanted an answer, and so she'd asked the question.

In writing.

And now, more than two weeks later, she'd received no answer except a bit of a cold shoulder at the last singing. She was embarrassed, sad, and so disappointed. And the cherry on top of that heartache was the fact that Micah's younger brother was causing trouble in her classroom.

Snapping her attention back to the present, she corralled all the children into place and cued the narrator. "Okay, Lizzie, let's go from the beginning."

"After Jesus was born in Bethlehem, three wise men from the east came searching for him. They wanted to bring him gifts." Lizzie's speech was clear and animated, just the right amount of expression. And Gott bless her, she had memorized it!

As Lizzie spoke, the three wise men moved forward, pretending to search.

"As they went on their way, a bright star rose from the east."

On cue, Truman rose up from behind the nativity scene and held his star high over the heads of the kneeling Mary and Joseph.

"The wise men were overjoyed when they saw the star shining bright in the night sky," said Lizzie. "They followed the star and it led them to the baby Jesus."

Suddenly Lena was standing beside Julie as the wise men made their way past shepherds and braying lambs to the pretend stable.

The wise men read their lines from index cards.

"We have followed this star for many miles," Buddy read aloud, "and at last, Gott has led us to the new leader of his people."

"We come bearing gifts. I have brought gold," said Ezra.

"And I have brought frankincense," Buddy said.

It was a sweet scene, the children trying their best.

Julie's throat felt thick from emotion. She blinked back tears as the children began to sing "We Three Kings." This was the lovely Christmas story. It was also the first year she would see it without Mem in the audience. And in that moment, she saw how something could be beautiful and sad at the same time.

Chapter 11

"Merry Christmas!" Rachel called to a customer leaving the shop with one hand on her shopping bag, the other on her granddaughter.

"Merry Christmas," the woman echoed. "It's just around the corner now. I can't tell you how much we enjoyed your shop. Right, Kylie?"

The little tyke nodded, her face lit with a smile. "We saw baby Jesus," the little girl said, and everyone within hearing range smiled.

"It's a statue of him, sweetie," said her grand-mother. "But such a good reminder of the meaning of Christmas. Thanks, again!"

"You have done such a wonderful job," the customer at the counter said. "I hadn't been to this shop in years, but this is my third time since you remodeled this summer."

"It just keeps getting better and better," another woman said from her place in line.

"Thank you," Rachel said, smiling over at Miriam, who was wrapping bulbs in tissue paper. "It's the friends and family members who've kept the place going. I couldn't do it alone." She added up the purchase on the old cash register, which jingled when the total popped up in the little window on top.

"Just keep doing what you're doing," the

customer said as she wrote a check for the purchase. "I was able to bring my mother here last week. It was a rare outing for her, but she loved it. I don't know if you remember the little woman in the red hat with a sprig of holly on it?"

"That was your mother? She was a charmer," Rachel said, pushing the two shopping bags toward the woman.

"Thank you for making our holiday special," the woman said.

And then, on to the next customer.

That had been the routine these days, ever since the week before Thanksgiving when the renovation of the store was nearly complete. Whether it was photos on the internet or word of mouth, the message had been spread that Star of Wonder made for the perfect Christmastime outing in Pennsylvania Dutch Country. The steady stream of customers had kept her busy and made it necessary for her to have at least one helper at all times—hence the seasonal hire of Miriam, who'd been game to take on a brief job and help out while all the other helpers were at school. When Luke was home, he spent most of Monday in the store, restocking items, going on supply runs for new ornaments, and charming the shoppers.

Rachel was delighted by the shop's success. With all the hoopla of the holiday, she believed this little shop fulfilled an important purpose in reminding folks of the true meaning and wonder

381

of Christmas. Yah, the busy days were tiring, but Star of Wonder was also an escape for her, a place to go where she could forget about the worry and weight of the decision she and Luke needed to make. Though the shop offered her comfort, the clock seemed to be ticking relentlessly to Christmas Day and decision time.

Just then the front doorbell jangled, and Aunt Madge entered with a robust woman who was even taller than Rachel. From the shape of her prayer cap, Rachel suspected she was Mennonite, a faith similar to Anabaptist but with a more modern lifestyle.

"Such a beautiful shop you have here," the woman said, her eyes opening wide with wonder.

"This is my friend, Hazel Decker," said Madge. "She's just here for the day, visiting from Bird-in-Hand." Madge introduced Rachel and Miriam, adding: "I'm going to take Hazel on a little tour of the shop."

"If you peek into the back room, don't mind the little girl playing there. My sister Polly," Rachel said.

"I'd love to meet her," Hazel said as they headed along the picket fence path.

Rachel lost track of time as she and Miriam kept moving the steady stream of customers along at the register. When at last they caught a bit of a break, Miriam gave a contented sigh and looked at the clock. "Grace will be here shortly to relieve me. In the meantime, I'm going to put some water in the electric pot and make a cup of tea. Would you like one?"

"That would be wonderful," Rachel said.

As Miriam headed to the back room, Madge and Hazel passed her.

"The shop is delightful. First-rate," Hazel said, rapping on the counter with her knuckles. "It offers a beautiful, meaningful Christmas experience."

"And Hazel is an expert," Aunt Madge said. "She owns a shop in Bird-in-Hand called Christmas Treasures. It's been around for a decade."

"We have our regular following," Hazel said. "But you've created something special here, Rachel. I'm surprised you're leaving it behind."

Rachel's eyes opened wide as she looked from Hazel to Madge. "Leaving? I mean, that was supposed to be a secret, and—"

"One of the boys slipped," Madge said. "Will or Eli, I don't know. But I wasn't surprised to hear it, with your husband living up in Maple Run." Madge touched her arm, reassuring her. "You've sacrificed a lot living apart, but no one expected you to sacrifice forever."

"I just . . . I wasn't ready to tell people." Rachel waved the subject off, pretending it didn't matter as she changed the subject. "Tell me about your shop, Hazel. Do you find that business drops off after the holidays?"

"A bit. Things slow down in January, and the winter months can be slow if snow keeps customers away. But the springtime always brings them back. And you'd be surprised at the summer traffic we get."

"Do you enjoy managing it?" Rachel asked.

"It's been a right good business through the years. My customers love Christmas, so they're generally a cheerful bunch. I think folks like to feel the joy of Christmas all year round."

Rachel nodded. "I've noticed that. A Christmas shop is such a pleasant place to be."

"Thanks to you," Aunt Madge said. "You turned this shop around, Rachel."

Hazel nodded approvingly. "I'm happy to take it on, whenever you're ready, Madge. I could write you a check today."

"I won't sell during the season," Madge said, "but let's get together in the New Year. Once the January lull comes along, we'll figure out a deal."

Rachel couldn't believe what she was hearing. "Aunt Madge, you're selling the shop?"

"In a few months," Madge said. "It's been a good season, but once you're gone, I've no interest in finding a new manager. The restaurant is enough for me to handle."

"I see," Rachel said, trying to process everything.

"I'm just going to go take a look at that manger

display one more time," Hazel said, heading deeper into the store.

Watching the woman move along the zigzag of picket fences, Rachel noticed the sparkling lights blur from the tears in her eyes. This shop had become such a big part of her life. It hurt her to think of letting it go, though that was what she and Luke were planning, wasn't it?

Just then the door opened, and in came two customers, followed by Grace, who was here to work her after-school shift, and Bethany, who'd come to pick up Polly. Rachel quickly dashed away her tears and tried to follow the conversations so that no one seemed to notice her distress.

Just then, Miriam appeared with a mug of tea for Rachel. Since she was on her way out, she agreed to give Bethany and Polly a ride home. Miriam whisked the girls out, and Aunt Madge and Hazel departed soon after.

As Grace helped the customers, Rachel was left staring at the charming Christmas shop and wondering how her life had turned down such a disappointing path. She had come to love this little shop, not so much in a material way, but in the joy and meaning it had brought to people's lives.

To her life.

But now she would be saying goodbye to the shop, goodbye to this town and her family. The weight of that choice was just too much to bear.

"I'll be in the back," she told Grace, taking her mug and heading down the path lined by sparkling white picket fences. She peeked into the backroom, but then thought it would be cloying. Instead, she pushed open the back door and stepped outside to the small loading area.

The cold air was a relief after the heat of her emotions, and she sat down on a brick stair, cupped the warm mug with both hands, and took a sip. Tea usually soothed her, but tonight it wasn't working.

Tipping her head back, she searched the dusky sky for their star. Although night hadn't fallen just yet, she found the star, bright as ever.

It should be reassuring: a warm cup of tea, a plan to be with Luke, their Christmas star. She should be happy. Joyous. Full of Christmas spirit.

But the burden in her heart was too heavy to bear. A sob escaped her throat as tears blurred her vision. She pressed a fist to her mouth as another sob rocked her. All she could do was cry. If she was making the right choice, why did it feel so wrong?

Chapter 12

When Miriam opened the back door of the shop in search of Rachel, her heart sank. She had not expected to see the young woman so distraught.

Granted, she had sensed that something was wrong when she'd left the shop. The odd feeling had haunted her until she'd turned the buggy around and come back to town. But she hadn't expected to find this dear girl sobbing.

"Is that you, Rachel?" She stepped out and went to the woman sitting in the gathering shadows. "It's just me."

Rachel twisted around to look up, her face glistening with tears. "I thought you were heading home."

"I went on my way, but I sensed that something was wrong. I dropped Bethany and Polly off and turned right back around." Miriam sat down on the cold brick step beside her. "Can you tell me what's wrong? Why are you crying?"

"I seem to be crying all the time, lately. Did you know that Aunt Madge is selling the shop?" Rachel asked in a squeaky voice.

"Oh, dear, no." Miriam put an arm over Rachel's shoulders and hugged her close. The young woman sorely needed some tender loving care. "Is that why the Mennonite woman was visiting?"

When Rachel nodded, Miriam sighed.

"Well, I'm sure Madge will change her mind if we talk to her. You can tell her how important the shop is, and that you want to stay on as manager."

"But I can't." Rachel sniffed, wiping at her wet cheek with the back of her hand. "I want to stay with the shop, but I have to move to Maple Run. There's no other way."

"You're moving?" This was news to Miriam. "Leaving us?"

"Luke and I have to go. We don't want to, but they'll give him a promotion, and our family needs the money, and we just can't live apart any longer!"

"I understand that. You two have endured a lot for a young couple." Miriam thought back to the last few years when Rachel and Luke had been planning their wedding. "We'll choose a date as soon as we know Mem is well enough for the big event," Rachel had said, so many times. A wedding season came and went, and then last year, as the time for Amish weddings rolled around, it was clear that Dara was not going to regain enough strength to see her oldest daughter marry Luke.

Such sad days. So many folks, young and old, had been heartbroken to lose Dara from this world.

"You and Luke take such good care of each other. He kept you on your feet when your mem died, and you're his rock now, supporting him from afar even while you take care of the little ones at home. You two haven't had a break from grief and sorrow. I know folks say you should move on, but they don't understand that grief is as real as a ham sandwich. You can't just wish it away."

Rachel's body shook with sobs that turned to laughter. "A ham sandwich?"

"It was the first thing that came to mind," Miriam said. Dinner hour was approaching and hunger was beginning to nip. "When was the last time you ate?"

"Breakfast. I brought sandwiches to share with Polly, but I couldn't muster the appetite."

Miriam assessed the young woman beside her. Something told her there was more going on here than sleep and a solid meal could fix. Still . . . "Let me give you a ride home. Grace can handle closing up the shop, and you and I can talk more in the buggy." She nudged Rachel playfully. "We need to give you a chance to let your tears flow before I return you to your family."

Seated beside Rachel in the buggy, the lap blanket tucked over their legs, Miriam poured on the mothering. Clearly, Gott had called her to be here for Rachel in this moment, and she felt blessed that she could stand in for her dear friend Dara and give the girl a shoulder to cry on.

Miriam had plenty of advice to dispense, but mostly she listened to Rachel's reasons why she didn't want to leave Joyful River.

She listened to Rachel's worries about her siblings, and how they'd be hurt by her move to Maple Run. Since Rachel's brief time away, Polly had been tearful at bedtime and Will had been having nightmares. The children had lost their mother last year, and now in the face of losing their sister and caretaker, they were frightened. Rightly so, the poor dears.

Miriam listened as Rachel shared her guilt over leaving her sister Julie and her father to manage without her.

She listened as Rachel worried she was a bad wife, sending her husband off to live alone while she stayed at home, surrounded by family.

Miriam let Rachel lament over the Christmas shop. How it broke her heart to leave the little store behind after pouring so much into it.

"Such a difficult situation," Miriam said when Rachel had run out of steam. "The way it stands now, I'm afraid that either way you decide will break a piece of your heart."

"I don't know what to do. I'm traveling to Maple Run Friday, so that I'll be there Christmas Day, but I don't know if I can bear to stay. I just hate to let down the people I love."

"You're trying to be so many things to so many people. But you're only human, Rachel." Miriam pulled back on the line and put the brakes on the buggy as the horse brought them in front of the Fisher home.

"I need to do the right thing," Rachel said.

"And you will. You must follow your heart on this, and I pray that your husband will agree."

"I don't know." Rachel rubbed her brow. "Luke wants to come home, I know he does, but he's trying to do the responsible thing."

"He's a good man. But you two are carrying around the weight of the world without realizing that there are folks all around you who want to help."

Rachel shook her head sadly. "That's kind of you to say, but I don't think there's anything you can do."

"I alone can't do much," Miriam said, "but working on a team, there's much we can accomplish."

"What team are you talking about?"

"Trust me on this," Miriam said. "Now, you need to go inside and have a nice dinner. Get the children to bed and get a good night's sleep yourself. I'll see you at the shop tomorrow afternoon, and of course there's the Christmas program tomorrow night."

"I almost forgot," Rachel said. "Truman is so excited to be the first Christmas star ever."

"And my Lizzie is the narrator. Memorized her lines in a week, though she could have read from a card. That one is an Amish schoolteacher in the making."

Chapter 13

L uke stepped out of the three-bedroom ranch
house and thanked the owner for showing
it to him after hours. He'd needed to wait until
his Tuesday shift ended at the factory. "It's a bit
more than we need," he told the man.

And the rent was a lot more than he was able to
spend each month. It was going to cost more to
rent a place here than he had expected. Another
strike against moving.

Not that he needed more convincing. He missed
Rach, Joyful River, the children, his friends. In
the few days he'd spent at home this month, he
could tell that Rachel wasn't completely ready to
leave home, though he sensed she was reluctant
to say so. Probably afraid he'd be hurt that she
wouldn't come north just for him.

Truth be told, Luke didn't want to be in Maple
Run, anyway.

He was ready to quit the job, pack it in, and
head home. It wasn't the most responsible choice,
but the alternatives were bleak.

If he brought Rachel up north, there'd be a new
round of expenses. The price of rental homes
had opened his eyes to that. He'd have a heart-
sick wife worried about the children at home.
And he'd be just as concerned about those young

ones. Polly, who was attached to Rachel as if she were her mother. The boys, who needed a woman at home who wasn't their schoolteacher. And Truman, who needed to be handled and encouraged in just the right way. A hired housekeeper wouldn't understand that these were special children, children who needed love and the security of knowing there was a woman at home looking out for them.

He debated the matter in his mind as he made the slow walk back to the boardinghouse. Should he call Rachel and leave a message in the phone shack? A lot of good that would do. She might not get it for days, and by then, she'd be on her way here for Christmas.

Would she be upset with him for quitting? He thought of their earlier conversations. As the husband, he played the role of consoler, telling her to have faith.

Have faith. If he was going to talk the talk, he needed to walk in faith, too.

As he passed through the neighborhood of small houses, he realized he was near the little park. Making a detour, he strode the few blocks to the hilltop, where he could see the lights of the town below, the smokestacks of the factory, and one very bright star.

Their Christmas star.

If ever he'd been looking for a sign from Gott, this was it.

Relief lightened his shoulders, and the cold air revitalized him as he mapped out his plan. He would go into work before dawn and start his shift at work, as usual. Then, during his break, he'd talk with his supervisor and give him the news.

He was taking action.

Luke was going home.

Chapter 14

W hen Rachel and the Fisher children arrived at the schoolhouse Wednesday evening, the little building was lit up and buzzing with conversation. Desks had been pushed to the walls of the large room, and chairs were now lined up in anticipation of guests who would make up their audience. Rachel had agreed to help the teachers corral the children, who were scuffling about excitedly with props and costumes.

"Rachel! Maybe you can work with Buddy," Julie said, waving Rachel over to where she and Lena were talking with the three boys playing the wise men.

"Buddy has been out of school sick," Lena said, "and he's nervous because he missed a few of the rehearsals. See here? Rachel will go over the part with you."

Buddy's lips were puckered, and he seemed to be holding back tears. "But I don't know any of the lines, and it's too late to learn."

"It's never too late," Julie said. "And it's just a few lines."

Buddy shook his head. "I can't do it." He pulled the dark green costume off over his head and stuffed it into Rachel's hands. "People will laugh when I mess up. I won't!" He turned away abruptly and bolted toward the door.

"But we need you!" Lena called after him. "There were three wise men, not two."

The other two wise men, Ezra and Jamie, stared at each other in a near panic.

"We can't do it without him," Ezra said.

Julie gave a pleading look, and Rachel nodded. "I'll go talk to him."

As Rachel headed out the door, Truman passed her and ran ahead. She didn't know what his hurry was until he caught up with Buddy.

"Hold on!" Truman called. "I'll help you."

"I don't need help," Buddy said, shrugging away from Truman. "I don't want to be in the show. I can't do it."

"Don't worry," Truman said. "I can help you."

"You can't teach me the lines."

"No. But I can take your place as a wise man." Truman's words made Buddy stop walking. "I'll do your part," said Truman.

Buddy looked up in disbelief. "How you gonna do that?"

"Easy," Truman said. "I know the lines for every part. I remember things like that. But if I do your part, you need to be the Christmas star. It's important, but much easier. No lines to speak."

"I don't want to. What if I make a mistake?"

"You won't. You just hold the star up over Mary and Joseph when Lizzie talks about it. Here's the switch to turn it on, see?" Truman showed it to Buddy. "Go on. Give it a try."

Buddy flicked it on and off a few times.

"That's it. You got this. You'll be a very good star."

Watching the two boys, Rachel was surprised by the way Truman nurtured Buddy through his insecurities. After all the teasing Buddy had done, Truman had forgiven him and found empathy; he had changed direction quickly to assist someone else.

It was truly a moment of growth, and she felt blessed to witness it.

"All right. I'll be the star," Buddy agreed.

Rachel handed Truman the emerald-green costume, and he pulled it over his head and smoothed it out.

As the two boys returned to the schoolhouse, Rachel hoped that a truce might be born of the situation. She longed to see Truman free of the taunting boys at school.

Back inside, she told Julie about the boys switching parts, and then helped some of the children slip on their green and red bibs for the "Merry Christmas" poem. While she'd been outside the seats had been filling up with family members, and there was an excited energy in the air. Rachel and the teachers started hushing the children and helping them get in place for the opening song.

" 'O, come, all ye faithful,' " the children sang in bright voice. " 'Joyful and triumphant!' " Julie had chosen to open the program with the carol because it spoke of everyone in the community coming together.

Standing in the back of the room, Rachel hugged her shawl closer around her and basked in the cheerful moment. Another busy day at the shop had helped keep her mind off Luke and their dilemma. She'd been a bit thrown that morning when Miriam had sent her oldest daughter, Essie, to work in her place, with a message telling Rachel to "Keep Faith."

"Do you know what your mem means by that?" Rachel had asked.

Essie had shrugged. "I didn't ask. When my mem is on a mission, the way she was this morning, I just try to stay out of her way."

Rachel and Essie had chuckled together at that, and then Rachel had given her a quick tour of the store. Essie had learned how to work the register quickly, and Rachel had been grateful for her help and company. That was the thing about her community in Joyful River. When she needed help, someone was there for her.

She was leaning against the back wall when the schoolhouse door opened off to her right. Someone slipped inside with a rush of cold air. Rachel looked over, expecting to see a harried parent.

Instead, it was Luke.

Luke was here from Maple Run, here in time for the Christmas program.

Her heart soared as she rushed to him and reached up, pressing her hands to the cool skin of his jaw, as if to make sure it was really him.

"What are you doing here?" she asked breathlessly. "How did you get off?

"I'm happy to see you, too," he teased.

Someone shushed them, and Rachel noticed that a few parents sitting at the back of the room had turned toward them.

She pressed a finger to her lips and Luke put an arm around her and ushered her out the door.

In the stillness of the cold night, under their glimmering star, Rachel looked up into her husband's eyes and sighed. "I don't know how you got off or how long you can stay, but I'm so happy to see you."

"And you, Rach," he breathed, "you are shining brighter than any star in the sky. Each night, I've been looking up at our Christmas star, thinking of you, but the truth is, nothing can replace being with you. We need to be together."

She pressed her palms to his chest, and he pulled them in under his coat.

"We've got to keep you warm," he said.

The cold was the least of her worries. "I don't know how long you can stay, but I have a confession to make. I can't move to Maple Run . . .

or any other town. Not right now, Luke. I've learned that I belong here in Joyful River. We belong here, together. My brothers and sisters need us, and I have a bustling shop to take care of, and this town is full of family and friends who love you and me." She nodded toward the schoolhouse, and then looked toward the fields and the purple hills that ringed their valley. "This is our home."

"That's exactly what I've been thinking since you left Maple Run," Luke said. "Worry was eating away at me like a lanternfly. I didn't want to fail you, but I couldn't stand to be apart anymore. And then, I realized we needed to take a leap of faith, you and I."

She nodded. "You told me to have faith."

"I did," he said. "I was planning to come home in the next day or two. I gave my notice at the factory today, but when I got home the landlady had a message from your Aunt Madge."

"A message?" Rachel couldn't imagine what her aunt wanted with Luke. "That's a mystery. What did she say? Did she find you a job?"

"The message said to come home immediately, that she'd meet me after the school Christmas program. So . . . here I am, home, at last. We'll find a way to pay off your family's debt and save for the future. We have a roof over our head in your dat's house, and I'm right comfortable with that for as long as we need it."

"And it comes with a built-in family," Rachel said.

"You know I love them all as if they were my own brothers and sisters. We'll stay on there and trust in Gott for what the future might bring."

Seeing genuine love in his eyes, Rachel burrowed her hands into the warmth of his coat. "It's a good thing you're planning to stay, because I won't be able to let you go, ever again," she said. "What a happy Christmas it will be!"

They held each other close for a good long minute, and Rachel felt herself relax against him.

"I don't want to let you go, either," he said, "but we need to get back inside. I can't have you freezing out here without a coat, and I admit, I'd like to see Truman's performance as a star."

"Actually, he's playing a wise man."

Luke feigned a look of shock. "I don't believe it!"

"I know. I was surprised, too, but I'll explain later."

As if floating on a cloud of joy, Rachel led him inside just as the nativity scene was coming together. When Mary, Joseph, and the child in the manger were in place, Buddy stepped up onto a crate, holding high the star prop that Truman was so delighted by. It was actually a twelve-inch star ornament from the store that they'd added foil streamers to, so it seemed to beam shimmering rays of light onto the manger.

At last, the three wise men moved across to the Christmas star. They joined the gathering of children playing shepherds, sheep, angels and the holy family. Wearing the emerald-green bib, Truman proceeded with great ceremony and delivered the first wise man's line.

"Thatta a boy," Luke whispered.

Rachel smiled. Truman had displayed such courage and empathy tonight, stepping into this role at the last minute. It was a good omen for his future, an opening for him to make a friend or two to help him find his way.

As the children sang "We Three Kings," Joseph and Mary kneeled down under the star, and little Tommy Kraybill sat up and gave a baby-faced yawn from his manger crib.

So cute! Rachel thought. This year the nativity scene was as lovely as a Christmas card.

At the song's chorus, many folks in the room joined in.

> O star of wonder, star of night,
> Star with royal beauty bright,
> Westward leading, still proceeding,
> Guide us to thy perfect light.

As Rachel held Luke's hand through the rest of the program, she thought of the star mentioned in the song. Gott had guided the wise men with a star. It seemed simple and yet profound. Gott was guiding all of his believers each and every day. And that was what had led Luke here tonight.

Faith.

It felt so good to have confidence in their decision to stay. Luke could help her in the shop until he found a full-time job. And if Aunt Madge sold the shop, well, they would both find something else. Gott's love was everlasting, like the sun, moon and stars in the sky.

After the songs and skits ended, the room was alive with conversation and cheer as neighbors chatted and parents and grandparents found their youngies and complimented them on a job well done.

Rachel and Luke moved toward the fray, where they found Truman returning the costume to Buddy and explaining, "If you ever need help again, I'm your man."

"Denki," Buddy said, handing over the illuminated star. "And that's a cool star. We should have one in the program every year."

Rachel gave Luke's arm a squeeze, and they backed away to let the boys continue their conversation.

They hugged Eli and Bethany, and then watched as Bethany called over to Buddy that he "did a right good job holding that star up."

Dat and Polly came around with compliments for all the children and genuine surprise at seeing Luke. Eli and Will patted Luke on the back as if he were the grown-up brother they'd always wanted.

"I couldn't stay away," Luke insisted. "I just couldn't spend Christmas away from my family."

Chapter 15

Y ou all did such a good job!" Julie said, bending down a bit to peer into the faces of her little first-grade angels.

"Denki, Teacher Julie," three of the girls said, almost in unison, before they skipped away to find their parents.

"Don't forget to thank your parents for coming tonight," Julie reminded them. As she straightened up, she found herself looking up at Micah Brubaker, his face so handsome in close proximity.

"I know it's a busy time for you," he said. "I don't mean to take you away from the children, but I do need to give you an answer. To your note, I mean."

"I can always spare a minute to talk," she said, hoping that the thudding of her heart wasn't rattling her voice.

He seemed a little nervous, and she could only think that meant that he hadn't liked the note. That he didn't think of her in a special way. That he didn't feel that certain spark between them.

"You know, Micah, I didn't mean to put you on the spot by writing to you. If you just want to forget about the whole thing, I really do understand."

"No, no! Your note was good. Awesome, actually. I mean, it was kind of like poetry."

Her throat tightened. "It was?" She didn't know how to take that.

"You're good with words. I mean, of course you are, since you're a teacher. Good with reading and writing. I was never so hot on learning that stuff."

"Everyone has their strong qualities," Julie said, staring into his soulful brown eyes. "The things you're learning from the wheelwright, building buggies and all that, I wouldn't know where to begin with something like that."

Micah shrugged. "It's not so hard."

"For you. And for me, teaching reading, writing, and arithmetic is where Gott wants me to be."

"I can see that." He nodded. "I wanted you to know that I've really enjoyed getting to know you. I mean, time just flies when we're together."

Was that a glimmer of hope? "I feel the same way."

"But I'm a pretty simple guy. I couldn't even begin to write back to you in any way that you wouldn't laugh at me."

"I would never do that."

"You'd probably correct my spelling and stuff."

"Micah! I would never . . . I'm not here to judge anyone. I try to teach my students, but I'm not grading you. You're a man with interesting things to say and . . . and I want to be around to hear you say them."

"You sure about that? Because I'd never want to disappoint you. I don't think a person like me deserves to court someone like you."

"I like you for who you are, Micah Brubaker," she assured him, realizing that "like" was a pretty watered-down version of how she felt, but no need to bowl him over just yet.

"Teacher Julie! Teacher Julie!" One of her students patted her arm to get her attention. Little Tommy Kraybill stood beside her holding up a cookie tin. "Mem told me to give you these and say Merry Christmas."

Julie held up a finger, signaling for Micah to wait as she thanked the little boy and told him to pass Christmas greetings on to his parents. When she looked up, Micah was stepping back.

"I know you're busy," he said.

"I am. But when things have settled down here, I'd like to talk." She tilted her head, wishing there was a way to let him know how much he made her heart stir when he was near. "Can you wait for me? Or come by my house a bit later?"

"I've got my buggy. If you want, I could give you a ride home."

"I'd really like that," she said as a tingly feeling of joy rippled down her spine. Really, really, really! "Just give me a half hour or so."

He nodded, his dark eyes gleaming with a new

confidence. Oh, how this young man filled her with joy, just by being nearby!

With a heart as light as the angels in the heavens, she joined her students in celebrating their hard work and best wishes for a happy Christmas.

Chapter 16

With her new sense of hope and well-being, Rachel scanned the folks still gathered in the schoolhouse. Her heart felt lightened by the smiles and giddy conversation around her. What a joy to be home for Christmas with Luke!

Over by the blackboard, Julie was talking with a handsome young man, the older brother of Buddy Brubaker. Buddy was now darting around, playing tag with Truman as Julie spoke with Micah. Taking it all in, Rachel suspected that Micah was the fella who'd been causing her sister some consternation lately. The young man's affections seemed to run hot and cold. Well, judging by the way he seemed mesmerized by her words, Rachel suspected that these two were talking things out.

"There you are!" Aunt Madge came trundling along, squeezing through the crowd to take Rachel and Luke aside. "A wonderful program, wasn't it? The children did so well."

Before Rachel could answer, her aunt ploughed on. "Good that you made it, Luke. I have a proposition for Rachel, and I believe it's something you should consider as a couple. Something this big needs to involve both husband and wife."

"I know we agree on that," said Luke.

"Of course. So I was looking at the accounts for the shop, trying to come up with a sales price for my friend Hazel. You know she wants to buy Star of Wonder. And when I went over the numbers, I couldn't get over what a huge profit the shop is making. It seems a shame to let it leave the family, but none of my children are interested in the shop. And I have my hands full with the diner. Gott has blessed me with a restaurant that does well, providing food and shelter and jobs for all my family. I was in the middle of this muddle when Miriam came to me with the answer."

"So you're not selling the shop?" Rachel asked, not quite sure what her aunt was trying to say.

"Oh, I'm selling it, but not to Hazel. To you, Rachel! You've worked so hard to create Star of Wonder. The shop was failing before you got involved, and you turned it all around. The profit should be yours. Of course, you'll have to take over the lease starting in January but the expenses are manageable. We can go over the accounting together after the holidays, but I'll draw up a little contract to make it all legal and official, starting this week."

"That's such a kind offer," Rachel said with a worried glance at Luke. "But we have very little money saved."

Madge waved off the concern. "I know you're using your savings to pay off the family debt. So I'm selling it to you for a dollar. Thanks to Gott's

411

blessings, I don't need the money. But I need the peace in my heart that comes only from sharing his plentiful gifts."

"A dollar?" Luke wrapped his arms around Rachel and said, "That's definitely in our price range."

The three of them laughed, and the deal was made. Rachel and Luke each hugged Madge, and then Madge's grandchildren interrupted, seeking hugs and praise for performances done well. "We'll talk details soon," Madge promised as the children led her away.

Giddy with happiness, Rachel looked up at Luke. "Did that really just happen? I think I'm dreaming."

"It happened. You worked your way into a business." He smiled, his eyes aglimmer with joy. "Do you think you could hire on a fella who's been looking for a job in Joyful River?"

"I don't know." She folded her arms. "Is he a family man? A hard worker? A kind person?"

Luke nodded. "Yes to all these things. And he's in love with the shop owner."

"Well, then, I think that could be arranged." She laughed and reached for his hand. "Come. Let's share the news!" They hurried back to the Fisher children, who were pulling on coats.

"We've just been touched by an angel, and we have a new family business!" Rachel announced to her family. "Turns out Luke and I are not moving away. You're stuck with us for good, here in Joyful River."

"You're staying?" Bethany exclaimed. "This is going to be a great Christmas!"

"A great Christmas!" Polly echoed.

The younger children encircled Rachel and Luke, laughing merrily.

Dat's face lit up when he heard the news. "That's the best Christmas present I've ever gotten!"

Over the next week, Luke became a seamless part of the Christmas shop. Rachel was especially glad to have him around, as she'd been feeling a little queasy lately and wasn't quite up to moving big boxes. At home, their family felt complete once again with Luke at the dinner table. In the last week before Christmas, the sales brought in enough profit to pay for the next three months of rent, with a generous amount to pay their salaries. They had found a secure business that employed both Luke and Rachel.

At the Christmas Eve gathering in the Lambrights' home, Rachel scanned the familiar faces of family and friends. How could she have considered spending Christmas anywhere else but here? She chatted with friends, but felt a little nauseous at the sight of the table heaped high with ham, chicken and casseroles. She passed by the table and took a seat over by one of the windows laden with pine boughs and fat candles. She found contentment watching a gentle flame when someone perched on the sofa beside her.

"Merry Christmas, dear Rachel." Miriam's smile glowed with her usual warmth and mirth.

"You've made this a wonderful Christmas. Denki for planting the seed with Aunt Madge."

"Oh, you've already thanked me, and really, you worked so hard. It was only right."

"It's a blessing," Rachel said. "And I'm grateful."

Miriam leaned in close and lowered her voice. "Luke's worried about you. He wants you to see a doctor."

"I'm fine," Rachel insisted.

"I think you're healthy," Miriam said. "And I think if you count back the weeks, you might find that it's not a doctor you need. It's a midwife."

"What?" Rachel struggled to think clearly as she thought back to her last monthly and did the math in her head. Eight weeks. "Eight weeks!" she gasped with joy. "Oh, Miriam!" She pressed her hands to her heart, which seemed full beyond measure this Christmas.

"I'm so happy for you," Miriam said. "I know your mem would be overjoyed."

The thought of Mem filled Rachel's heart with emotion, though this time it was more tenderness than regret. "She was a good mother to us. She loved us so, and she always let us know it. I don't know how I'll follow in her footsteps."

"You will, Rachel." Miriam patted her shoulder. "You will find your way, as all mothers do."

That night, when the bedroom door was closed and Rachel and Luke were in their private cocoon, she shared the news.

"A baby? A child!" Luke was all smiles. "This is a Christmas full of wonder!"

"To be starting our own family . . . I can barely imagine it." Rachel's eyes filled with tears. "At least this explains why I've been crying so much lately."

"Tears of joy?" asked Luke.

Rachel nodded as she moved into the warmth of his arms. "Tears of joy."

Holding her close, Luke wiped her tears with a gentle fingertip, then kissed her cheeks. "I don't know which gift is greater—finding our way home, or learning that a baby is on the way."

"Who could decide?" Rachel relaxed against him, warm and secure. "This Christmas, we're doubly blessed."

Center Point Large Print
600 Brooks Road / PO Box 1
Thorndike, ME 04986-0001 USA

(207) 568-3717

US & Canada:
1 800 929-9108
www.centerpointlargeprint.com